HUNTED

HUNTED

N.M. BROWNE

BLOOMSBURY

Published by Bloomsbury, New York and London
Distributed to the trade by Holtzbrinck Publishers
Library of Congress Cataloging-in-Publication Data
Browne, N. M.
Hunted / by N. M. Browne.
p. cm.
Summary: A young woman in a coma becomes a magical red fox in another space
and time, where she plays a vital role in a rebellion against the king.
ISBN 1-58234-759-X (hc)
ISBN 1-58234-903-7 (ppk)
[1. Space and time--Fiction. 2. Coma--Fiction. 3. Supernatural--Fiction.
4. Foxes--Fiction. 5. Adventure and adventurers--Fiction.]
PZ7.B82215 Hu 2002
[Fic]--dc21
2001043903

Printed in the U.S.A.

3 5 7 9 10 8 6 4 2

Bloomsbury USA Children's Books
175 Fifth Avenue
New York, NY 10010

All papers used by Bloomsbury Publishing are natural, recyclable products made from
wood grown in well-managed forests. The manufacturing processes conform to the
environmental regulations of the country of origin.

For my mum

Chapter 1

At Bay: Day 1

She ran. There was a roaring in her ears. Her legs moved leadenly. She willed them to move faster, but they merely staggered uselessly. Fear had robbed her of coordination. Time slowed. She was shaking. She knew she wouldn't get away, couldn't get away. Tina pushed her. She stumbled backwards, legs trembling. There was nowhere to go. Her fear was a kind of sickness in her mouth. Tina's thin, pinched face was contorted into a mask of spite. Tina's face was centimetres from her own face. It blotted out everything. Tina grabbed a hank of hair, right near the scalp. It shocked her; the rough hands, the strength of Tina's hands.

They were all round her now, six or seven of them shouting at her. The sound of their taunts and the opening of their mouths got somehow separated in her head. 'Karen, you slag! You should've left my Billy alone.' The mouths moved vicious and red, like animals snarling. It made no sense. It hurt when she fell. It was a stinging kind of quick pain, like a childhood graze. The kick hurt more. Her flesh felt thin as a peach skin, unbelievably vulnerable. She shrank from their boots and tried to disappear. She curled up like a baby in a womb and tried to protect her head. There was blood everywhere, in her mouth as she sobbed, 'Please stop! I never ...' Her voice sounded pathetic even to her. The roaring in her ears turned to a kind of ringing and she slipped into a fuzzy black space of silence and darkness and hot pain. They were still there when the light came back.

'She's come round.'

'She's not going to get away with it that easy!'

They had dragged her somewhere near the canal. There was no one else around. They could murder her here and no one would find her for months. She felt damp and did not know if it was from the ground or if she had wet herself. Her school skirt had ridden up high to show her pale freckled thighs. Her skin was so white it looked blue where the veins coursed. Livid purple bruises were already forming. Mel and Cindy were laughing and pointing. Tina's smile was a leer of triumph. It made Karen realise with cold certainty that the worst was yet to come. She did not want to face whatever came next. There had to be an escape. They might kill her. She staggered to her feet and began to run while they laughed. They let her go a few metres until, whooping with the pleasure of it, they caught her and pushed her into the mud, screaming obscenities. She had a picture in her mind of a fox set upon by slavering hounds. She hung on to that thought as they punched and kicked her until the darkness engulfed her again.

It was dark when she woke. Everyone had gone. She moved cautiously. She had a memory of pain, sharp pain, searing pain, sudden pain that obliterated the sun for a minute. She only allowed herself to remember the horror of it for an instant, no more than that. She slammed shut the cage door on her memory. She would deal with that later.

She found that her limbs moved easily enough and so staggered to her feet. The scent of blood was strong. She wrinkled her nose. It was a damp night. The stench was pungent, canal water, urine and fear. She made almost no sound as she padded along the muddy towpath. She did not want to go home. She knew she was in a mess. Just for the moment she could not quite remember where home was. That did not worry her. The further from the scene of the attack she went the better the air smelled. She would find home by first light. She was sure that she had a home, but she could not go there straight away. She had to get away. She did not want to answer any questions. There would be questions she knew, because something had happened to her. Something bad had happened to her and she did not want to think about it.

She wanted only the cleansing wind blowing round her in the quiet night. And solitude, she wanted solitude most of all. She did not usually like the dark but the moon was bright and she found she could see quite clearly. There were no houses nearby, only the lock-keeper's cottage, long uninhabited. It was a heritage ice-cream and gift shop in the summer. It smelled stale and musty and she passed it swiftly. She could go anywhere. What could hurt her more than she had been hurt already? She sniffed the air, revelling in the unexpected multiplicity of the scents that surrounded her: damp mould on wood, wet leaves and sweet grasses, the strong odour of the earth and the still water, reeking a little of oil. She felt a great surge of energy and delight and started to run, more swiftly than she had imagined she could, while the cool wind ruffled her hair and brought the promise of other places in its fragrant wake. Freedom. For now there was just the night and her lean little body pounding along the moonlit towpath. There was no other word for it. This was freedom.

It did not strike her as odd that her senses were abnormally acute that night, nor that she ran with an unusual speed and rhythm. Perhaps it was the shock of her experience but she accepted all this strangeness unhesitatingly. It did not even strike her as odd that she wished to run through cold fields far from home, after what had probably been the worst afternoon of her life. None of her normal concerns broke through her ebullience. Karen cared only for the intoxicating odours in the night air and the wild pleasure of her own loping, ground-eating stride. It carried her swiftly from the scene of her humiliation.

She was quite lost. Not normally adventurous, she had always avoided walking near the canal. It was a lonely path and it was possible to walk many miles and see no one but the occasional dog walker or hiker *en route* to the distant hills. This part of the canal crossed wasteland. Beyond the canal there was only open country for several miles. For Karen, this was uncharted ground. She neither noticed nor cared.

The countryside was not lush. Even the valleys were not so sheltered that they would interest much apart from sheep. It had been moorland before industrialisation and even where cultivated, trees were still wind-beaten into stunted deformity. She ran on through fields and over small brooks, over stony outcrops, always keeping well away from the sprawl of buildings. Nowhere where there were people was safe.

Her feet pounded the ground, beating time to her heart's rhythm, urging her on. She ran further and found herself running through a forest of giant trees, straight limbed, unbowed and perfect as a fairy tale. She had never seen them before. The air smelled clearer, cleaner without its undertone of carbon monoxide. She must be far from town here. She stopped. She stood panting, her body shuddering, in a kind of wonder. Her heart's wild beating slowed. Why had no one told her of this great forest? There was something subtly different about the way it smelled; the earth here somehow had a different flavour. She was warmer too and not just because of her exertions. For the first time she had an intimation of strangeness. Things did not seem quite right. The piles of decaying leaves were quite deep in places, almost up to her chest. That should not be. For the first time since she had woken by the bank of the canal she began to think. Perhaps she had suffered some kind of concussion. What was she doing running around like this? She brought her hand to her head. The movement was awkward. She had to lower her head to meet her inexplicably inflexible arm. Had she broken it? She had felt no pain. No, it was worse than that. She had no hand. No scream escaped from her throat, but only because her vocal chords would not obey her. Panic nearly overwhelmed her. Her whole body trembled. She closed her eyes. She had made a mistake. She must be hallucinating. She must be suffering from shock. She opened her eyes. She still had no hand. Though it was dark in the forest, her keen eyes had no trouble recognising the unmistakable form of an animal's paw. She had no hand, only a paw. It could not be true. She was positive that she had not always had a paw. She had not been expecting that.

Somehow she had become something else. Yet there was no sense that this experience was in any way unreal, indeed nothing had ever seemed more real. She breathed deeply. This was no dream. The lightest of breezes frilled the thick hairs of her winter coat. The sensation was pleasurable and quite unlike anything else she'd ever felt. She had not always been like this. She had not always had this dark red fur. It was all wrong. She struggled to remember what she had been expecting. She had not been expecting this. She could smell the moist mustiness of the fermenting leaves, the loam of a fecund earth. Even in the darkness each variation in texture in the tree bark and each small gradation of colour in the fallen leaves was acutely visible as if she viewed everything through a portable microscope. This was beyond her imagination. She should have had hands, that was it, she should have had hands and so how could she have a paw where a hand should be?

Something made a great howl of anguish. It was a terrible, tortured cry. As her body's reflexes took over and the bunched muscle of her haunches tensed, ready to run, she realised that the something was herself. It was the only noise her inhuman throat could make. Something like despair sapped even her lively animal body of energy. What could have happened to her? How could this have happened? What could she do? Things were badly wrong she knew that. Beaten and bemused she slunk towards a leaf-filled hollow. She buried her nose under her hind legs. How could such an animal muzzle be *her* nose? How could she have hind legs? She wrapped her fine brush of a tail around her. How did she get a tail? That was wrong too. She had not always had a tail. It was all part of a terrible wrongness. Desolation dampened her fox body's instinct for preservation. Karen wanted only the oblivion of sleep. In spite of everything it came swiftly. Oblivion was her only answer to the unanswerable 'Why?'

There were reprisals of a sort. Not enough as far as her family were concerned. After a long night ringing round the local hospitals, her grandfather had discovered that a dog walker had found her battered, unconscious body by the canal bank. He had gone straight to the police. Tina and the others had been charged with 'actual bodily harm' or something like that. It made little difference. The gang were given suspended sentences. Women's violence was not taken that seriously. Karen remained suspended in no man's land, in hospital. The bruises faded, doctors set her broken bones and no one could explain why she failed to recover consciousness. They called it a coma.

To begin with there were lots of letters to the local paper bemoaning her fate and that of the country, that such a thing could happen in an ordinary town. The national press got hold of the story just as it had run its natural course in her home town. They made much of the tragic tale. Readers of one of the tabloids sent money, cards and an embarrassment of small soft toys to her bedside. Nothing worked. Karen remained oblivious to them all.

Chapter 2

Running on Instinct: Day 2

Karen woke with the first wan light of dawn. It was raining. She was cold and rapidly becoming wet. She shivered. Any hope that her memory had misled her was dashed by the first involuntary flick of her white-tipped, alien tail. She tried to remember why she was so sure this was not right. She knew that this was not the way she was meant to be. She was sure that she had not always been a fox. Yet her body was unmistakably that of a sleek, red fox and an extremely hungry red fox at that. That was another strange thing, this hunger was new to her, this desperate, urgent craving for food that filled her mind with a single imperative; eat! What could foxes eat? It was not a rhetorical question. She hoped that whatever force had transformed her into a fox had transformed her into a fox with good instincts. She shied away from consideration of what could have happened to turn her into a fox. She could not understand who or what could have done such a thing. She tried to think but her thoughts kept skittering away. Was this an act of God? Surely he was not prone to such arbitrary, pointless miracles and no law of physics she had ever come across could account for it. She could remember laws of physics, or at least that there were such things. She found it hard to think at all with every part of her shrieking 'Eat!'

She nosed around in the now wet leaves searching for the source of a sweet smell of decay and found the remains of some largish bird. The meat was high but edible and before Karen had time to register disgust, she found that she had eaten it. So much for instinct. When she realised what she had done she thought she might be sick, the taste was as powerful as the stench had been, but her fox body steadfastly refused to give up a source of calories. She kept it down and found that the screaming void that had been her empty stomach was silenced. The body now demanded water. She found a shallow puddle of muddy rainwater and lapped it gratefully. Mud had its own, not unpleasant, flavour. It was only then that her mind was free to attempt to think. What did she do now? She sniffed the air in the way that now seemed natural to her. A new scent was carried by the wind. She recognised it. Even without the augmented senses of a fox, she would have known the distinctive smell of horses and dogs. She found that she had begun to run. Her body knew what to do. She could hear the pounding of hooves and the baying of hounds. They were not far behind. She was sure they were after her. She was certain of it in her bones.

There was no pleasure now in the neat, economical pace of her fox self. There was only fear coursing like poison through every fibre of her. The fox did not stagger or falter. She had slipped once, somewhere, not long ago. She remembered the feeling, and an echo of fear. The fox did not slip or slide on the slippery rain-sodden leaves. Fear made her fox self faster. Every whisker, every hair was alert for information that could help her in her desperate flight. Her heart pumped so hard it hurt. She did not know how she breathed as the air flowed round her like a slipstream. Paws pounded, senses strained, her whole physical being was focused on escape. Only Karen's mind faltered. She had no sense of where she was going. Where could she run? Who could she go to? She could imagine no one who would give her protection. There was not much time for thought. She hurtled sure-footedly through the forest dodging trees and fallen branches, leaping awkward obstacles, looking for somewhere to hide. The excited yapping of the dogs spurred her on. It was hard to override instinct. She wanted to stop and think, but the hounds were drawing closer.

She could hear the shouts of men and a hunting horn, clear and loud, resonating through the forest. The sound was as loud as a klaxon and seemed as unmusical, a flat, ugly, man-made noise disrupting the very air. Birds flew away as the hunt approached. Her thinking mind determined to cross water to disguise her scent. Her fleet fox body was already there. At some unconscious level she had sensed the nearness of the trickling brook. She raced towards it. Even swollen with rain it was not much. She splashed through it at speed. It was cold on her underbelly. She did not care. It was only a narrow, shallow stream; would it be enough? The hounds were closer. She could smell their wet coats, their excitement, their eagerness for the kill. Her chest hurt with the effort she was expending. What did pain matter? She could not slow even for an instant. The men and horses sounded like an army charging through the trees. There was now only open ground ahead. There they would gain, unhampered by the obstacles of the forest floor, the soft ground and the inconvenient brushwood. Death was snapping at her heels. She tried not to think of what it would be like to be between the sharp-toothed jaws of dogs. She knew of nowhere to go to ground. The country was unknown, unfamiliar as a foreign land. She ran on. The fields were waterlogged in places and thick with mud near stiles and places of heavy use. Mud splattered her pelt till she was black with it. She ran on. The rain was driving down through the grey morning. It was hardly light and visibility was poor. It made no difference. She ran on. That klaxon call sounded again. It was much closer now. She was beginning to tremble with the exertion. Could a fox burst its heart with running? Breathing was hard but she kept on doing it. Nothing mattered. She just ran on. Everything Karen had ever been was pared down into this small desperate form of the hunted fox. She would survive. They would not get her. She had to survive.

There was some kind of building ahead, a strange-looking whitewashed construction that made no sense to her fox's eye level. It was rich in the stinking odours of human habitation. Would they disguise her own pungent scent of fox? She did not know. She had to make a decision. She did not know how much further she could run. Every moment of open country gave the hunters an advantage. She knew that the trembling in her muscles was not a good sign. She did not know what lay ahead. She would take her chance to lose them in the stench of men. She ran towards what looked like outbuildings and smelled of hay. There did not seem to be anyone around. She was wrong. A figure stood just outside. It was a man, a young man; a young man watching her. For some reason she felt as if he had been watching her for some time. He looked straight at her, grey eyes meeting her own. Silently, he opened the door to the hayloft. Fearing a trap, she hesitated, one paw raised. Her body shuddered and shook with exhaustion. The hounds bayed in the distance. It was warm and dry inside. Her fox's instinct said run, take your chance in the wet wilds outdoors. Her human perception thought the man had a kind face. She trusted that and slunk cautiously inside. She cowered behind some bales of hay and waited.

She did not have to wait long before she heard snuffling and the clatter of horses' hooves and hounds' paws on the wet impacted ground outside the hayloft. The hounds must have lost her scent because none came close. There were voices. She could not make out clear speech but her human intelligence surmised that the horses' riders spoke with the young man. There was the sound of hearty male laughter and then the sound of hooves and hounds receding. They were gone; but did that make her safe? She waited many pounding heartbeats, scarcely breathing, resting lightly, ready to run. The man came inside. He carried a misshapen pottery bowl of water and some slices of cold cooked ham in his huge hands. He approached cautiously as if she were a wild animal, which perhaps she was. She was salivating. Hunger was obviously part of being a fox. The void of her stomach was screaming again. The ham smelled better than the finest meal she'd ever eaten. She had run a long way on the incomplete remains of a dead bird.

The man crooned softly under his breath. She bared her teeth but did not move. She wanted to but the trembling in her limbs hampered her. She smelled no taint in the meat or the water to suggest it might have been poisoned, but what did she know? He did not come close enough to touch her. He stopped about a metre away and laid his offering on the ground. Her nose quivered, everything quivered. What was the right move now? From her position crouched ready to run, the man looked enormous. Karen could see that he was still quite young, tall but a little skinny for his height. He had a beard, but it was rather fine and insubstantial, a pale shadow in a shade between gold and copper, like his hair. He smelled of sweat and milk and meat. His clothes, which were like nothing Karen had seen before, smelled stalely of dirt, old sweat, dust and sheep.

She made a decision and crept forward, her eyes never leaving the man's face. It hurt to walk and for the first time she was aware that something was stuck in the soft part of her paw, a sliver of thorn or a splinter of wood. It laid a trail of blood as she limped forward. She saw the man register it but he said nothing. He squatted down on his haunches so their eyes were almost level. Even close-to he still looked kind. Dare she trust his food? Once more, her hunger answered her before she had really put the question. The flavour of ham, salty and strong, filled her senses. She ate ravenously of the ham and drank deeply of the water. Her last thought as her body collapsed under her was, 'So it was poisoned, after all.'

Chapter 3

Meaningless Jabber: Day 3 (Morning)

Waking somewhere unknown and dark was becoming a habit. Karen opened her eyes. Her head hurt. There was very little light. She was lying on dry straw in what looked like a stone igloo but smelled like a sheep pen. The roof felt low even to a fox. It was like a tomb. The young man lay beside her wrapped in a rank-smelling blanket. He snapped awake as she opened her eyes. She was ready for him. Her teeth were bared and a warning growl issued involuntarily from her throat. The man struggled to sit up, keeping his head low so as not to crack it on the stone ceiling. In the confined space his stink was overpowering. The word 'vagrant' popped into her head. That's what you called people who looked like him. There were other words too, 'tramp', 'beggar'. How could she know that and yet not know where she had come from? There was a dark patch of unknowing in her head, thicker than a cloud, more like a hole or a tear in her memory. It distracted her for a moment. She made herself focus on the matter in hand. What was this man and what was he playing at? Neither her imagination nor her limited fox experience could suggest any reason for his having poisoned or drugged her. The exit from the igloo or cave that they were in was blocked by a small boulder. It was within the reach of his arm and the man dislodged it with a push. The pale light of early morning spilled through the small aperture. Early morning! She had lost a whole day to this man's food. She weighed up the possibility of escape through the hole. The man could reach over and stop her too easily. His eyes stared at her intently as a miser views his gold. It was not a look to make her comfortable.

She got ready. There would be an opportunity. She did not like that look in his eyes. Muscles tensed ready for flight. She tried to hold his disconcerting gaze. They looked at each other for what seemed like a long time then, at last, the man spoke and she felt her fox blood run cold. It seemed that she had lost the capacity to understand speech.

That was another wrongness. She knew she should be able to understand, had been able to understand things – before, in the time she couldn't remember. Perhaps this man spoke gibberish, albeit in a calm voice with normal conversational inflection. Somehow she knew he did not. She felt her muscles sag. She felt more lost than ever. What was happening to her? Despair at this new revelation, robbed her of the urge to tear out his throat. Her fox mind knew that he outweighed her anyway and that she was unlikely to come off best in a fight. She cowered back away from him, while he talked. Meaningless syllables tripped earnestly off his tongue. She shook her ears as if that might help her to make sense of his words. It didn't. Not one word seemed to her to approximate familiar speech. If she had not already accepted the impossible several times over, this terrifying loss of comprehension might have unhinged her. As it was she gave a mental shrug and tried to gain as much as possible from what she could understand. His tone was apologetic. His hands were spread wide in a pleading gesture. It seemed that he had not intended to hurt her. She noted for the first time that her injured paw had been roughly bandaged. The clean straw may have been laid for her benefit, for the man lay on several greasy sheepskins sewn together. So what now? What did he want with her? She found herself considering options. If he had wanted to kill her he could have done so easily and he probably wouldn't have bandaged her paw. Did he want her as a pet? She had digested the poisoned meal and her stomach felt empty again. It rumbled hungrily, reminding her of the essential needs of her existence. She did not know how to hunt or scavenge for herself. Had she known once and just forgotten? She did not think so. Pets were fed. She knew that. She even had a mental picture of a dog, a pet of some woman she must have once known. If he would feed her until she could discover what had happened to her and what to do about it, then she could probably refrain from biting him. If she could work out what the man was saying she could probably manage to give him the minimum return of affection and obedience expected of a pet. She stopped growling. She eyed the leather satchel on which he had rested his head. There was food there; she knew it. The man was not stupid because it seemed that he read her thoughts. With deliberate movements, keeping his hands visible almost as if she were some threat to him, he took the satchel. From within it he produced two apples, a lump of cheese and half a loaf of tough-looking dark bread. Karen licked her lips. She could not stop herself. Her eyes could not move from the food, and her nose quivered. Still talking his unhelpful gobbledegook, the man bit into an apple before proffering the rest to the fox. He must think her a fool. She retreated. The man leant forward and placed the apple on the ground between them. She forced herself to wait. Still watching her he took a long, hooked stick she had not noticed before and pushed the apple towards her. She was glad she'd not attacked him. The presence of that stick would have given her less than no chance against him. With one part of her mind she berated herself for failing to notice it earlier. She ate the apple and the cheese and the bread he offered her, but only after he had tasted it first. It struck her that this man expected a high degree of understanding from a fox, indeed that he treated her with a strange deference, apart from attempting to drug or poison her, of course.

After the meal the man pointed firmly at his own chest and repeatedly made the sound 'Mowl,' as if it was his name. He pronounced it like 'owl'. Was he actually saying something quite different like 'Mark' that merely sounded like 'Mowl' to her fox senses? She could not say. He then pointed at her fox self and said 'Fewg' several times. She thought he was trying to name her but couldn't be sure. He paused and seemed to wait for some reaction from her. She was almost tempted to try to repeat the name, but she knew that would have been seriously weird behaviour for a fox. Instead, she bowed her head in acknowledgement of the naming. That was probably in itself uncharacteristic fox behaviour but she was on untested ground here, for which her fox reactions were inadequate and her half forgotten experience unhelpful. After this they looked at each other for a while and Karen became aware of another urgent animal need. Never taking her eyes off the man, 'Fowl Owl' as she named him, she slunk out of the shelter and into the sweet air of outdoors. Fowl Owl stayed close to her. He was less than a hand's-breadth away. After she had relieved herself she found it easy to see why. They were up in the hills surrounded by grazing sheep. Her fox self found that very interesting. They were on high ground. She took the opportunity to try and get her bearings. Nestling in the valley some distance below she could just make out the cluster of buildings she had run towards in her flight from the hounds. She was a little suspicious of the distorting effect of the lower perspective of her fox-eyed perception, but they still looked like nothing she had ever seen before. There seemed to be one large thatched structure against which a number of other thatched triangular buildings leant. The whole thing was low lying, no more than a single storey. Wisps of blue-grey smoke drifted from chimneyless apertures above the roof. It did not look like a permanent structure and yet she was sure it was. From her vantage point she could see clearly a large number of round, thatched outbuildings that seemed to suggest permanence, and a round stone well. Where the hell was she? Should she recognise this landscape or was it really as unknown as it seemed? She shook her fox head. She could not worry about that now. She had a more immediate concern, to run or not to run? Fowl Owl looked at her questioningly. She would have loved to leave, a part of her wanted to run very badly. But she was totally lost. She did not even recognise the shape of the hills. From the hilltop she could see no road, no electricity pylons, no farmhouse other than the ramshackle thatched affair below her. That was a wrongness too. She knew such things ought to have been there.

The man turned away from her as she surveyed the view, almost as if he was offering her the courtesy of privacy. Using his large hooked stick as a staff he walked on. After a brief moment she followed him, trotting a few paces behind. She could not see his face but she knew he was smiling. Was that good?

Karen's grandmother shifted her bulk on the uncomfortable plastic chair and put down her knitting to take the proffered coffee.

'It's supposed to be *cappuccino* from one of them machines.' Her husband's tone said it all. The best this hospital could come up with was undrinkable coffee with a foreign name and a verdict of 'stable' for his granddaughter. It was a battle to force himself to look at her, lying still as a sculpted knight on a marble tomb. Karen's skin looked almost translucent, paler than the white sheets. Underneath her lids, where the network of blue veins was finer than filigree, her eyes were still. Her long red hair had been carefully plaited and pinned in braids on the top of her head like a Tyrolean girl from the newsreels of his youth. He knew it was to keep it from tangling but it still looked odd to him. Karen in life—

No, he must stop thinking that. He corrected himself; normally, Karen had not been much for fancy hairdos.

'She's not dying, you know,' his wife said as if she had caught his thought, scarcely formed, that she was as near dead as made no difference. 'Something is going on in that head of hers. Something important.'

The tear that rolled down her plump cheek, still smooth in spite of her age, belied the steadiness of her voice.

'I'd like to get the bastards that—'

'Don't, George. It won't help. We've got to put that behind us.'

George unclenched his fist, and murmured, 'They want shooting,' under his breath. He meant it. Grace knew he meant it and silently she both understood and disapproved. She had spent a long life resolutely looking on the bright side. It took a lot of energy; she had none left over for hate.

'That boy came in. That Billy,' she continued, brightly, sipping the cappuccino absently.

'The one it was all about?'

Grace nodded. 'He brought them roses.'

She indicated the bedside table where a dozen pink roses with an abundance of gypsophila and rather stiff greenery had been awkwardly stuffed into a grubby vase, as if they had just been unwrapped from their cellophane.

'They will have cost him, them,' said George grudgingly.

Grace nodded. 'It weren't his fault. I remembered him when I saw him. I taught him once, only for a few weeks or I'd have remembered him straight off. He said they'd only spoken once – him and Karen – about me. He said he thought she seemed sad, a bit lost – he'd wanted to cheer her up.' Grace paused. 'D'you think she was sad, still, after all this time?' Her eyes brimmed over with tears but her voice was as bright and steady as before.

'I don't know, love. She never said much – it weren't her way.'

'She were like her granddad there,' said Grace with a quick, sharp look at her husband. 'It doesn't mean she didn't feel as much as everyone else. Does it?'

George said nothing. What would talking do? Instead, he fought the urge to pull out the blessed tubes that kept Karen with them in this bleach-scented nightmare, and just let her go. His hands trembled, so urgent was the urge to free her and them from this terrible no man's land. The loud ticking of the clock on the wall, which remained ten minutes slow, and the hum of the machinery drove him mad. They were trapped, both of them, watching her breathe, each breath a moment lost that none of them would ever have again, lost to this undertaker's waiting room. Grace resumed her knitting and the rhythmic click of her needles was more than he could take. He knew by some quality in the way she knitted, even in the way she breathed, that she expected him to go and would not mind if he went; they had been together a long time.

He could feel unreasoning anger rising. He had to get away. 'If you're right here, I think I'll go outside and take a turn round the block. I could do with a blow in the fresh air.'

Grace's lips twitched into a sad, affectionate, near smile. She waited till the sound of his echoing footsteps had all but disappeared. Her voice shook a little for the first time, as whispering, she turned to touch her granddaughter's still form.

'I know you're there, Karen. Don't you fret. I'll find a way to get through to you yet. I've not given up on you. I've lost a daughter and a son-in-law – I'm not letting you go without a fight.'

As a nurse hovered into view, Grace spoke in a louder more conversational voice.

'That Billy is quite a nice lad really. I thought it were good of him to come again. The nurse, Lynne, the pretty one, she said that's the sixth lot of flowers he's brought you already …'

Meaningless chatter, but the grim-faced specialist had said that it might help. If it would help Karen she'd jabber on till doomsday.

Chapter 4

Quarry: Day 3 (Morning)

The man, Mowl, observed Karen Fox slyly out of the corner of his eye. He was right. The vixen was an arl. He gave a great spontaneous smile. To have seen and spoken to an arl! Against the white sky and grey winter hills, the vivid russet of the fox's coat seemed to glow as if lit from within. The fox was the only bright spot in a world leached of colour: the only real thing in a world of shadows. He was quite sure he was right. Such a perfect fox could not be of this world. As a shepherd, he had spent time enough protecting his flock against wild animals. He recognised one when he saw one. This fox was not a wild animal, nor was she exactly tame. She was something else, a something else with such a sense of latent power about her that it made the hairs stand erect on the back of his neck. The fox carried with her the pungent scent of elsewhere. He closed his eyes and, as he had been taught, he searched the ether with his mind for spiritual emanations.

He had always been sensitive to such things. He sensed nothing but her strangeness and that was enough to make his innards churn with an excitement that was not far short of fear. What great cataclysm could the presence of an arl, here on the farmstead, portend?

He walked a little further, the unwild fox following. Her presence gave him something new to think about on the lonely hillside. It was like the old days when Dake Varl, for whom he worked, had hired a scholar from the Schools of Court for his daughters. Mowl had been allowed to study with them and had enjoyed mulling over what he had been taught, practising his spiritual exercises for long hours at a time. His mind worked best to the beat of his feet as he patrolled the hills, caring for his flock. He had been a good student, mastering the languages spoken throughout the six kingdoms and showing a talent for all of the six tiers of philosophy – the numerical, rhetorical, categorical, natural, spiritual and magical. He had always been especially fascinated by the arcane study of arls, unborn souls from another tier of being, the Plane of Ede, where the spirits of men took non-human form. What was an unborn soul? Did it know things that he did not about the other planes of being? Did it know about the tier of being after death as well as the tier of being before human life? He hadn't thought of those things for a long time.

When he had been a boy he had liked to imagine that he was a powerful Adept, able to hear the thoughts of men and arls. He never believed he would ever meet an arl. He was older now but his daydreams had not moved on very far. Now he imagined studying the arl, maybe writing a paper to send to the Convocation of Scholars at Maybury! If he could do something like that, the ignominy of his status would not matter. He could travel the world as a scholar. The fox might be a way out for him, a way to leave the Varl clan that would not dishonour himself or them. His smile grew broader still.

Distantly, a horse whickered and brought him back to himself and the windswept hillside. The fox had stopped, uncertainty clear on her face, ready to run. There was a rustle in the grass a long way off; the wind or someone coming? Mowl turned to investigate. Someone was coming. He could hear unnaturally loud and ragged breathing. He held out a hand in a signal to stay the fox. He sensed her struggling against the instinct to run, and for a disorienting moment it was as if he shared her fear, her prescience of danger. His own heart started to beat more raggedly. He could not demand she stay by his side feeling like that. With a sharp pang of regret he found himself whispering, 'Go, noble arl. If you are afraid, run!' He did not watch her go. He did not know if she would come back. He too was curious as to who could be climbing the hills towards them, but he had no reason to be afraid. He moved in the direction of the sound. It was still early. He had missed the Varl morning prayers to the Keeper, but no one would rush to find him just for that. The sound was getting closer. He could see a figure struggling with the encumbrance of thick woollen skirts and some kind of bundle, clambering over the tussocks of coarse grass. His heart leapt. It was Leva, Dake Varl's eldest daughter.

'Leva!' His cry was of unadulterated joy. 'You can't guess what I've discovered!'

'Shh!' The woman flashed dark eyes at him and he fell silent. Something was wrong. He ran to help her. She steadied herself on his arm.

'Mowl. You have to go. Now!'

'But Leva, I've found an arl!'

Leva shook her head savagely, holding her side where she'd developed a stitch, panting for breath. Her angry voice came in gasps.

'You've got to go, Mowl! Now! You're in terrible danger.'

Mowl went cold. As he got close to her he noticed that she had dressed in extreme haste and that her eyes were puffy and red. She had run all the way from the farmhouse in her stockinged feet. It was a steep climb and Leva was a woman now and no longer ran around the hillside as she once had. She was out of practice and painfully out of breath. Something very bad must have happened to make her run like that. What if Dake Varl had found out about them?

'Has your father— ? '

'He knows.' The blunt words turned Mowl's world upside-down. 'I'm to be married next week – to Jenn Doka; his family have come up with the bride price – but it's not that.' With a small wave of her hand, she dismissed the one thing they had both feared above all else.

Mowl was stunned. He could not imagine anything worse. Their fear of her father's anger if he discovered their relationship had hung over them for the last few months like the sharp edge of a guillotine, poised to fall.

'My father sent Dorren to Maybury to add your name to the list for King Flane's new Militia.'

That was not so bad. It was quite fair of her father. He could have sent a clan-less shepherd out of his lands to live as a vagrant for the rest of his days for dallying with the Varl daughter-heir. Mowl breathed again. Leva saw that some of the tension had left Mowl's face.

'No, you don't understand, the sergeant saw your name on the list and declared your life forfeit. Mowl, they say your father was a traitor!'

Mowl looked at her without understanding. His mind seemed almost frozen, the flow of his thoughts stuck in shocked rigidity.

'What do you mean?'

'Your father was a Speare, a soldier – they say he killed

King Rufin; you're his nearest blood relative and your life is forfeit. Mowl, stop being so stupid! You have to run. Now! The messenger is some kind of distant kin to mother, married into the Second Household. Mother will stall him, but there's not much time. Please Mowl!' Leva's dark eyes were unexpectedly moist and frightened. 'It's over for you here anyway. Father knows. You must run, but not to Maybury – go to Deworth. There are boats there that can take you over the sea, away from Loyrenton altogether. You might be able to make a new life – in another place.'

What new life? Clan-less men without a place were vagrants. They were unwelcome even outside the boundaries of Loyrenton. That knowledge hung, unspoken between them.

'Here, take these. It's all we can give you. Now go!'

She thrust her bundle into his arms and turned away at a run. He thought she was crying but in the harsh wind it was hard to tell. He could not get his faculties to function, but his legs obeyed some wiser, life-preserving impulse and he ran for the shelter to pick up his satchel and bedding. The arl was there, waiting, her intelligent triangular head turned towards him. It was difficult not to read a question in her eyes. His thoughts thawed sufficiently for him to feel an unexpected twinge of pleasure. She had not run away. Did it matter? He could never now study the arl and learn her language – he would never address the Convocation of Maybury. He was to become what he had always feared, a vagrant and, worse than that, a vagrant with a polluted bloodline. He was the last relative of a traitor. His heart felt dead as a stone and cold within him. He spoke softly to the arl, fearful of frightening her further. He could see that she was trembling.

'Noble arl, I have to go – you are welcome to join me in my flight but I cannot save you from the King's men again. Now we are both quarry!'

Chapter 5

Moving on: Day 3 (Morning)

Fowl Owl looked distressed – that was clear enough to Fox. More than that he reeked of fear. His hands, moving rapidly to secure his blanket and sheepskin to his satchel, were shaking. The man's face was taut with worry. She could see that his height and beard had deceived her; he was even younger than she had first thought. She followed him out of the stone shelter. He struggled clumsily with his possessions. He abandoned his shepherd's stick, unwrapped a large metal sword from a bundle and grimly strapped it to his hips by means of a leather harness. Karen Fox liked neither the smell of the oiled metal, an acrid bitterness that caught in her throat, nor the scent of fear that emanated from the man. That sword was a wrongness. This man-boy did not look or dress as he ought to and swords belonged in museums. She knew that and the knowledge made her more afraid. The cold wind brought the scent of horse to her receptive nostrils and she quickened her pace. Had the hunters returned?

It began to rain and the hillside exploded with a dizzying variety of new smells. Their multiplicity was dazzling to her acute fox senses, like fireworks for the nose. Making sense of this perceptual assault distracted her and made thinking difficult. She was a fox in trouble. She was hungry again. She smelled things in the undergrowth but was too confused to even begin to think about hunting. She was not sure she had the strength to outrun the hunters if they had indeed returned. This man might help her. She moved closer to his side and fell in step. He was striding across the hillside, moving so fast she had to run to keep up. He was so lost in his own thoughts he didn't seem to notice her.

Whatever was going on in that shaggy head of his, Mowl offered her the best chance of survival she'd got.

Karen Fox strained to hear any sign of danger. This state of hyper-alertness seemed to be part of what it was to be a fox. Her heart pumped fear around her body as efficiently and as constantly as it pumped blood. Far away she heard a horse whinny. She bolted for the cover of some scrubby trees. Mowl followed. He moved more quickly and more efficiently than she had expected. His breathing was ragged. She knew or thought she knew what she was running from. What was Mowl running from? What had he done?

The whinny had come from some distance behind

them. There was no path or road of any sort that a horse and rider might follow. The wind was now in the wrong direction for her to glean more than a hint of a scent of a horse. She crouched down behind the tree and quivered. Mowl was whispering to her in a way he obviously thought was reassuring. She wished he'd shut up. She was listening for any further sound to indicate the presence of a horseman who might also be a huntsman. She was not interested in reassurance. She was interested in survival.

The rain falling on the leaves of the bush sounded thunderous to her fox's ears. Mowl's low murmur sounded clamorous. After a time, after many rapid fox heartbeats but perhaps not many minutes, Mowl shifted his weight and cautiously scrambled to his feet. They had heard nothing to suggest they were being followed. Cautiously, Karen Fox followed Mowl as he ran down the hillside. She trusted his senses less than she trusted her own. As for his sense – there was a large question mark over the rationality of a youth with a sword who spoke to foxes. Nonetheless she followed him, hanging her head a little to keep the rain out of her eyes. Her tail twitched behind her, mirroring her edginess and irritation. She did not like the rain. The sodden bandage round her injured paw unravelled and was trampled in the mud. Mowl stank of damp wool and dirt and misery. Before that moment she had not known that misery had its own distinctive smell.

Mowl gathered his cloak more tightly round him. It made no difference. An endless sheet of rain soaked through it until he was drenched and cold almost to his bones. A mist had settled in the hollow between the hills. It was an all-encompassing greyness. The fox remained by his side. Her small, red, somehow disgruntled, form was the only source of comfort in a world bereft of it. Water dripped off his nose. Some of the water was salty.

He had stopped running. He had a stitch in his side. Common sense told him he could not run as far as Deworth. He walked now, as fast as he could without the stitch returning. His ears strained constantly for sounds of pursuit. It was hard to hurry. The rain had turned the soft earth to grey mud of the most congealing, adhesive kind. Mowl's feet were now truly made of clay. His wooden clogs were twice their normal weight with mud. His spirits felt as heavy as his feet.

Predictably Fox heard them first; distant hooves and the shouts of a man, spurring on his horse. She had raised a paw and turned to question the wind. Watching her he felt again the dizzying illusion that he could sense what she sensed. It was sure to be an illusion. He could clearly read her indecision, her fear and then her certainty. With a quick glance up at his face she turned and ran up the hillside to the only cover around, a lichen-covered limestone outcrop. He ducked in an unsuccessful attempt to diminish his gangly height and lurched after her. He was shaking as much from fear as from cold. Sound carried a long way in the narrow valley. He feared that his ragged breathing could be heard a mile away. The fox's quick glance seemed to suggest the same concern. He had the most bizarre sensation that if she could have shushed him she would have. With a desperate effort of will he focused on the nature of Balance that held all life in equilibrium. He pictured the web-fine skeins of order that held all worlds in place. He calmed his unruly breathing and had the satisfaction of seeing a flicker of approval (could it be?) in the eyes of the fox. He managed to keep his breathing calm as the rider came closer. He only just kept panic at bay.

Dake Varl bowed his head before the small shrine in the courtyard and contemplated the symbol crudely scratched on the wall, a hand holding an evenly balanced set of hand scales, the symbol of the Keeper. He licked his finger to trace the symbol. 'May all that issues from me serve equilibrium.' He began the common prayer of the day but stopped, unable to continue. Had he served equilibrium? It seemed as if he might have better served himself.

It had begun when Yani had whispered that she had overheard Leva giggling with her cousins and sisters about Mowl. He knew he had paled because Yani had told him and forced a restorative tincture of something or other down his throat. Yani had been annoyed that Leva had so foolishly risked her reputation before a bride price had been agreed with a suitable family. But when she saw her husband's face, she had clapped her hand to her mouth in horror. 'He has to go away before anything comes of it,' she had said firmly, and Dake had nodded. 'He can join the King's Militiamen. It will give him a living.' She had decided and he had nodded, pleased to find a way out that did not involve him killing the boy. For at that one moment he had wanted to.

They ought to have known better.

Now the King's man, a courtier, had come to take Mowl to the gallows at Maybury for treason at one remove. Dake felt cold at the thought of it. He had ushered the guest into the smoky interior of the homestead. Yani had hastily dressed herself in the lace headdress and stole of her rank. She looked uncomfortable, an unfamiliar stranger reeking of mothballs. When he'd heard her fluency in the sibilant court tongue, her deft circumlocutions, her precise use of complex honorifics, his pride in her swelled. He had known that she could make the encounter last for as long as they needed. He had run then; faster than an old man ought to, faster than was good for him, to retrieve the precious, hidden bundle from the storehouse, a sword wrapped in a woollen cloak. He had been an excellent runner in his youth; not all his strength had left him.

His daughter had been working indoors. She came at his bidding, hesitant and afraid. She had not forgotten his cold anger when he had heard of her relationship with Mowl, the shepherd. She was unused to his anger. It didn't matter now.

'Leva, listen!' He had hissed at her in an urgent whisper to get her full attention. And he told her of Mowl's danger. The look of horror on her face was one he never wanted to see again. Stunned, she had accepted the parcel. Her face had drained of blood when she recognised that it was a weapon. She had bowed her head in confused acknowledgement of the gift and ducked briefly back inside the homestead to grab some things. She had not paused even for her outdoor shoes, but had run at full pelt for the hills. She was a good girl, practical like her mother. He watched her go. They were not giving Mowl much of a chance to get away, but it would have to be enough.

'May his father's sword bring him more luck than it brought to my brother.' Dake was startled to hear himself speak the words out loud.

If Mowl were more like Leva, Dake would worry less about his chances of survival. Leva had inherited all of Yani's strength while her cousin had inherited all his mother's feyness. Dake winced inwardly as he recalled Leva and Mowl's liaison, but the two were blameless. He only blamed himself and maybe Tira, Mowl's mother –

for dying in childbirth. Mowl irked him and always had. Mowl's father Mant would never have been content to live Mowl's life, accepting the charity of the Varls, tending sheep in the godforsaken bleakness of the Varl clan lands. He could not help despising his nephew's strange passivity, but he still felt a coward and a traitor to his brother's memory for not immediately claiming his kinship with Mant and Mowl. Yani had been against it. King Flane would as likely kill them both as let Mowl free. It made sense, as Yani's opinions always did. She had forbidden him to reveal his relationship to Mant Speare, pulling rank as she never had before in the long years of their partnership. He was ashamed, not because she had invoked her rights as the Goodwife of the Varls, but because he had felt grateful. His ears burned with the red heat of his shame. Would Mant have let it rest there? He thought not. His brother had been a brave man. But how could he really know? When he died, Mant had been scarcely older than Mowl was now. Age changed things. He did not think it had changed him for the better, he had once burned to fight injustice. Where had his passion gone? He stood for a while, lost in his regretful thoughts, until he heard a footfall behind him.

'I thought I'd find you here.' It was Yani.

'Has he gone?'

'Yes, he's well on his way by now. Sar Hanse, the King's man complimented me on my perfect command of the courtier's tongue – he had feared he might have to sully his mouth with the vulgar speech. He rode off to inform his liege that Mowl left here months ago and that we were ignorant of his background.' Yani's voice reverberated with contempt. She spat vehemently on the ground as if to cleanse her mouth of the sour taste of the lie. 'Flane's a fool to encourage such men. Did Leva warn Mowl?'

'I saw her go. I did not see her return. You're sure she's not …?'

'Dake, it's fine. There will be no babe. Jenn Doka and she will be wed before the moon's third quarter. Her heart is bruised but not broken. She will be fine. I wish I could feel as hopeful for Mowl.'

Dake nodded grimly and patted her briefly on the shoulder.

'You did well. I did not know you had such a subtle command of the old court snake-tongue.'

Yani grinned. 'I was schooled in it from the age of three. And birched when I made a mistake!' She grabbed his arm and forced him to meet her eye. His were moist. 'We did right, Dake. There was no gain in letting them know about you. Why jeopardise everything? No one remembers who you were before you came here. We have built something here to be proud of. Would you risk our children's safety too?'

She held his gaze, her own dark eyes unwavering and

compelling. Yani was never uncertain. He loved her for it, but he had to look away.

'I came here to pray.' He took his knife from his belt and nicked his finger till it bled, then traced the shape of the symbol in his own blood. His voice was bitter when he spoke. 'May the Keeper of Balances keep Mowl safe, for I, his uncle-in-blood, have not.'

Chapter 6

Pursued: Day 3 (Afternoon)

Grace stirred on the plastic seat and jolted into wakefulness, dry-mouthed, her heart banging, her nerves jangling – Karen. Karen was in danger. She'd dreamed that Karen was in danger. It took her a moment to remember where she was, then it all came flooding back. She lurched towards Karen's hospital bed. Her granddaughter lay serenely on the bed. Her green eyes were opened wide and unseeing.

'Karen, Karen, love, can you hear me?' Something about the hospital air had dried her throat and lips so that her panicked cry was more of a hoarse croak. She licked her lips and pushed the red button by Karen's bed to alert the nurse. Karen was still breathing, she'd checked. At least when Karen's eyes were closed it was possible to imagine that she slept. Those strange unseeing eyes were almost corpse-like, as if the life and spirit had already gone from her, as if she were not her Karen.

Grace suppressed her sob before it had gathered enough momentum to break from her. The nurse took a long time in coming. When she did come she seemed unconcerned.

'Don't worry, it's involuntary. It doesn't mean anything. Sometimes they move, or seem to see you, but it's just a muscular spasm.' She modified her brusque tone when she saw Grace's face. 'I'm sorry. I didn't mean that the way it sounded. Don't worry. She's no worse. I don't think she's any better but I might be wrong. We'll get the doctor in tomorrow to assess her. Look, I'll just put the screen round for a minute and make sure she's comfortable. Why don't you go to the canteen, get something to eat? They've got some lovely cakes in today. I just had one for my break.' The nurse was only young. She couldn't be expected to know what it felt like and if she did know would she still work here? So much pain was contained in these bright, dry rooms. Grace wondered if it would ever be possible for her to smell disinfectant again without knowing this doomed, sick, fluttering of fear.

Fox and Mowl stayed crouched behind the boulder until the rider passed them. The man was elaborately dressed in the purple and green livery of the Second Household, the King's aristocratic courtiers. The rain had soaked the feathers in his plumed hat and they got a glimpse of the rivulets of green dye running down his clenched face as he rode fast. From his expression he liked rain less than Fox. He did not see them, nor did he seem to be looking for anyone. He just rode. Mowl wondered if the man were an Adept of some sort, trained to know men by their emanations. It was a rare talent but he wished to take no chances. Why otherwise would the King send such a fop to arrest him? Mowl tried to control his fearful thoughts just in case. He could not quite believe it when the man just rode past. Mowl was in no doubt that the man had ridden from the Varl farmstead.

Mowl and Fox waited, hunched behind the rocky outcrop, too fearful to move. Perhaps their pursuer was trying to trick them, perhaps he would return on foot to catch them when they ventured out to walk again in the open. They listened until the regular muffled thud of hoof against grass receded. Even Fox could no longer hear it. Mowl found himself quite unable to move. His hands shook. He had eaten little since daybreak. From his satchel he produced the things Leva had thrust into his hand. The midnight blue cloak, which had wrapped the sword, was already draped over his shoulders, the sword was at his hip, and, in less than a heartbeat, the food she had brought him was in his mouth. In spite of the dampness of the day his throat was as dry as cornhusk. It almost hurt to swallow. He shared what he had with the fox, who ate ravenously. It helped. His thinking parts worked a little better after the warm bread and sour goat's cheese. It was true. All that Leva said was true. He was a hunted man. It was not just a ruse of Yani Varl's to get him away from her daughter and away from the farm-stead. He was a wanted man. He could not believe it. He was no one now, a fugitive, homeless, alone but for Fox. Just this morning he had been full of hope. Now the King himself wanted him dead. It was not fair. It was not just. It was simply the truth. He rooted further in his satchel and was pleased to discover a small flask of beer – good, unwatered beer; Leva must have grabbed it from Dake Varl's own store. He would save it for a bleaker moment. There was a small pouch of coins too. He recognised the embroidered leather bag. It was Leva's own. She would be in trouble for that. He didn't want to think about Leva. They had been friends all his life. She was his only friend long before she became something more to him. He would miss her. He let out a sigh, shaky and unsteady. He felt stronger for the food but was still afraid to leave the shelter of the rock. There was no sign of the King's man. Would the King send others? How badly did the King want him caught? He got stiffly and clumsily to his feet. He had not been captured yet. With a shake of her rain-drenched pelt, Fox followed him, back on to the road to Deworth.

He had been to Deworth only twice before, once on

market day, when they were shorthanded and once with Dake Varl. That had been a strange occasion. Dake Varl had insisted that he carry both sword and belt dagger and dress in borrowed finery for the occasion. He had visited amongst others an old family friend, an Adept of magical philosophy, a woman with an aura of power. He had been afraid of her then. He would never forget the way she'd looked at him, with a cold penetrating eye, as if she saw to the core of his soul and was unimpressed. Would he still be afraid of her now? The thought of her still chilled him, but she was not the King's Militia. What had he to be afraid of? She wasn't likely to want him dead. Perhaps he could speak to her about the fox arl? He might learn something before he made his escape from Loyrenton for ever. He quickened his step. He would rather hurry towards some goal, however vague, than hurry from Leva and the only life he had ever known.

The path between the Varl clan lands and Deworth was little more than a grassy track, well-marked by the churned mud of hoof prints and tracks of the cart. It was a half-day's walk regularly undertaken. The Varls rarely missed a market day. The landscape changed as Mowl walked on, the coarse grass of the fell became the more fertile lowland of their nearest neighbours, the Drays, the Corners and the Hayns. He was almost at the outskirts of the Drays' land before he was stopped in his tracks by the thought. Would the King's men have warned these farmers about him? He had forgotten just how close the path passed to their homesteads. It went almost through their farmyards. He felt his stomach knot again. Were there soldiers waiting for him there? There was nowhere to hide. He removed his midnight blue cloak. It was very bright against the muted colours of the autumn landscape. He dropped to his belly where the grass was high. Fox flopped down beside him. He could see men at a distance preparing the fields for the cold season seeding. He was annoyed with himself for not thinking more like a hunted man. Should he leave the path and trespass on the fields or risk the path and whatever that might bring? There were farm dogs too, half-trained, half-wild mongrel/wolf hybrids, noisy more than vicious. Their hysterical barking could be heard for a good distance. Mowl trusted that they were tied up to protect the farmstead. Mowl could hear them now. By the Keeper! He hadn't the wit of a child. Fox shivered at the sound of dogs. He gave a quick sideways look. The dogs would go wild when they scented her. They had no choice but to skirt the farms and avoid the farm workers as best they could. He slunk on hands and knees in a broad arc around the farmsteads. Mowl was caked in mud; Fox too was grey with it. The rain had stopped. It did not seem to matter. They still made slow progress. Fox kept careful pace with Mowl's own slow advance.

Just before midday, workers trooped in from the field

to the farmstead for lunch. As far as Mowl could tell there was no evidence of the Militia. They made better speed, crawling through the fields readied for planting. Their tracks were all too plain in the dark earth. What could he do? Trying not to leave handprints he slithered along the ground, supporting his weight on his forearms. He did not know what the farmers would make of it. He had never been so dirty or so wet.

They crawled to the road. His arms and knees had started to bleed and his back ached. He had to stand up to ease his limbs and stretch. He had to gamble that they were too far away from the farmstead to be seen. They were well camouflaged now, the same grey brown as the track, mud-caked from head to foot. It was not long before he smelled Deworth. Even to his human senses it was rank with the scent of chimney smoke and cooking smells, the village dung heap and the pungent aroma of fermenting hops. He smelled it long before he saw the first of the thatched homesteads. The cart track habitually used by the Varls was a kind of back door approach to Deworth. The village nestled in the hollow of the valley, unseen until Mowl reached the brow of the tree-covered hill. It was clearly visible then, lying in the shelter of the gently sloping hill, like a lamb huddled against its mother's flanks. There were perhaps twenty dwellings in the valley, arranged to face a central patch of open ground, which served as the market on market days. The buildings were not arranged in an orderly way, and from Mowl's vantage point seemed to sprawl in a ramshackle patchwork of crumbling lime wash, thatched roofs, vegetable gardens and outhouses, all surrounded by muddy paths or stepping stones. Yani Varl would have ordered things better. The same river that Mowl had fished from the safety of the Varl lands flowed here more sluggishly and was broad enough to take small craft. Two of the low thatched buildings bordering the marketplace, backed on to the river. One of them, he was sure, had offered food and drink to the market day visitors. He remembered coveting those houses, close to the market with all the excitement of visiting traders to talk to, and yet right next to the wide river and its promise of quiet solitude. It looked different today, hostile and unwelcoming. Today, he was a vagrant and a fugitive from the King's justice.

He hadn't remembered the village layout quite as well as he thought he had. He had remembered that the fishermen and less prosperous villagers lived in the troglodyte caves that pockmarked the orange-tinted cliffs of the region. He had been fascinated by the haphazard arrangements of steps and the irregular doors and windows that characterised them. What he'd forgotten was that they lay on the opposite side of the wide river, a boat ride away. He had thought they were nearer. It would be difficult to cross the river without being seen. He had a sudden flash of recollection – the Adept with her aura of power and strangeness – standing in the doorway of just such a cave. How had he forgotten that detail? He had no memory of crossing the river, and yet he must have done so. What else had he forgotten about that visit?

Now that he had reached Deworth he felt more than a little lost. He didn't want to crawl into the village; he was not sure his torn elbows and grazed knees would bear his weight, but he dare not walk there either. He was too tall, too muddy, too much a stranger, far too conspicuous. He was also too far away to see more than the broad outlines of the settlement. He needed to get a better view, but did not want to be seen until he had a better idea of what to do. Leva had said to get a boat; well, that was fine but how did one go about it? Nothing in his extensive studies and sheltered life was of much use to him.

He glanced at the fox, who was watching him with a strangely intense stare. Maybe the Adept would help him? *If* he could reach her. He had only met her for a moment, two or three summers previously, yet he had felt the impact of her presence in the very marrow of his bones. She had looked him right in the eye and said something in the southern language he had not known well at that time. He remembered the hairs on his neck rising in her presence as iron filings lift in the presence of a lodestone. Perhaps he could use his own small talent to reach her in the ether. Perhaps if she knew he was there she might help? She was a person of power, and he had never felt more powerless. It was a measure of his desperation and his exhaustion that he even thought that way. He felt cold at the thought of seeing her again, but had no other ideas. He crossed his stiff legs and began to breathe deeply in an effort to sense the spiritual emanations of her presence. He almost gasped at the force of what he felt. It was like a lightning bolt in his head, a sudden pain behind his eyes that made him dizzy and sick. If he had not been sitting down he would have thought he was about to fall over. Nothing like that had ever happened to him before. Was this the Adept's doing? Was this the force of the Adept's spirit? He felt as though his thoughts, feelings, his very self, had been raked over like an empty field, in the space of a heartbeat. He had shut his eyes at the brutal intensity of it and when he opened them he saw that Fox was gone from his side. The shock of the force of his experience dimmed his vision, as if he'd just looked into the sun. His eyes watered. When his sight recovered he saw why Fox had gone. A man in the livery of the Militia, scarlet and blue, was striding powerfully uphill towards him. His queasiness intensified. He stood up awkwardly though his knees threatened to buckle under him. He would at least meet his fate, upright, like a man. Was he done for so soon?

Chapter 7

Deworth: Day 3 (Evening)

Fox watched the large bearded stranger close in on Mowl. Should she run? She noted the long sword at his waist and the conical metal helmet he wore over a scarlet balaclava. The balaclava was covered in small metal rings. There was a word for that kind of thing, a word she knew – chain mail. She felt a swift flicker of pleasure at her cleverness in remembering the word. The man wore a lot of chain mail. He was wearing a knee-length tunic of the stuff over the top of a long, scarlet, woollen shirt. He had dark greyish-blue woollen stockings and short leather boots. A long and damp cloak of a faded midnight blue was draped over his broad shoulders. The cloak was embroidered with some kind of crest, but she could make no sense of the symbol. Karen had never seen anyone dressed like that before. She was certain of it. Her memory was less than perfect but she was certain of it. His costume was a uniform and the uniform was military. In her experience soldiers carried guns not swords and wore combat fatigues not chain mail. This was a very great wrongness. Her fox's heart raced. The world spun round her. She was very afraid. There were too many discrepancies between what was and what she was sure should be. The number of burning, unanswered questions was rising all the time: Who was she? Where was she? What was she doing here? A fourth question flitted transiently across her agitated thoughts. When was she? Her fox self was not interested in questions and could not form hypotheses. She hesitated only for a moment, straining to hear what the man said to Mowl, eager to hear what was going on, anxious to hide from danger, torn between curiosity and vulpine caution. It was an unequal battle; her mind was slave to her fox body. The soldier might hurt her. She ran for the cover of the bushes. She was very hungry. Maybe when she had eaten she would be able to work it out. She could hear the commanding voice of the scarlet stranger even in her temporary retreat. She could not understand his words either. She had truly lost the power to understand human speech. Only the sharpness of hunger distracted her from a poignant sense of loss.

'You are late, Sar. We've been waiting for you.' The soldier looked Mowl up and down. He saw a tall, lean-framed spectre, grey with mud, wet and stinking with it. 'You're not what I expected. I hope you've got your own stuff with you because there's nothing here and our orders were to wait for you before we got under way. There will be no time to clean yourself up.'

The man was talking gibberish. Mowl, shocked, could not make sense of it. He gaped at the man, uncomprehending. He understood the words but they made no sense. He had run and walked and crawled from the Varl lands only to find himself before the very thing he'd been striving to avoid; a King's man. In the part of his mind that still worked he was shocked that there were Militiamen in Deworth; it was an important local centre but what were soldiers doing here? He was confused by the amicable way the man addressed him. He'd imagined a very different confrontation, a swift arrest and then the gallows. Even the thought made him swallow hard. He was bemused. Then it struck him. The soldier was expecting someone and assumed that Mowl was that someone. Should he, could he play along? Fortunately, the soldier did not demand any response from him but led the way down the hill towards the shore of the river. He talked about the arrival of stone blocks and masons from Genden as if it was relevant to Mowl. Mowl followed with an unsteady, stumbling gait. Mowl's limbs were stiff and awkward. He was still trying to work out what was going on. They skirted the village, walking instead towards some flat stony land bordering the river, the flood plain of the River Varla, from which the Varls had taken their name.

Something was going on. There was the sound of raised voices. At least twenty soldiers blocked Mowl's view. They lounged around the pebble shale of the riverbank, watching as one of their number argued with some older workmen from the village. The soldiers looked relaxed, amused even, but Mowl noted that they all wore mail shirts and helmets and that their swords gleamed at their hips. They could afford to look amused. They jumped to their feet when they heard Mowl's companion coming. Their smiles disappeared like pictures in the sand. The lone soldier arguing with the villagers looked uncomfortable. There was a red flush to his neck. He looked no older than Mowl himself. Two of the workmen were standing so close to the soldier that he had to keep stepping back so that the pebbles rattled under his feet. He looked out of his depth. Mowl could sense the edge of violence in the salty air. A cold wind blew in from the estuary. He shivered. Everyone stopped when they saw Mowl and the bearded soldier.

'Sergeant Kreek, Sar, I was just explaining ...'

Kreek waved the young man away. He slunk gratefully back to the ranks of his companions, though the angry flush of his face took a while to cool. Kreek had everyone's attention. His voice as he addressed the gathering was not loud but rang with authority.

'I've found our man. This is Sar Venish, the scribe

63

from Devonbourne. I have a full set of instructions here, which Sar Venish can relate to us. On the King's instructions we will be building temples throughout the region – they will all be built to the same pattern and the quantity and price of all requirements has been worked out on the tariff sheet by the King's own adviser, Hale Garnem. Sar Venish, here, is also empowered to levy the temple tax from Deworth and its outlying farms, and don't be taken in by his youth – we are here to make sure that it all goes smoothly.' At this point he glanced meaningfully at the soldiers, now in line, silent and alert. 'We are prepared to use local labour and pay a standard rate of two grunen a day plus a quart of ale and soldier's rations. Tomorrow, Sar Venish will inspect the village to work out the tax due. It will be taken in goods or grunen – talen if any have such coins. It will be collected fairly and in proportion to your means. Go back to your homes and spread the news through the village.'

The workmen did not move, but their indecision was evident in their posture. The muscled bulk of Sergeant Kreek and his cold, dispassionate eyes had a persuasive authority. They were afraid of him. Mowl needed no special sensitivity to see that. They weren't alone in their fear either – Sergeant Kreek emanated well-controlled but violent potency. He rooted in a large, official-looking saddlebag on the ground and pulled out a rolled parchment. He raised his voice again.

'Here is the proclamation sealed with the royal seal.'

One of the villagers stepped forward to inspect the design stamped in sealing wax, the colour of dried blood. Mowl recognised the man, he was a carpenter and well-regarded as a skilled craftsmen. He had made the Goodwife's chairs at the farm. The carpenter studied the seal carefully and then nodded at the other villagers.

'It's his seal right enough, but what does it say?' He was uneasy at this invasion of his village but much less inclined to argue with the sergeant than with his men. Kreek handed the parchment to Mowl. If there had been a moment to explain that Mowl was not Sar Venish, that moment was gone. Who else could he claim to be? He could not admit to being Mowl Speare that was certain. Mowl's courage failed under Sergeant Kreek's ice-blue gaze. He wiped his muddy hands on his jerkin and squinted at the parchment, taking care to raise it so that he could not meet the carpenter's anxious eyes. He could only hope that the carpenter would not recognise him as Dake Varl's one-time shepherd. What would he do when the real Sar Venish arrived? He could not think about that now. He became aware of the terrible, attentive silence as everyone present waited for him. Mowl licked dry lips. Both the townspeople and the soldiers looked at him respectfully, ignoring his mud-soaked garments and filthy face. Mowl carefully broke the seal of the parchment and cleared his suddenly parched throat. What else could he do?

The scroll was written, rather unhelpfully, in High Loyren, the language of the court. He read it through aloud. He was hesitant at first. His voice sounded very thin and solitary in the open air but then he warmed to his task and did the best job he could. The blank expressions on the faces of the villagers confirmed his suspicion. No one in Deworth spoke High Loyren. From the look on the sergeant's face, he was little wiser than the villagers. It was an almost too extraordinary coincidence that the delayed Sar Venish was a scribe, for there was no other skill at which Mowl so excelled. He could not have posed as a stonemason or even a soldier with any conviction, but this, this he could do well. He took a deep breath and began again.

'That is to say, in the common tongue: By order of King Flane of the United Kingdoms of Loyrenton, henceforth to be known as "His Highness the King Keeper of the Purple Path", all inhabitants of Loyrenton will be taxed according to their standing and estate to fund the building of temples throughout the land to the glory of the Keeper and the Purple Path.' There was a lot of additional courtly long-windedness, which Mowl refrained from translating. That was the crux of it and that was quite bad enough in the eyes of the villagers. The doctrine of the Purple Path was a minority philosophy, derived from the work of the largely ignored scholar, Capetan. It held that the only tier of existence that counted for anything was the tier of the natural man. Mowl knew about it, of course, from his studies but it was not the belief of the people of Loyrenton, especially not in Deworth. The villagers looked scarcely less bemused than they had before. They looked at one another as if for reassurance. Fear and concern clouded their faces as they began to recognise that they were utterly at the mercy of these armed men. Most men made a living in Deworth but not a rich living. In a hard winter many would be hungry until spring. It was obvious to all of them that if their meagre goods were taxed then some of them would die. Mowl saw that realisation in their grim looks, their tight-lipped expressions. The carpenter did not know what to say. At length he blurted out: 'Does the Goodwife know of this?'

Goodwife Linton owned the large, fertile estate, which stretched from Deworth across as far as Heverby. For years the Lintons had run Deworth as part of their private fiefdom. If the Goodwife did not want her village to pay tax to the King then she would make sure that they did not.

The sergeant made eye contact with each of the villagers in turn before speaking. They all shifted a little under his uncompromising stare. 'Sar Linton is installed at the Castle of Maybury, at the Queen's pleasure. I believe the Goodwife is busy trying to arrange for a Royal pardon.'

There was an audible angry gasp from the villagers. Mowl found that he was speaking. Where was his wisdom? But he shared the villager's outrage.

'What is the charge?'

The sergeant turned to look at him, one dark eyebrow slightly raised.

'But surely, even in Devonbourne, you hear the news. He is accused of treason against the King and apostasy against the Purple Path.' Kreek gave Mowl a hard look. 'Perhaps you were travelling when the news came?'

Mowl felt foolish. He was in too much danger to ally himself with these villagers. Mowl hated to see the beaten expressions on their faces as they realised their impotence. If the Goodwife could not help them no one could. This should not be happening. He couldn't help them, he knew that, and they wouldn't help him. He was on his own and he had to find a way to get away before Kreek found out who he really was. First he needed to find Fox. She was in danger so close to the village. He was distracted by that thought. He even forgot his own exposed position for a moment. He jumped when Kreek spoke. Kreek noticed. He had very penetrating eyes. Mowl was certain that he knew he was a fraud.

'I suppose you'll be needing a drink and, perhaps, a wash. I have some private papers for you here, which you will need to see before tomorrow. I believe there is an inn of sorts here where you can stay.' Mowl nodded dumbly. Though he was sure the real Sar Venish would have responded less nervously, Kreek's fearsome presence seemed to rob Mowl of his wits. Kreek's eyes bored into Mowl's. 'I will call for you at daybreak.'

Kreek indicated the house, which Mowl had visited before. Mowl wished he had a hat to pull over his eyes, anything more substantial than a mere layer of dirt to disguise him. He was shaking again and he was certain that Kreek would notice. Mowl felt sure that if he were to be recognised anywhere it would be at the inn. He accepted the papers Kreek gave him with a quick nod of acknowledgement and a tremor of panic in his guts. Every thing he did as Sar Venish got him into further trouble. He wished he'd been quick enough to pretend to be someone else, not Mowl Speare obviously, but some innocent who could have passed through Deworth quietly and without fuss and now be on the way to the south. Leva used to say 'If wishes were grain, we'd all want for nothing.' Leva! She wouldn't have got herself into such a mess. She had too much sense. He bowed his head, as much from sudden homesickness as from an urge to disguise himself, and made his way to the village inn.

Chapter 8

The Adept Acts: Day 3 (Night) – Day 4 (Dawn)

Karen Fox dozed under a bush until darkness fell. By then her whole world had shrunk to the size of the gaping hole in her belly. She had to eat. There was plenty of food about. The smell of stew on the cold air, the warm poultry smell of chickens, the rotten, putrid smell of carrion all made her crazed and careless. There was water trapped on a shallow indentation on the rock. It had the musty taste of lichen. She did not care. She slunk on her empty belly towards the nearest smallholding. It was quite dark. No neon lights bled away the blackness of the night to turn it plum-coloured. The only light leaking from the shuttered windows was the warm yellow candlelight, which flickered like a TV screen. This was a wrongness too but it was a beautiful wrongness. She had not thought foxes could see colour, but *she* could. Even the monochrome night was not really monochrome, but a visual feast of great subtlety. Not that any of that mattered. She needed food. It was awkward, unlatching the door to the raised wooden hen house without hands. Her paws were useless, stiff and inflexible, but the soft parts of her mouth and tongue were pliable and, if she was prepared to tolerate the bitterness of the taste of wood and the risk of splinters, she knew she could work it free. She was prepared to risk almost anything to be rid of the tyrant, hunger. There. She broke the neck of the bird with one swift bite and warm, metallic-tasting blood and feathers filled her mouth. Adrenalin sang through her body as she ran for her hideout before the men came to see what the fuss was about. She felt a surge of wild happiness at the thought of her feast and the taste of it and the smell of it and the richness of the night and her own fleet feet.

Mowl sat by the fire, his eyes streaming as the woodsmoke from damp timbers filled the small room. He'd never spent much time indoors. As far as he could see it offered few advantages. He had washed the worst of the mud off in the river and was drying by the fire, but he still felt cold – inside as well as out. It could not be long before his lie would be discovered. Perhaps Sergeant Kreek had power enough to hang him on his own authority. Would it be any more terrible to end his days dropped from a Deworth tree than to hang in some other place? He should run away into the night, but he would not go without Fox. It was a simple truth and Mowl did not know how it had come about, but in the brief time he had spent with the arl she had become more important to him than he could reasonably explain, even by his interest in all things of the spiritual tier. He did not try to explain it. He could not go without Fox and he did not know where she was. So he would stay in Deworth and in danger until he found her. He tried to disguise his discomfort and did his best to impersonate Sar Venish.

The room had a table and stool but the combined light of fire and candle did little to help his tired eyes decipher the messages to Sar Venish. They were in none of the languages he knew. He suspected they were in code but the large meal he'd eaten and the good ale he'd drunk had made his mind slow. The innkeeper's daughter was not as pretty as Leva, few girls were, but she smiled at him coquettishly. He'd drunk more than he'd wanted to because she'd kept filling up his tankard. The sounds of conversation grew more distant and confused in his mind. He thought he heard the carpenter's friend say, between puffs on his pipe, that there was a fox nearby that had got one of his chickens. He wanted to ask about what had happened, find out if the fox was all right, but his tongue felt heavy and clumsy in his mouth. He'd been drugged, as he'd drugged Fox. There was balance in that. By the time he recognised his symptoms it was too late. He should have known no loyal daughter of Deworth would smile so invitingly at King Flane's tax collector.

When he came round his head hurt dully. He almost cried out when he tried to move it; a piercing pain behind his eyes left him breathless. It made him keep very still. There was a strong smell of salt, fish and warm decay. His arms were bound. He opened his eyes fractionally, and tried to take in as much as he could without moving his head. He was in a cave. A huge wood fire burned in a grate, but no smoke filled the chamber. The air was damp and clear. Strings of herbs and salted fish hung from the ceiling like creepers hanging from a tree. Cautiously, he tried to attune himself to emanations, but his thinking muscles felt fatigued and strangely tender as if they had been under some attack while he had slept. The pain in his head got worse. He did not groan. He did not want to show that he was awake. By the Keeper, what was going on now?

'You're awake then, Sar Speare?' The mocking tone and title told him that he was recognised. Technically, he was Sar Speare, the only survivor of the Speare family, heir to a traitor and the death penalty. He swallowed hard and painfully. What was his captor going to do to him?

Mowl said nothing in reply. He didn't recognise the voice. It was female and not young. He did not want to compromise himself further. He felt horribly vulnerable, tied up and groggy. There was a bitter taste in his mouth and sickness not far behind.

He became accustomed to the gloom. He could identify three figures, the pipe-smoking carpenter's friend, the carpenter and a woman, the Adept, the friend of Dake Varl. It was her voice that he'd heard. His fear intensified. He had not forgotten his experience on the hillside. If the Adept were the source of that lightning bolt emanation that had so raked his whole being, he would almost rather face Sergeant Kreek's sword than the Adept's ire. Why was she against him? He had hoped she might help him for Dake Varl's sake. What was he going to do now? Nothing obvious presented itself. He struggled to remain still and silent under the twin assaults of hopelessness and fear.

The Adept was speaking again, this time to her two companions. Her voice was low but angry. Mowl strained to hear what she said.

'Go home! You can't take such foolish risks again with the Militia everywhere. You'll get us all killed. Go home and stay low. You'd better come back at dawn – say your wife needs a poultice or something – I might have worked out what to do with him. Don't risk anything like this again. The King and Hale Garnem are nervous already – any hint of organised resistance and a lot more people will die. This isn't even King Flane's man. I'm surprised you didn't recognise him. He's gained a few spans and a beard, but surely you can see – his eyes are unchanged. This is Sar Varl's shepherd! He's no tax collector and I want to know what he thinks he's up to, pretending to be one. I don't like this at all. Go home!'

With a worried, anxious glance at Mowl the men left. The Adept dismissed the men from her mind as surely as she dismissed them from her presence. Mowl was her problem now. Mowl's skills had grown as she thought they might, years ago when she had first met him. She did not need an untrained talent around. She had to guard her thoughts too closely when there were other Adepts around. More than that she had heard of his inherited conviction for treachery. She made it her job to hear all such things. She did not need a convicted traitor pretending to be a King's man in her village. There were too many secrets there already. By the Keeper, what should she do with him, Mant Speare's son? She strained the herbal drink she had made for herself and sipped it absently. She was getting older and it took a lot of strength to blunt the young man's sensitivities so that he would not sense her emanations as she sensed his. Was there a way to let him live and have him help her? If there was she could not think of it. In war there were casualties, but some were to be regretted more than others.

'Mowl Speare, do you remember me?'

Mowl nodded, his throat still too dry from the drugged ale for him to speak easily. He coughed and did his best. 'I met you when I was with Dake Varl. I was going to look for you. I'm wanted for treason. I thought you might be able to help me get away and...' His voice croaked. He hesitated for a moment. Should he trust her? 'I found a fox.' He had to say it. This woman was an Adept, she could not harm an arl. Adepts were by oath dedicated to the protection of all souls, incarnated or otherwise. It was hard to speak. He was terribly thirsty.

'A fox?'

'I think she's an arl. I wanted to bring her to you. Dake Varl said you studied at the Boyaine. I thought you might know?'

The Adept Laine was stunned. This she had not expected. She poured him a tankard of cold water and helped him drink it so that he could continue. She was not ready to free him yet.

'Where is this ... *arl*?'

Mowl drank deeply of the cool liquid, poured somewhat ineptly down his throat and chin.

'She was here, in the village – I don't know where she is now. I hope she's safe.'

'What made you think she was an arl?'

Mowl paused; now that he tried to define that something in her essential substance that was different, he struggled to find the words.

'I cannot say, maybe it was her emanations – I just knew.' He did not wish to say more. He did not want to confess his lifetime fascination with arls in case this woman thought he had persuaded himself he'd found one just because he wanted to. Fox *was* an arl. He knew it. Belatedly, he regretted mentioning Fox. Why could he discern no emanations here? He should have done – had she blocked his perceptions? Why would an Adept do that? He didn't think that they were allowed to do that. It was wrong, as wrong as invading another's thoughts. Sluggish though he was, he recognised that this Adept was a very dangerous woman – an Adept who did not play by the rules. The thought sent a further chill through him. What did she want from him?

He tried to keep himself outwardly calm and relaxed while she paced the cave. He knew that when faced with a dangerous creature it was foolish to show fear. He schooled his face into impassivity – that was the proper way to behave in front of such a one as the Adept. He made himself pretend that he trusted this woman. He forced himself to be calm. At length she stopped her pacing and sat cross-legged before the fire, in the position of deepest contemplation. It was the position his tutor had taught him to adopt to find the equilibrium within. He saw her face go blank and wondered if he too looked so slack-faced and vulnerable when seeking to feel the emanations of the spiritual plane. Even through his strange numbness he sensed her strength. He had made a mistake to tell her about Fox.

Mowl struggled fruitlessly against his bonds until his shoulders ached. There was no escape. Eventually, he fell into a light doze. In his half conscious state he sensed the Adept listening to some distant emanation he could not quite perceive. He dreamed that he heard the lost, lonely cry of an abandoned lamb. The lamb was deep in a crevasse and he could not reach her. His hand was only a span away from touching her, freeing her, and his own voice whispered, 'It's all right, I'll find a way to save you.'

He woke with a start to find the fire all but burnt out and the Adept uncrossing her legs and stretching. She gave him a calculating look.

'I found your fox. You are right. She is no ordinary fox. I cannot honestly say if she is an arl. She is a spirit trapped and somehow hurt. I do not think that her current form is her natural incarnation, and each moment she lives as a fox, her true spirit weakens further. I sense a deep sickness within her. At Boyaine they taught us that an arl can live only twenty-four days without Transformation. An arl that cannot Transform dies.' She sounded regretful. Dawn must have been breaking because he could see her face emerging from the gloom of the cave. She did not look dangerous but old, worn with exhaustion and grey as a spectre from the tier of the unmanifest. She spoke softly. 'I am not an expert on these matters, I abandoned my studies a long time ago to concentrate on less recondite matters. There is a Succeptor in Lerry. You know what a Succeptor is?'

Mowl had studied such things but dare not speak, for fear of saying the wrong thing. He shrugged minutely, hoping she would carry on.

'A boy like you should not be so ignorant.' She clicked her tongue in irritation but she did continue. 'An Adept is adept at hearing the spiritual emanations of many creatures. A Succeptor is a healer who heals through unique sympathy with those emanations. A Succeptor feels what the patient feels and knows what must be done to heal them through uniquely secret rituals and magicks. It's an ability so rare that, in the whole of Loyrenton, only Georgil of Lerry can truly claim the gift. He is the only one who might help you. If you could get this "fox" to him fast enough you might have a chance to save her, but even then she may be too damaged to Transform.' The Adept looked sad. 'I did not know arls too could suffer.' The Adept stood up. 'I'm going to give you a chance, Mant Speare's son. You must run away as fast as you can; while you stay here, you put dear friends and important plans at risk. You are in great danger and I cannot protect you. Take Sar Venish's papers – I want nothing of them. Find your arl, she is in the bushes on the hill above the village, and head for

Lerry.' She hesitated and Mowl had the distinct impression that she wrestled with her conscience. 'You are not in alignment, you two, but I think you could find the right resonance. If you each drink two or three drops of this, it might help, but it must be taken in a place of safety because it will make you sleep. She may be an arl or she may be something else. The Succeptor may help or he may not. The Keeper of Balances will use you as is fitting in the cause of equilibrium. He will keep you safe or he will not. That is all my faith. Hurry!' She pressed a small bottle into Mowl's hand and pushed him out of the cave.

The light was poor. Paddles were breaking the still waters with a musical, scarcely audible, splash – someone was coming! He clambered down the steep steps, carved from the rock like the Adept's cave and, keeping to the deeper darkness of the cliff's shadow, crept away. He was not dead yet. He could not quite believe his good fortune. His head still felt muzzy, his thinking slow, but he could remember the Adept's words clearly. Was it luck or the benisons of the Keeper that had brought him to the Adept's cave? He had a purpose now – to live, yes, but to live to find Georgil, the Succeptor of Lerry and save Fox.

Chapter 9

The Sergeant Acts: Days 4 – 5

S ergeant Kreek was angry. Sar Venish had vanished. The villagers claimed to know nothing of his disappearance, but something was going on. The carpenter, who seemed to be the villagers' unofficial spokesman, had suggested that he speak to the Adept Laine. The sergeant mistrusted wise women almost as much as he distrusted priests. While he toyed with meeting the first, a fine example of the second had ridden into the village, all purple cloak and haughty manners. He came with orders from the King's High Priest to begin his ministry immediately with or without a temple. Kreek liked neither the priest nor his orders. There was a time when he'd been proud to be a soldier. He'd fought for Queen Lin and the freedom of Loyrenton; villagers had cheered when he rode by. He did not like the way these villagers looked at him now.

His mood was not improved when the youthful priest,

Domus Cantus, brimming with self-importance, demanded to accompany him to the Adept's cave. No one who knew Kreek would ever call him sensitive, except in his uncanny gift for predicting trouble, but he needed no uncommon skill to see that the villagers were unlikely to be impressed by Domus Cantus. It was a wet morning. The priest's finery was already looking bedraggled if not a little ridiculous. Kreek carefully wrapped his own cloak over his mail coat. Driving rain and salt air played havoc with the metal. He checked his sword to be certain that it still slid easily from its sheath even in the bad weather. It moved freely with a familiar rasp. The sound was obscurely comforting. He did not have a good feeling about this visit. With growing trepidation, he and the priest stepped into the small wooden ferry that would take them across the river.

The priest curled his nose at the strong reek of fish and damp timber. He lifted his long cloak to prevent it trailing in the small heap of entrails lying on the shale. Someone had been gutting fish. That's what they did here. Kreek watched the gesture with contempt. The priest was a courtier all right. Kreek had come across the type before – useless except for fermenting trouble. Not for the first time Kreek earnestly wished that he had been posted somewhere else.

The Adept had been expecting them. Adepts had that gift. It was one of the reasons Kreek mistrusted them.

The cave was warm and dry. The Adept Laine greeted them with great cordiality, speaking to the priest in High Loyren. She was clearly a well-educated woman. They refused the drink she offered, though it was tempting. Kreek did not yet know her loyalties, and a young man, Sar Venish, had disappeared. The sergeant's neck hair prickled in the woman's presence, an augury of trouble. He took charge.

'Sorry for calling on you uninvited but the villagers thought you might know where the tax collector is? Sar Venish they call him – young, scurvy-looking. Have you seen him?'

The woman smiled so that previously unnoticed wrinkles creased her face. There was little humour in her smile.

'I have never met Sar Venish.'

The priest looked around the small cave with evident distaste.

'She is an Adept. They have no use for truth. She lies!' He spat the accusation with so much venom, it surprised Kreek. It was not considered seemly to show emotion in courtly circles. The priest should have displayed better self-control.

The Adept turned hard eyes on Domus Cantus and spoke in a voice of creditable calm.

'I assure you, Sar, that I serve the Keeper in all things, and lies never accomplish his will.'

Kreek responded. 'So you have not seen the young man who arrived here yesterday?'

'That is not what I said.'

'See how these superstitious witches twist the very words they use!' The priest's vehement interjection was most extraordinary, but Kreek chose to ignore it.

The priest's face was crimson with emotion. A vein pulsed in his temple like a fat, purple worm.

'Would you explain?' Kreek asked the Adept in the same even tone that she had adopted.

The Adept smiled again. 'Isn't it obvious? That young man was not Sar Venish.'

'Go on.'

The Adept paused. She was not anxious to see Mowl die but she dared not protect him. There was too much else at stake. She had done what she could to give him a chance at survival. If the Keeper wished to use him, she commended him to his hands, the Adept of Deworth could do no more for him.

'Sergeant, you do not seem as well-informed as I might have expected. The young man who arrived yesterday was the renegade, Mowl Speare. Before you leap after him in hot pursuit, I would urge caution – it may be that he is, in some way, protected by the Keeper. It would not be good to kill such a one. He travels with an arl – an extraordinary sign of favour, don't you think?'

She smiled, a confident, knowing smile to hide her uncertainty. May the Keeper forgive her if she'd done wrong.

'She lies! There are no arls; the tiers of the unborn are children's tales. She is an evil witch, consecrated to superstition. She is condemned from her own mouth!'

The priest screamed the words with manic fervour and, before Kreek was fully aware of the danger, had unsheathed his belt knife. It glinted, orange in the light of the fire. The priest leaped nimbly forward, crossing in two strides the small space between himself and the woman. He grabbed her. With one wiry arm he had caught the woman round her chest and pulled her against him, so that her bony back was held tight and hard against his own chest. Her head thrashed briefly and feebly, just catching the priest's chin. The woman scarcely had time to scream before in one unexpectedly deft motion, the priest slit her throat with his free hand. Blood spurted everywhere. She fell in a ragged red-streaked heap at Kreek's feet. Her dead eyes showed only surprise. Kreek moved instinctively, but too late. He disarmed the priest and locked his arms behind his back. The priest's small frame was wiry with the strength of youth, but he was easily overpowered by the large sergeant.

'What did you do that for?' Kreek was shocked and angrier than he could remember being for a long time.

He had to fight the urge to teach the priest a violent lesson of his own.

'Orders from the High Priest. We are to usher in a new era, without superstition, without Adepts and their flummery. I serve the glory of His Highness the King, Keeper of the Purple Path.'

Kreek let the madman go. It was likely that he told the truth. He controlled his fury at the priest, his order and the regime they served. He was only a soldier after all and orders were orders.

'Do not draw a weapon in my presence again or I cannot guarantee that it will not next be sheathed in your own person.' The sergeant's formal speech, level tone and cold eyes cooled the fervour of the priest. Kreek noted that the youth's hand shook a little and he could not look at the face of his victim.

'Do priests of the Purple Path perform burial rites?'

'Of course.'

'Good, then you can ready this body for burial. I will send some of my men to help you. I must leave in search of this Mowl Speare. The Adept gave us good information – she might have helped us further.' Kreek surveyed the bloody mess on the floor. 'There is not much more that can be done here anyway before the arrival of the real Sar Venish.'

'But I must begin to meet my congregation. I cannot stay here.' Horror was in the priest's voice.

'I'm sure your congregation will flock to meet *you*, Sar, when they hear of what you've done to their revered Adept.'

'She was a treacherous witch!'

Kreek said nothing.

The young priest looked a little pale. He seemed to have trouble focusing on the Adept's remains. His startled eyes kept straying away from his handiwork, as if reluctant to acknowledge what lay there. It was one thing to kill an evil witch, quite another to clean the blood from the corpse of an old woman. She looked frail and ordinary in death. A sack of bones, simply dressed, white hair like thistledown, loose around her face. Her small mouth was slightly open. The priest's expensive purple cloak was soaked with dark blood. The floor of the cave was slick with it where the woman had fallen.

A sudden thought struck Kreek as he turned to leave.

'May I ask you, priest, where is the Adept now?'

'What do you mean?'

'I have killed many men, but I have always believed that each of them crossed to the tier of the unmanifest. What do you say?'

The priest swallowed hard. 'I would say that she is dead. There is no tier of the unmanifest.'

'Is that what you will tell the villagers?'

The young man nodded.

'And you think this will make you … popular?'

'It makes me right. That's all that matters.'

Mowl was hungry, tired, thirsty and lost. He had walked
a way upstream to the ford. It was not far but he had
made heavy work of it. He was afraid that by the time
he'd crossed back to Fox's side of the river she might
have gone, fearing herself abandoned by him. Maybe she
had been killed for stealing chickens or killed just in case
she stole chickens? Thinking of her vulnerability made
him less frightened for himself. He had to save her. His
head still did not feel properly affixed to his shoulders.
The drug the serving girl had given him had left him
with a powerful hangover. It was late afternoon by the
time he'd crossed the ford. He found a handful of berries
in the thorn bushes. They were the kind that he'd only
ever eaten cooked before. He dared not stop to light a
fire though their bitterness raw made them an unpleasant snack. By the time he'd drunk something from the
river and resumed his furtive progress in the cover of the
trees, he realised why those particular berries were
always eaten cooked. He was violently and spectacularly
ill – sicker than he had ever been in his life. He was afraid
to be seen and he could not go on so he crawled into a
shallow hollow under a hedgerow. It was close and dry
and he could shelter there until the pain and sickness
ceased. He was still there when darkness came. Weak
from the emetic effect of the berries and bent double to

ease the griping pains in his belly, he spent the cold night in exhausted, disturbed slumber. He was in despair. He needed to get away quickly and could do nothing but lie there weaker than a new-born lamb. In his dreams he had himself become a fox running chest-deep through mud while Kreek and a pack of ravening wolves pursued him.

He woke with a start. His neck was stiff. He was cold and the acrid taste and sour stench of his own dried vomit drove him to stagger to his feet and wash his face in the river. The clean, icy water helped. He was a little unsteady on his feet but he could stand and shiver and maybe walk a little further. Dare he beg for food at one of the farmhouses he knew were not far away? He was tempted to seek out the distinctive strangeness of the fox's emanations but he was afraid. The Adept might hear him and though she had let him go he knew that she was not his friend. He would have to trust to Fox's superior perceptions to find him, if she had a mind to. He thought she would seek him out, but why he thought that he did not know. Thinking of Fox and the Adept made him shiver all the more. Perhaps he should risk setting a fire. He walked back to the copse of trees and bushes where he had spent the night. There was plenty of wood around though most of it was still wet from yesterday's rain. He knew all too well the dangers of becoming too cold. He was hardy and strong but he knew that if he did not find food and warmth soon he would not survive the journey to Lerry. His stomach felt sore and empty – apart from the berries, he had not eaten since the drugged meal in the inn two nights ago and he had not eaten well for the day before that. A noise in the bushes alerted him to danger; his hand strayed to his sword's hilt, not that he was in any state to fight. He loosened it a little in its scabbard with one hand while the other went for his belt knife. Dake Varl had trained him in the arts of war, as part of the farm defence corps. He'd practised with a sword and knife every day of his life. Dake Varl did not believe in shields and had encouraged him to fight with either hand. The branches of the trees and bushes were too dense for sword work. His knife would be more use though it was not as sharp. His breathing was too loud. It sounded as if he'd been running across hard ground for half a day. He held his breath and controlled the palsied shaking in his knees and hands. Someone else was breathing raggedly, panting. It was coming closer. He prayed to the Keeper and balanced his weight a little better, ready to lunge forward and pre-empt an attack. Here it was!

Fox! She looked less sleek, less perfect than she had looked before. Her coat glowed less brightly; she looked more like a fox of the natural tier, but she was still Fox. He felt an unexpected lump in his throat as he fell to his knees to stroke her intelligent head. She did not prevent him and even brushed against his legs as a domesticated dog might do.

'Fox,' he whispered, 'I was so afraid you were lost.'

He wanted to hug her to him but was worried he might startle her. She tilted her head as if straining to understand him. They stayed like that for a moment just looking at each other. He was so relieved to see her, though what Fox thought he couldn't judge. Now she was here they could try to get away. He was grateful not to have to return to Deworth. He did not really see how he could have evaded capture there. With Fox found, escape seemed possible again.

Mowl found another secluded spot screened from the river by foliage. He gathered the driest wood he could find and knew that he was favoured by the Keeper when he managed to tickle a fat grountfish almost at once. Mowl took the risk of building a small fire to cook the fish and warm his still shaking body. Fox feasted on carrion. Mowl could smell the decay on her breath but did not care. When he had eaten he felt better, more resolute, though he still did not feel strong. They ought to move on, put miles between them and Deworth as the Adept had said. Then he remembered the small bottle the Adept had given him. What would the liquid do to attune them? Might it bond the arl to him in some way? Would it be right to try to bind her? He opened it and sniffed it suspiciously. It had a strange and bitter perfume. He placed three drops in the palm of his hand and licked it off his palm, and repeated the gesture, offering it to the fox. She sniffed it cautiously, then followed his lead and licked it clean. He felt that she knew what she was doing. They looked at each other. Nothing happened. Fox sneezed. The liquid numbed Mowl's tongue a little, its taste as sour as the fruit that had made him so ill. The fox's eyes seemed a little glassy-looking. She closed them and lay down at his feet. He hoped that she was not hurt. He lay down beside her and, covering them both with the midnight blue cloak from his satchel, he gave himself up to sleep.

Horse's hooves woke him. Horse's hooves galloping nearby. He staggered to his feet, groping for his knife, trying to remember where he was and what was going on. It was dusk. Fox was gone. He was totally disoriented and moved groggily towards the galloping hooves. Maybe it was Leva bringing him food after a hard day's lambing. Within a heartbeat he'd realised his mistake. It was Sergeant Kreek bringing only his sword after a hard day's tracking. Kreek's voice was low and deeply menacing.

'You lied to me, lad. No one lies to me.'

The man dismounted. He was very heavily built, much as Dake Varl would have been in his prime. He had long arms and a long reach. Mowl had no time to be afraid. He gathered his wits remarkably quickly.

Sergeant Kreek wanted to kill him. It was written plainly in his eyes. It would take Mowl all his skill and courage to stop him. He prayed fervently and silently that he had recovered his strength sufficiently to defend himself. He unsheathed his sword. It was well weighted and finely made. It was a better sword than he had ever used before. Maybe that would make a difference.

Chapter 10

First Understanding: Day 5

Karen Fox felt strange. She had woken in a state of total disorientation. There was a brief moment of shock when she saw the fox paws in front of her and for a split second she almost remembered what other thing she had once been. The shock was swiftly replaced with relief. She did not want to have to deal with any more change. She was just beginning to get the hang of things as they were. Mowl had lain sleeping, a half smile on his face. It struck her that he must feel cold with all that pale, hairless skin exposed. Even with his wispy beard his face seemed very naked and vulnerable. This observation made her feel oddly protective towards him. It was not an emotion she had time to consider. She had slipped out from under his cloak, quietly so as not to wake him, to see what she could find to eat. The succulent flesh of the chicken she had caught at Deworth was a high point in her new life. The taste memory had brought a rush of saliva to her mouth, but she could not live on memories.

She had been about to explore the scent scape around her for something with which to fill her belly when she had heard the rumble of horse's hooves. With a flash of her white-tipped tail she had run for cover. From her safe place she had seen the arrival of the sergeant. She had seen Mowl's staggering awakening and felt a strange mixture of emotions; part contempt, part sympathy for his clumsy ineptness. He would be too easy for the hard-faced soldier to kill. He wore his youth and confusion like a badge, a badge that said 'victim, kick me'. He reminded her of someone. She could not remember who. Her response was involuntary. She slunk back further under the bushes and watched.

The sergeant dismounted. He was a heavy man and Fox could sense the vibrations of his footfalls under her sensitive paws. The sight of him made her want to run away, but she felt a bizarre loyalty to Fowl Owl, a need to know what happened to him. The sergeant smelled of stale ale and human sweat, of unwashed wool, and bitter metal, and underneath it all ran a base note scent of blood and death. Most worryingly of all, Fox's acute sense of smell could detect no hint of fear. Mowl, suddenly conscious of his danger, stank of it. In spite of that, Fox was surprised to see that his hands were steady on his sword hilt. The sergeant swung his sword and lunged. He seemed surprised when Mowl countered the attack. Metal clanged against metal, a sound to make Fox cringe and retreat. She made herself stay. She thought it would be over quickly but it was not. This was not the kind of sword fighting she had expected. Somewhere she had seen men fight with light rapiers, with rapid strokes and flamboyant gestures. This fight was not like that. These swords were heavy. The big man swung his around his head to build up a fearful momentum. Kreek slashed at Mowl, then without pausing used the constant fluid motion of the sword to rain blow after brutal blow on the younger man. Mowl parried each attack with unexpected speed so that the clang of the swords meeting resonated like a cracked bell. It seemed clear, even to Fox, that both men knew what they were doing and that Mowl was fighting for his life. He was not as strong as his opponent but he was lithe and quick and powerful enough to handle his long sword with considerable conviction. He dodged what would have been a fatal blow more than once, but he was tiring. Fox with her predator's instincts could see the slight trembling in his legs, a slowing of his reactions. Kreek's blade sliced his left arm and blood welled up and stained his sheepskin jerkin. Mowl ignored it and struck back, managing a glancing blow off his attacker's chest. Kreek's mail shirt protected him, but the Sergeant sensed Mowl's fatigue too. He only had to wait. Suddenly Mowl slipped. The damp ground had become quite churned up by their footwork and Mowl's clogs were less tightly fitting than the soldier's metal-cleated boots. Mowl fought to retain his balance but fell to the ground. The big man's arm rose to deal Mowl his deathblow. Time slowed. Karen fought her vulpine instincts. She wanted to run away. She found herself running, but towards Mowl. She did not know what she was going to do – she didn't know what she could do. But she had to do something before the great sword could fall. She did not expect the sergeant's reaction. His eyes widened when he saw her. His scent soured with the acrid stench of fear. He stepped backwards away from Mowl. His sword arm fell but not as she had feared across Mowl's exposed chest.

'The arl!' he said and, almost falling in his effort to get away, sheathed his sword and remounted his horse. 'Noble arl, forgive me.' He muttered under his breath, his face suddenly white and strained. He turned his horse with one furtive, fearful look in her direction and galloped away.

What was an arl? Mowl lay where he had fallen, his weathered face now very pale. Mud streaked his blood-sodden tunic. Blood pumped from his wound at such a rate that Fox knew he would die from its loss if she could not do something. She remembered something about first aid, though where from she could not begin to imagine. She needed a tourniquet to stem the blood loss. She knew that at one time she could have made such a thing. She needed to tear some cloth to wrap around him. Even using both paws and teeth she could find nothing suitable. She needed help. Mowl's eyes were closed but she knew he was not yet dead. She nudged him with her nose. She licked his face; he tasted of salt and earth. He opened his eyes. His eyes had a lost bewildered look. Concussion? Unlikely – he had not hit his head. Shock? Maybe.

'Mowl. You're losing blood. We have to staunch it.'

Mowl nodded. He managed to move into a half recumbent position supported by his right elbow. He tried feebly to remove his sword belt but it was too stiff. There had to be some scrap of cloth they could try. In desperation Fox pressed her paw against the injury then her whole head to try to stem the flow. Mowl was drifting off and appeared not to notice. He spoke in a musing voice of quiet amusement.

'I know I'm dying, Fox, because I thought you spoke to me.'

Fox was shocked to discover that she could both understand what Mowl was saying and know that what he said was true. How had she spoken to him? Her mouth, teeth and tongue wouldn't make words, yet she had communicated with him somehow.

She tried to say, 'It's OK, don't worry,' in the language she knew was her own. Her fox's muscles would not, could not make those noises. How could she have spoken to Mowl? How had it happened? There was a word for mind to mind communication, it flashed into her head bringing with it a tantalising impression of some other world she had once known, another creature she had once been – whatever it was it was gone swiftly, leaving just the word 'telepathy'. Who or what had she once been that she knew such words, understood things that a fox could not know? The mystery of it made her head hurt. She was very hungry and needed to eat. She fought the urge to pursue quarry, dinner that she knew was just out of sight. She could sense warm-blooded creatures, big enough to make good eating, scuffling in the under-growth. She could smell the sweet pungency of carrion in the grass not far away. She forced her hunger to the back of her mind, even though a fox's mind didn't seem to have much depth and 'back' wasn't very far away. She would wait with this man, this companion until he died. The thought brought regret – was that a fox thing, regret? Karen Fox thought not. Karen Fox knew he couldn't live long. Mowl patted her head, with a rather feeble gesture. She flinched instinctively at the touch but did not jerk her head away.

'Goodbye, dear arl,' he muttered and fell heavily back down to the earth. Again she was sure that she did now understand him. Those sounds he made had a meaning they had not had before. Even if she had not understood the words she would have understood their import. Her only friend was dying. She could not help him. She felt a terrible frustration with her fox body. Once she could have helped him. What had gone wrong? Seeing Mowl this way hurt her in some part of herself for which she had no name. She closed her eyes and slept lightly, her body still pressing down on Mowl's injured limb, her senses still alert for danger or worse, for change.

Chapter II

Resignation: Day 6

Grace woke to the sound of the nurse's quick sharp footsteps echoing down the corridor. She glanced at Karen and noted the lack of change, straightened her cardigan and skirt which had got all twisted and sipped some flat, saccharine-sweet lemonade. There was a second set of footsteps coming her way. They were not George's. He could not stand to be there much. Maybe they belonged to the doctor. Grace tried to organise her chaotic thoughts, tried to lock her grief away so that she would be able to ask sensible questions. It was a disappointment when it was not the doctor. It was Billy.

'Mrs Rennard.' He nodded at her awkwardly. He had an unusual face, dark with large, bovine eyes and a generous, sensual mouth. Strong features, big features that sometimes looked unfeasibly handsome and at other times almost plain. He smiled nervously and his face settled into handsome mould. He had beautiful, strong, white teeth.

'There's no change then?' He handed her a bunch of luminously pink roses.

'No, love. She opened her eyes for a bit, but it meant nothing. I keep talking to her but …' Grace trailed off. The hospital sapped her of her spirit. Her optimism was slowly withering away. She forced herself into brightness. 'It was nice of you to come.'

'Well, I … I … keep wondering, like. What if it were all my fault?'

'Did you beat her unconscious?'

'No.'

'Well then, of course it wasn't your fault.'

'No, but it were my fault that Tina did it.'

'Did you tell her to?'

'No!' He sounded angry even at the suggestion.

'Billy, it's not your fault. Your girlfriend, Tina.' It was hard for Grace to say the name. 'Tina did it.'

'We'd had a row.'

'You and …'

He nodded. 'Tina wanted to know why I'd been talking to … to Karen. I said she was a nice girl and she talked to me like a person, not a, well not like an enemy – I don't know what. Tina was always trying to make me do stuff, say things, be different, she'd never let me be.'

Grace felt the only fellow feeling she'd ever felt for

Tina. Hadn't she spent the best part of fifty years trying to make George be different? It had taken her that long to realise it was pointless.

'Tina got right mad, ballistic. She said why didn't I go out with Karen then, and I said I might just do that, if she'd let me. I shouldn't have said nothing. I knew about Tina's temper. I didn't want to go out with Karen. I mean I liked her and everything but I knew Karen wasn't, well, Karen didn't seem like she'd go out with anyone. D'you know? I can't explain. She was always, somewhere else.'

It was true then. Billy had felt it too. Karen had been such a lively vibrant baby until her parents died and then she became this little shadow creature, grave and quiet and pale. Grace had tried so hard to make it up to her – to be mother and father to her but she'd never done it. All these years on Karen still missed them, was still only half in the world, the other half gone with her mother.

'She missed her mother,' said Grace in a voice laden with loss.

'Well, I wanted to say sorry for any of it that was my fault. I stopped going out with her, with Tina I mean, but she wrote to me and, and I think I might go back out with her again.'

Grace suddenly realised the point of this conversation.

'Billy, it's up to you who you go out with. It's nothing to do with me. I'm not going to say it's OK. What's happened has happened. Will your Tina beat up some other girl, if you look at her sideways? Will you blame yourself then too? Do what you want. I've got enough problems of my own.'

Billy hung his head. He looked ugly, sullen and dull-eyed. What did he want from her? Forgiveness?

'I'll come back next week.' He walked away, his shoulders hunched and dejected. Grace found she had been holding the stems of the roses so tightly that the thorns had torn her hands and made them bleed. She watched the dark red bead of blood trickle down her hand. What did it matter? What did any of it matter? It was all too difficult.

Karen Fox dozed where she lay. She was woken some unmeasured span of time later by the sound of someone approaching, noisily. It was a man driving a cart, struggling a little to guide two massive dray horses over the uneven ground. He must have followed the sergeant's tracks because they were far from the road. Karen Fox wondered why he had bothered. The man had the bearing of a soldier. Karen Fox was beginning to recognise the air of physical confidence. He was a large man, corpulent even, smelling faintly of male sweat, sweet wine and red meat. He got down from his seat clumsily and limped to Mowl's prostrate form. He felt Mowl's pulse with calm efficiency and shooed Fox away from the wound. His strong hands did what her paws could not. He fashioned a tourniquet and half dragged, half lifted Mowl's unconscious form to the cart. Karen Fox did not like the way Mowl's limp arm grazed the sides of the wooden cart, or the way his head thumped along the bottom of the cart as the older man manhandled him. Fox could neither help nor hinder. She backed away and watched with growing concern. The man carefully disarmed Mowl, an action that made more sense to Karen now that she'd seen him fight. He took a long look at the sword, then searched Mowl carefully. Was the man a thief? It gave Karen an uncomfortable feeling to see her companion treated in this way. She did not know what she could do about it. Mowl's satchel was still in the bushes where they had rested along with a pile of tattered parchment. It was within Fox's power to drag it out into the open. Would that help Mowl? Was there anything there that might encourage this man to treat Mowl well? Surely a person did not bandage a man he intended to harm? Fox had heard the clink of coins in the bag. Would money help? The man was continuing his methodical search of Mowl's clothing. Fox took a decision and slunk back to their hiding place, returning a moment later with Mowl's satchel. She left the parchment behind.

'What have we got here then?' The man's voice was deep and musical, a pleasant voice. 'Clever fox!' He picked up the satchel and his huge ham-like hands began to empty the contents carefully on to the cart. He examined the midnight blue cloak very carefully, even checking the lining, though what for Fox could not imagine. He weighed the bag of coins in his hand and counted out the contents. The coins were unfamiliar to Karen but by the man's low whistle she surmised that they were worth something. Perhaps she had done right to bring out the satchel. It was difficult to know. Karen Fox leaped on to the cart and took a position beside Mowl. He looked and felt clammy, his pale hair, damp with sweat, stuck like lank rat's tails around his face. His was the only face Karen knew. She did not want him to die.

The man brought the satchel back to the cart. He rolled the sheepskin to make a pillow, which he placed gently under Mowl's leaden head. He covered him with the blue cloak. Fox noticed for the first time that it was decorated with a small insignia in gold embroidery, something like a heraldic crest. It meant nothing to Karen Fox.

The man spoke to Mowl before he remounted the cart and took up his reins.

'Well, young man, every picture tells a story and I'll find out yours or my name's not Fenn Dale!' His speech seemed loud and incongruous in the quietness of the morning. It must have struck him as odd too for he did not speak again.

Fox kept watch on Mowl. She watched his waxen face

for any sign of awareness, listened out for his every breath. The cart jolted and shuddered along the open country until they reached a crude cart track. Fox winced as at every bump blood seeped from Mowl's wound. She licked it clean. They crossed the river at a humpback bridge, taking the road that led away from Deworth. When the sun hit its zenith in a heavy grey sky they stopped. The man lit a fire and shared some cooked rabbit with the fox. He drizzled some water on to Mowl's unmoving lips. They drove on until darkness fell, when the man again shared his rations. After eating, the man, who had named himself Fenn Dale, rolled himself in a blanket and snored by the dying fire until dawn, then they set off again. Through it all, against all instinct, Karen stayed by Mowl's side and waited. It was simple really. He would either live or die.

Chapter 12

Friend or Foe?: Days 7 – 9

By dawn of the next day it was clear that Mowl was no better and was not getting any better. Fenn Dale acted. He washed Mowl's wound; his large, powerful hands performed the task with unexpected gentleness and Karen Fox envied him his dexterity. He took a small metal needle and some thick thread, like a violin string from his kitbag on the floor of the cart. He lit a fire, boiled water for an infusion and heated the needle on a flat stone. He spooned some of the hot liquid into Mowl's mouth, lifting his head a little to make it easier for him to swallow. The smell of it made Karen shiver. It was a bad smell, an unnatural smell. After Mowl had drunk it he looked even less alive than before. When the needle had cooled, the man sewed back together the flaps of skin and vein that the sergeant's sword had so brutally divided.

Watching it made Fox shudder, which was strange given what she had become, a greedy dismemberer of small animals. Her teeth did as much violence as the sergeant's sword. She had not expected to find herself squeamish about surgery. Mowl thrashed about a little but not enough to interfere with the task. When the man had finished, the blood no longer flowed so freely and Mowl's injured arm felt warmer to the touch. Overnight Mowl's colour improved and for the first time Fox believed that he might actually survive.

By the time they reached the outskirts of Maybury Fox had decided three things; that Mowl was going to be all right, that she had never been anywhere like Maybury before and that she did not entirely trust Fenn Dale. Mowl had sat up briefly or at least propped himself up on his good elbow, stroked her head and murmured 'fox' under his breath in an affectionate mumble, before drifting away from awareness. It was odd how much that pleased her.

Maybury started as a shamble of cottages and narrow lanes, like a more compacted, more orderly Deworth, but it soon became a fantastical walled city of towering stone buildings, carved with elaborate designs and painted every colour she had ever seen. Every stone building, and she saw about ten, was not only as garishly painted as a fairground, but was full of stained glass, glowing with rainbow brightness in patterns of unimaginable complexity. Yet somehow, there was a kind of harmony about it. The more she looked the more she could see a kind of order in the vivid kaleido-scopic colour. This was matched by at least as vivid a cor-nucopia of smells and sounds. She slunk under Mowl's cloak for protection, shivering with excitement and ter-ror. She tried to focus only on what was immediately around her. It was then that her nascent suspicion of Mowl's rescuer was fully roused.

The arched, stone portal to the city was manned with soldiers in the same red and blue livery as Mowl's attacker. Fox cowered against Mowl. He slept still and was impervious to danger. She was sure that these men were somehow Mowl's enemy. Mowl's enemy was her enemy. Her fur bristled with fear. Should she wake Mowl?

A young soldier stopped Fenn Dale's cart, barring the route with a lethal-looking, steel-tipped pike. Although there was more noise than Fox had become used to, she heard Fenn Dale's confident command with crystal clarity. 'Fenn Dale – Don't salute me here, fool! – I have a message for the King. See that he gets it.'

Poking her nose out from under the cloak, Karen Fox saw Fenn Dale slip a rolled parchment into the soldier's hand. The soldier's hand hovered on the brink of a salute before falling uncomfortably to his side. He gave a kind of bow and waved them through without a glance at the contents of the cart. It took Karen Fox some time to stop shaking. If the King's soldiers were Mowl's enemy, what did that make Fenn Dale?

The road they travelled through the city was roughly cobbled, which was just as well as rivers of effluent ran around the stones. The air was full of the smell of many people and unwashed wool, with sweat and excrement and freshly baked bread; with roasting pig, and urine, with rosemary, lavender, cloves and sour milk. She tried to shut down her nose but it was impossible. There were too many people bustling around; she was gripped by a kind of claustrophobia. Though she remembered seeing busier places in that somewhere else that kept haunting her, she did not remember the stink that now assaulted her. She wanted to explore the myriad smells in all their wonderful and astonishing combinations, but she was as overwhelmed by the intensity of it as she was exhilarated by its richness. Too many bodies clustered round the cart; the pungency of their scent was a powerful pleasure. Fox delighted in it, her nostrils quivering, but when she realised that many of those running on rag-bound feet beside the cart were children, her delight turned to horror. The crowd were pushing one another to get close to Fenn Dale, palms outstretched, begging. One small girl looked nearly starved, her thin arms were blue with cold. Fox heard her shrill cry of, 'Alms for the Keeper's children, Sar.' She saw Fenn Dale push her casually aside with the toe of his boot and drive on.

They drove through the jostling crowd until they

came to a large, partially timbered building with a thatched roof. It reeked of pigeons and horses and the piquant flavour of meat stew. She followed at Fenn Dale's heels like a well-trained hound. While he shouted instructions for Mowl to be taken to a good chamber, Karen Fox looked warily about her. She was determined to learn more about what was going on, make some kind of sense of it, ensure that Mowl and she were safe. In the bustle of what was obviously a thriving tavern, no one gave Fox a second glance. She followed Fenn Dale into a large, limewashed room, redolent of ale, animal grease and the sweetness of herb-strewn rushes. It had a huge open fire, with a stone hearth and a chimney breast decorated with a painted fresco of a hunt. Just looking at it chilled Fox's blood. Fenn Dale ordered ale and found a seat at one of the several wooden tables about the room. He sighed loudly, loosened his belt and stretched his legs out in front of him in a very theatrical display of contentment and ease. Fox curled herself at his feet, hiding her tail and trying to appear as dog-like and inconspicuous as possible. Fortunately, there were no real dogs at the inn.

Although Fenn Dale appeared relaxed, his scent was spiced with wariness. A man dressed like a farmer and smelling of the flat, bitterness of metal sat with him chatting, apparently idly, about grain prices and the unseasonably wet weather. To Karen Fox's acute senses they seemed furtive and ill at ease. She listened carefully.

'Weather's been bad in Deworth.'

'Yes?'

'Someone harvested the Adept – heard it from a good friend.'

'The Adept, eh? That's sad news. I've heard there's more bad weather coming and Deworth is in the thick of it '

Karen Fox strained to make sense of the cryptic conversation. There was more of the same. Three other men joined Fenn Dale over the course of the evening, each sat and chatted in the same oblique manner while notes were passed under the table. What was going on and what did it mean for Mowl and herself?

She thought a little better of Fenn Dale when he ordered a large portion of stew and threw choice scraps to her under the table. She was confident that Mowl was safe for the moment and she allowed herself to relax a little in the warmth of the fire. Lazily she toyed with pursuing the interesting scent trails that marked the room. Nothing in her memory smelled so powerfully of life; her memory was of a shadow place. She liked it better here.

Mowl woke after what seemed like a very long time to a sharp pain below his left shoulder and a profound relief. He was still alive. He had not thought to live to see another sunset when the bulky Sergeant Kreek had unsheathed his sword. He remembered the moment of terrible fear when he'd slipped on the muddy ground, and Fox, Fox had helped him. Thank the Keeper of Balances that he had survived!

He was lying somewhere quite unknown on a raised bed with linen sheets. There was even a bolster on which to lay his head. It smelled of lavender and poultry feathers. It was dark but for the eldritch blue light from the window, which was glazed with cobalt blue glass. He wished the moonlight had been brighter, the better to see such a marvel. He had heard of such things and knew that they were not uncommon in Maybury. Was that then where he was? How long had he been here?

He tried to leave the bed to touch the glass, but the bed was far too high. He felt weak and his arm pained him. He sank back into the softness and luxury of the bed and waited to find out where he was and what he was doing there. He had not the energy for anything else.

He did not have to wait long. He had only shut his eyes for a moment when Fenn Dale arrived with a lantern and tray of bread, cheese and ale. Mowl recognised Fenn Dale as the large if hazy presence who had tended him through his sickness. Fox trotted into the room behind him and Mowl felt a surge of unexpected joy at seeing her. To him she glowed even in the darkness with a weird inner light, a light of strangeness. She looked well but for how much longer would she remain that way? How many days had he been ill? He had to get her to the Succeptor at Lerry before the twenty-fourth day of her fox incarnation was over.

He was suddenly conscious of his manners. Mindful of Yani's instructions on etiquette, he addressed his benefactor in High Loyren, as he appeared to be of some status in the world.

'Sar, I am deeply grateful for the care you have taken with my person. I will be forever in your debt.'

Fenn Dale's reply took him aback.

'You can save your fancy words. I know who you are, Mowl Speare. I would know your father's cloak and sword anywhere. Just what, by the Balance, are you playing at?'

Mowl found it suddenly hard to swallow.

'Sar, I don't know what you mean – the sword was a gift. I don't know anything about it.' Mowl did not try to deny his name. His previous attempt at subterfuge had not ended well.

Fenn Dale laughed, a short burst of derision. 'Of course you know nothing about the sword, any more than you know that you have been wearing the cloak of the Personal Guard of King Rufin!' Fenn Dale's sarcasm was heavy and decidedly unfriendly. 'I am not a patient man, Sar Mowl, and in a few short days you have jeopardised what we have been working towards for years!'

Fenn Dale sat down heavily on the only seat in the room. He reached over and grabbed a tankard of ale from Mowl's tray.

Mowl used the time to try to make some sense of what he was hearing. Why would Leva have a sword and cloak that belonged to his father?

Fenn Dale looked at him as if he expected an explanation. Mowl spoke slowly, gathering his thoughts as he went.

'I am Mowl Speare, that much is true, but I know nothing of my father. Le— a friend gave me money, the sword, and a cloak for my journey when I heard that I was wanted for treason.' Mowl was careful not to name the source of the gifts. It occurred to him, rather late in the day, that the Varls might be in serious trouble for protecting him and helping his escape. What did Fenn Dale want from him? He had acted as a friend but had he patched him up only to hand him over to the authorities? He was afraid again. He was sweating and his stomach churned.

Fenn Dale looked at Mowl thoughtfully.

'What do you know of your father?'

'I thought he was a soldier of King Rufin's guard. I heard that my mother died bearing me and my father died soon after. I assumed that it happened in battle, as he was a soldier. Then I heard he was wanted for treason for killing the old King.'

'And you believe that? Have you never wanted to know more?'

Mowl gave Fenn Dale a hard look. 'I used to imagine that he was a very brave and wonderful man but I've never seen him. My mother's dead – how could I find out more? Who could I have asked? I don't even know if he was a good soldier or a good man. What do you want me to say? That I don't believe a man I know nothing about could have committed treason just because he happened to father me?' Mowl's voice was coloured by bitterness and an unexpected anger.

Karen Fox listened carefully with her new-found understanding. Poor Mowl, growing up fatherless and motherless. She felt a surge of unexpected empathy. Fenn Dale looked at Mowl for a moment without the slightest trace of sympathy. His voice was cold.

'Why did you claim to be Sar Venish?'

'How do you know about that? I'm grateful for your care of me, but I don't have to answer your questions.'

Fenn Dale's hand went immediately to his belt knife, and in spite of his limp, he was at Mowl's bedside in one stride. He rested the knife lightly against Mowl's throat.

'Listen, pup. I served with your father and he was a fine man. I've been searching for you since I heard your name had been spotted on the Militia lists. I've risked imprisonment and worse to save you. I repeat, I'm not a patient man and if I think you're unworthy of your father's name, make no mistake, I'll risk nothing further for your sake. Have you got that?'

Mowl nodded, his face white with the shock of the sudden attack. Fox bared her teeth in a low-throated growl, but did not know what else to do.

Fenn Dale sheathed the knife and, limped back to his stool and took another long draught of his ale. His voice when he spoke again was soft and his tone conversational.

'Now, why did you pretend to be Sar Venish?'

Mowl waited until he was sure that he could keep his voice steady before replying.

'It was a misunderstanding – they thought I was Sar Venish – I did not want to be arrested.'

'Well, the good Sergeant Kreek of Deworth, with a little help from that popinjay priest, Domus Cantus, decided that you probably killed Sar Venish, and posed in his place as a spy. They believe you were involved in a conspiracy. Even as we speak, King's men are setting the countryside alight searching for spies and traitors under every haystack, poking their nose into every midden they can find, aye, and they are finding them too.'

Fenn Dale's voice rose again, fury plain in the reddening of his fleshy face.

Mowl struggled to think of something appropriate to say. He had nothing to do with spies or murder. The world beyond the Varl estate was more confusing and fraught with danger than he had ever imagined. He calmed his breathing, sought his equilibrium, determined not to show his fear, his weakness. He looked around the room as casually as possible, trying to give the impression of thoughtful bemusement, while searching desperately for his father's sword. This Fenn Dale was too much like the Adept, unpredictable, unreadable, and of uncertain loyalties. He was clearly a very dangerous man.

Chapter 13

Truth or Lies?: Day 9 (Night)

Fenn Dale did not speak for a while, merely supped his ale. His anger seemed to abate in another sudden change of mood. When he spoke again it was softly, even confidingly.

'There are some things you should know, Mowl Speare.' Fenn Dale looked down to examine the neat nails of his huge, pink hands. 'Your father was no traitor. I was a friend of Mant Speare. He was a great favourite of Rufin – he was a good huntsman, but also a good companion, witty and amusing.' He took another noisy slurp of ale before continuing. 'King Rufin had asked particularly that he accompany him on a wild boar hunt but Mant was anxious to get back to his wife who was due to have their first child.' Fenn Dale looked at Mowl with a calculating look. 'I suppose that was you. Anyway it was agreed that I would meet him at a favoured camping spot at noon on the day of the hunt to take over his duties so that he could ride on home. We'd arranged that I was to ride up bringing news that your mother, Tir, needed him. As it happened that was too true, though neither of us knew it then. Mant didn't mind breaking the odd rule where necessary, the King would have understood. In those days Hale Garnem's chief official responsibility was to do the duty roster, and he wouldn't change it unless you paid him – Mant wouldn't play that game.' Fenn Dale's voice grew softer as he reminisced. 'It was a very bright autumn day, a perfect day for a hunt. I regretted that I'd not been invited along and hoped that they'd be successful and we'd feast on roast boar that night. I had less of an instinct for danger then. I rode cheerfully into an abandoned battlefield. Two guardsmen I knew slightly were dead from sword wounds. One had lost his right arm. It lay beside him, severed at the shoulder. Blood stained the grass and crows were gathering. I could see two more prostrate figures. I dismounted and the full horror of it became clearer. Mant Speare lay dead. I knew it without checking his pulse. It was warm for autumn and flies were already buzzing round the corpse. A guardsman's spear had pierced his chest. He was no longer Mant Speare. His face was frozen in a terrible rictus, his soul had moved on. The King lay near him, his body twisted as if he too was dead. He would have died if I hadn't come along. I was a Hean before my marriage, we've been surgeons for generations. I always carry a tin of medical necessities wherever I go. There was nothing I could do for Mant but I was able to help the King. (You see there was Balance in my finding you!) The King revived a little when I moistened his lips with water. He told me that he had been attacked by the other guardsmen, without warning, that Mant had thrown himself in the path of the spear aimed at the King. He fought like a manticore and all the other beasts of the sphere magical to protect the King, but his lifeblood drained from his wounds and he fell.' Fenn Dale choked a little on his words. 'The traitors had fled at my approach, presuming that the King was dead. I could not carry both the injured King and Mant so I burned Mant's body in accordance with the soldier's rites in battle. It was properly done and all the forms were respected. There was not the time to bury him. The King had to be helped. I took Mant's sword and cloak, which was all he had of value on him, to give to his wife. The King struggled to croak out his wishes – that I lay the King's own ring upon the burnt body as a sign and seal of his loyalty so that he might enter the realm of the unmanifest as a Royal soul.' Fenn Dale paused to clear his throat and Fox was surprised to see tears in Fenn Dale's eyes. He paused as though picturing the scene. When he continued it was with a brisker tone. 'I took the King to my home, to Lerry where there was a gifted healer, a Succeptor. There had been rumours at court as there always were, about this or that faction wishing to replace King Rufin with Flane and I was afraid Rufin would surely be murdered if I returned him to court. That was a mistake. When I finally returned, I learned that Mant had been blamed for the murder of the King, and his body falsely identified as Rufin's. One thing I will say is that I don't think Flane was involved in the plot. Hale Garnem, now our first Minister, he was involved, I'd stake my life on it, but not Flane. Garnem worked on Queen Lin for months, persuading her that it was her duty to take a new husband. Hale Garnem favoured Flane, because he was weak, and in the end the Queen married Flane. Succession has always been through the female line and the Queen's husband is King – suitable or not. Rufin made his escape and stayed with relatives of mine until he was well. Rufin had no great desire to rule again – he wasn't much interested in affairs of state even when he was king, I would have to admit that – but he's older now and doesn't like what Flane's doing with this Purple Path business. It's another way for Garnem to increase his power, I'm sure of it. We're going to bring Rufin back. He is, finally, willing to reclaim the throne. He would not accept that Flane was a worse King than he himself had been. But now – Hale Garnem has altogether too much power, he has overstepped himself – good men destroyed, taxation … ' Fenn Dale waved his arms around as though words finally failed him. He leaned forward, alight with passion. 'On the day of your father's murder, when I thought Rufin was also dead, I made a vow – a holy vow of vengeance. I made an altar to the Keeper and made his mark in blood, spit and dung, in the old way. I made my oath then – to bring down the ones who did this. What I need to know is – are you with us?'

Mowl looked at Fenn Dale in astonishment. He had not expected that.

'What do you mean?'

'Will you fight on the side of the true King as your father's son and rid the Kingdom of the scourge that Flane has become?'

Mowl did not know what to say or what to think. Was Fenn Dale quite mad?

Mowl sank back on his pillow. What kind of a response could he give? Karen Fox was suspicious. She had seen enough of Fenn Dale to distrust him. She knew she didn't fully understand what was going on. She was becoming used to that. But she could understand that if Mowl was already wanted for treason, agreeing to support a former King might constitute proof of treason. Mowl needed to be very careful and in his current state he was in no position to think very clearly, if at all. She felt an intimation of danger in her fox's bones.

'Don't say anything.' She willed Mowl to hear her. He suddenly looked at her.

'Fox?'

Fenn Dale turned to Mowl in surprise.

'What do you mean, "Fox"? Don't go wool-gathering now boy, are you with us?'

Mowl glanced at Fox who tried again to make him hear her.

'It might be a trap.' Fox willed that Mowl might understand her. She did not know what she was doing besides thinking as loudly as she possibly could and very much wanting Mowl to hear her. Had he heard her?

'My arm hurts,' Mowl said shortly. 'I cannot talk about fighting at the moment.' Then, remembering his training, he added more courteously, 'I would wish some time to consider the grave import of all you have told me.'

Fenn Dale stood up and for a moment Fox and Mowl both feared the swift reappearance of his belt knife. He gave Mowl a searching look, but his tone when he spoke again was courtly.

'Forgive me, Sar Speare, you need to rest. It is not every day a son hears details of his father's murder.'

Mowl nodded, eagerly. 'There is much to think of, Sar Dale. Thank you for telling me. I am sure my father would have wanted me to know.'

He did not have to feign the small break in his voice that occurred when he said the word 'father'. It was a powerful word of great resonance. How would his life have been different if his father had lived? He would have had a place in the world instead of being dependent on the charity of the Varls; he would have had a status; he would perhaps have had sufficient wealth for a bride price and a chance to marry into one of the major clans. He thought fleetingly and painfully of Leva. He could not imagine what his relationship might have been with this, his lifetime dead father. It was too far beyond his experience.

Fenn Dale heaved himself to his feet, limped to Mowl's side and patted him, brusquely on his good arm. His voice was soft and somehow sad. 'Good-night, boy, I am glad to have spoken with you. You have been on my conscience for many a year.'

Mowl waited until he had left the room before he allowed himself to relax. Even without Fox's warning he did not entirely trust Fenn Dale. He had not dared seek out his spiritual emanations but it was unnecessary anyway; it was enough that Fenn Dale was too quick with that knife of his, too unpredictable, too brutal.

Mowl let out a long, deep breath of relief that was almost a sigh. He *was* glad about his father. It was good to know that the blood that flowed through his veins was not traitor's blood and there was more good news than that – Fox had spoken to him three times now. He could hear the voice of an arl! That was remarkable. Had he, Mowl, developed the gift of interpreting her spiritual emanations, as the Adepts were believed to do? He remembered the Adept's potion, the taste of the three bitter drops of liquid in his mouth. It had worked.

Fox jumped on to the bed and looked him straight in the eye. Her odd luminescence seemed even brighter now.

'*Can you hear me?*'

He nodded in bemusement.

'*If you can hear me, stroke my head three times and touch the tip of my tail.*' It was stupid but Karen Fox needed some tangible proof that she was not imagining this strange new power. She wanted a proof that could not be accounted for by Mowl's arbitrary movements. Mowl very deliberately stroked her head three times and touched her tail. His eyes never left her face.

Karen felt a surge of elation. She could make him hear! They could communicate! She knew that communication had once been part of her life, whatever that life had been. Something in her sang with sudden joy at being able to speak to someone again. Her joy turned to shock when she heard Mowl's voice in her own mind. '*Noble arl, I am three times blessed to know you, to hear you and to speak to one who transcends their own tier of existence. I am overwhelmed.*'

Mowl's lips did not move but she knew she had heard his thoughts as clearly as if he had spoken. It was deeply disturbing but their shared danger left her with no time

127

to think about this gift they shared.

'*Mowl, I don't really understand what you mean by all that. I only know that we're in danger. Fenn Dale is involved with the Militia. I heard him talk to a Militiaman while you slept. He sent a note to the King, the King now, I mean. I think you should get out of here.*'

He didn't argue or pause to ask her the plethora of questions she could almost watch forming behind his eyes. He believed her. He trusted her. He struggled to his feet. It cost him dear. She could see that. Blood seeped from the wound and Mowl's white face paled further.

'I know of nowhere in Maybury where we can hide.' Mowl whispered as he gathered the items of his pack together. He found that his sword had been laid under his bed with his cloak. Mowl wrapped the warm cloak around his shoulders, taking care that King Rufin's insignia was hidden. He stopped shivering. He strapped the sword to his belt with some difficulty, wincing with the pain. Fox remained on the bed and tried to assist him in lifting his satchel to his shoulder. She did not have the strength; neither did Mowl. '*I'll have to leave it behind.*' His voice was tinged with regret and Fox recognised that it was all Mowl had from his former life.

There was nothing helpful Fox could say.

Mowl's movements were awkward; he was in obvious pain. The wooden door to their room creaked on its hinges. Downstairs men slept, slumped over tables. Fox could smell them. Stale stew flavoured the air and the warm fug of smoke and ale made her want to sneeze. She fought against it. Mowl could hear the reverberant snoring of the men and the clumping footfalls of the serving girl's outdoor clogs, as she still moved about the room tending the fire and sweeping the rushes. There was no way they could escape unseen. The glazed window in the bedroom did not open. Mowl would have found it hard to smash its wondrous blue glass in order to make his escape. He might have steeled himself to do it, but it would have made too much noise.

Fox and Mowl both hesitated at the door. What did they do now?

Chapter 14

Running: Day 9 (Night)

Mowl struggled to stand in spite of his dizziness and the pain in his wound. He did not think he had the strength for this. Luckily, Fox was indefatigable. She almost pulsed with nervous, animal energy. Thank the Keeper for Fox.

'*I could create a diversion.*' Fox put all her will into communicating with Mowl as clearly as she could. She was not certain Mowl understood. Pain contorted his features and sweat gleamed on his forehead. Fox did not think he could remain upright for long. She made a decision and hoped that Mowl still retained the wit to take advantage of it. She raced down the crude wooden stairs, as noisily as possible and deliberately ran at one of the table legs, overturning the table and pitching ale and cold stew into the lap of one of the sleeping, snoring guests. The serving girl shrieked in surprise, and tried to hit Fox with her broom. This woke the other dozing occupants of the room while Fox ran under tables and stools creating havoc in her wake. When she considered she had given Mowl sufficient time to stagger through the door, she ran out through the still unlatched door; good, Mowl had left it open for her. He had still got his wits about him. She headed for the shadows. She found Mowl there leaning against a stone wall, breathing heavily. Sweat now streamed down his face; a growing bloodstain darkened his tunic. Neither was a good sign. Fox sniffed the night air. The wind was blowing from the south and its clean, salt tang told Fox that the sea lay not too far from them. Could they stow away on a boat? Could Mowl walk as far as a boat?

She feared that she might have made enough noise to wake Fenn Dale. What if he chose to betray them now? Mowl could not run and she knew nowhere to hide. She wondered if she should have trusted Fenn Dale a little longer and given Mowl's wound a few more days to heal. Mowl's eyes were shut tight. After a while he spoke softly, trusting to Fox's sharp ears.

'I think Dorren is here.'

Who or what was Dorren? Fox waited for Mowl to say more. She had to wait for a long moment before Mowl managed to speak again.

'Dorren is the Goodwife's brother, Leva's uncle. Leva used to say he was not quite the full talen. He's not yet wed – he's got a twisted back. He drives the covered cart and trades Varl wool and cloth around the country. I know he's close by. Sometimes I can sense things. If we could find the cart I could hide until I'm stronger. Dorren wouldn't betray me. He's got no interest in the King's business.' He spoke breathlessly, his voice so low even Karen Fox had to strain to hear it.

She accepted this explanation with bemusement. Did he mean he could smell Dorren? She did not understand what he meant, but if he found her somewhere safe she didn't care. She hoped that he would lead the way.

Mowl tried to. It was very dark and his night vision was poor. He nearly stumbled many times on the uneven cobbles, or slipped in the streams of wet refuse that trickled along the thoroughfare. Fox was frustrated. If she had known what Dorren smelled like she could have found him. Mowl's 'sense' of Dorren was too elusive; some directions were cold and others hot, some hot trails turned cold and vice versa. Mowl did not have the strength for this blind staggering about and she did not have the patience. At least no one followed them. Mowl had unsheathed his sword and was using it as he'd once used his shepherd's stick, surely he would blunt its edge? The sound of its metallic scraping against the cobbles set her teeth on edge. He made too much noise but he need-ed its support. Once they heard footsteps. Mowl pressed himself against the wall of a large stone building and allowed himself to be engulfed by its shadow. Fox just stood as still as a wild creature can when flight is impossible and fight is unrealistic. Two men approached in soldier's livery – the Watch. The men were talking about a bet and their voices rang through the damp darkness; stealth was clearly not part of their job. One of them carried a storm lantern, which blinded them to the deeper shadows. Fox and Mowl held their breath and the men walked past them, arguing amicably about the relative merits of two different card games. Mowl scarcely waited for them to be out of earshot before pointing excitedly in the direction of a crumbling building. It seemed pretty unremarkable to Fox; it smelled sourly of stale ale and vomit, men and horses. There were a couple of horses whickering under the meagre shelter of a makeshift wooden lean-to. Then she saw the cart. It was shaped like an old-fashioned gypsy caravan, but plain and without windows. It had one door at the back hinged at the bottom so that it could be lowered to form a ramp. It was half open. It smelled of sheep. It reminded Fox of her sharp hunger. Mowl was right. It did have the faint scent of the grassy hillside of the Varl lands.

Mowl did not wait for her. He ran unsteadily for the cart, as if it was an oasis in a barren land. The metal of his sword scraped the cobbles and somehow became entangled with his legs. He slipped on the greasy layer of damp filth that filmed the stones and fell headlong on to the ground. He let out an involuntary yelp as the movement jarred his wounded arm.

Suddenly, Mowl, in all his awkwardness, was bathed in the warm yellow light of the storm lantern. The Watch had returned. The two Militiamen walked deliberately towards Mowl. Fox hesitated – what should she do? Mowl struggled to his feet, hiding his longsword behind his back. He smiled sheepishly at the soldiers, trying to ignore the sickening pain in his arm and the rising panic in the rest of him. The soldiers spoke roughly.

'Hey you! Who are you? What are you doing breaking the curfew?'

Mowl answered in an exaggerated country burr, which even to Fox sounded theatrical.

'I'm new to these parts – I didn't know about no curfew, I was visiting this girl, see ...'

The Militiamen did not see. It was a brave if unconvincing performance. Stony-faced they moved towards him.

'Well, wherever you're from you can explain it to our sergeant. No one is allowed out during the night watch.'

Mowl swayed slightly. Fox did not know if he was about to fall or if he was pretending drunkenness. The smaller of the two Militiamen reached to take his arm and Mowl sprang. In one unbroken movement he moved his sword from behind his back and hefted it two-handed into the air where he swung it in a powerful arc to land flat-bladed, hard against the soldier's back, knocking him forward. Mowl moved very quickly and Fox did not want to consider what it cost him in pain. The second soldier reacted slowly. He had not been expecting trouble. He grappled with his own sword, but the flat of Mowl's blade knocked him off his feet. Mowl was obviously wary of drawing blood, recoiling from murder. The first man got to his feet and drew his sword. He was dazed from the fall and Mowl knocked his sword easily from his hand. It clattered loudly where it fell, a sound loud enough to wake the dead. The soldier realised that he didn't stand a chance. Mowl, even injured, was a good swordsman.

'Go! Take him too!' Mowl pushed the fallen man with his foot. 'If you go now I'll let you live. Raise the alarm and I will follow you and kill you like a festival pig.' He spoke grimly. Even Fox believed him, though she knew he could scarcely walk let alone run. As he spoke he kicked over the storm lantern, plunging them all into darkness. The soldiers ran, stumbling, falling over each other in their haste to get away. Mowl did not run. Fox doubted that he had the strength. Instead, when he was sure the men had gone, he walked unsteadily towards the tailgate of the Varl cart. He did not look back. Fox emerged from the shadows and followed him at a trot, uncertain whether she had witnessed a display of great integrity or great foolishness. Her fox self did not approve of half measures; kill or be killed, that was the way things were, or so it seemed to her. She jumped up at the tailgate of the covered cart despite a strong feeling that she was entering a trap. She ignored instinct and for Mowl's sake followed him into the enclosed darkness. Someone threw a sack over her head and Mowl screamed.

Mowl's scream sounded like an echo of Karen Fox's own fear. It was so easy to die here. The thing over her head smelled bad and she thrashed around to release herself, instinct usurping reason. She made herself stop. She made herself listen and think. Mowl was fighting someone or something heavy. It smelled like a man, even filtered as it was through the heady scent of sheep from the sack on her head. She forced away the taste memory of lamb stew. She could sense grunts of effort, heavy breathing, the smell of sweat. The cart rocked with their weight. Mowl was definitely in a fight.

'Dorren, is that you? Stop it! I need your help!' Mowl's voice was breathless and weak-sounding. His arm was not up to any more fighting.

'Mowl? By the Keeper! I feared you were dead!'

The other voice was breathless too and deep, as if the cart itself spoke rather than a man.

'Is this your hound?' Something removed the sack from Karen Fox's head. Fox could just discern the broad outline of a huge, crouching figure.

'Dorren, the Militia's after me. I just fought the Watch. Can you get us away, Dorren?' Mowl's voice was pain-filled and sickly to Karen's ears.

'The roads are full of Militia looking for you, Mowl,' the deep-voiced stranger sighed. 'I'll get us out of Maybury but I don't know if we can avoid the Militia entirely. They're searching every cart on the road for you and other so-called traitors. I don't know what this country's come to.' His voice broke and Fox wondered at the grief in it. 'Stay under cover. We'll try and make as much ground as we can before dawn.'

Now that Fox's keen eyes had adapted to the darkness of the cart she could see Dorren's large, misshapen body stoop to leave the cart. As he went he patted Mowl lightly on his shoulder.

'I'm glad you've found me. I've been praying that you at least still lived. Don't worry, I'll find a way to keep you safe. No one knows the byways of Loyrenton like me.'

He was gone before Mowl could reply. He fastened the ramp securely and, more quietly than could have been expected, readied the horses. Within a surprisingly short time they were on their way. The only witness to their leaving was the man hidden in the shadows by the ramshackle inn. He watched until they were out of sight, then turned and limped back down the midnight street.

Chapter 15

Learning: Days 9 – 10

T he young priest's face flushed a deep, angry, pink. The real Sar Venish sat opposite him in the Deworth tavern. Sar Venish looked much the worse for wear, having been discovered very much alive, if dead drunk in a certain house a little north of Maybury, a house with a very unsavoury reputation. His eyes were bloodshot and his clothing dishevelled.

'So, did you kill the impostor with the temerity to pretend to my elevated rank?' His voice, an affected drawl, even without the slurring effect of alcohol, marked him as a member of the Second Household, the aristocracy.

Sergeant Kreek shifted uncomfortably behind the young priest.

'Not exactly.' The priest's tone was scathing. 'The sergeant believes him protected by an arl. The very superstition we are charged to root out!'

Sar Venish sipped his ale with greater relish than

was normally expected in a courtier.

'So what did they teach you about arls at the priest school?' The scribe's voice was faintly mocking. It was evident that they had taught the young priest comparatively little or there would be no need of his own services.

The priest reddened further. 'A Priest of the Purple Path is not obliged to speak of the mysteries with any drunken sot who asks him.'

'Ah! A zealot. Well, it takes all sorts to make this sad little world swing in balance with the rest. Oh! Sorry! You of the Purple Path believe this sad little world is all there is, don't you? If memory serves, it's all derived from the heresy of Capetan. Nice to see it making the rounds again. No doubt you have read him in the original?'

'I don't have to have read anything to know the truth!' The young priest was easily goaded, and hissed his response. Kreek kept a watchful eye on his hands. The young man had a temper. He did not want another body to deal with.

'Mmmmm, well, if you want a debate about truth … better not, eh? Our good King has cause to worry about that. There are some very spicy rumours doing the rounds of the taverns in Maybury, an honest man couldn't of course repeat them, but still …'

Sar Venish finished his drink and looked around expectantly for a refill.

'Sar Venish, I believe your presence is required at the temple site. The villagers wish to meet with you to discuss the level of their taxes.' Sergeant Kreek's words were quiet but firm and Sar Venish was not quite the fool he appeared; he straightened his clothing and stood up, ready to follow the sergeant.

'Well, we must all do the work of His Highness the King, Keeper of the Purple Path.' He stood as though to leave, then paused. 'I don't suppose you caught this so-called arl, did you? I'm sure the King would be grateful if such a creature was not roaming the countryside, inspiring the peasantry to religious fervour and the like.' Kreek watched the flicker of satisfaction in Sar Venish's eyes when he saw the priest's eager expression. A clever man, Sar Venish, who knew which field his wheat was in. He antagonised the priest enough to satisfy his desire for mischief and then gave him an idea, which could gain the ambitious priest the preferment he craved. It would also undoubtedly free Sar Venish from his own unwelcome supervision – Kreek would bet talen on it. Sergeant Kreek almost smiled when, on cue, the young priest turned to him.

'I have been thinking, Kreek. I do not for one moment believe that this creature you saw was an arl, for no such creatures exist, but Sar Venish is right. It would greatly please His Majesty to have an opportunity to prove that such creatures are nothing more than frauds to gull the

140

gullible. As the King's representative in matters of religion, I order you to track this creature and dispatch it immediately to the King with my best wishes. Sar Venish, please write an appropriate accompanying letter!'

Sergeant Kreek's almost-smile faded as he felt the dread chill which presaged trouble, and Sar Venish grinned.

Dorren drove the horses hard. It was not long before they left the heady scent of Maybury far behind. Karen Fox was worried about Mowl. His breath was ragged and he felt clammy. She tried to speak to him but he did not hear her. He had lapsed into unconsciousness again. Fox sniffed at the wound and cleaned up the dried blood with her tongue. It still smelled clean, though the stitches had burst. She hoped that it was just exhaustion and pain that afflicted him. She did her best to wrap his cloak around him and lay close beside him in the cart to lend him her warmth. She slept fitfully, always aware of Mowl's breathing, keeping vigil as best she could. Were they safe with Dorren? Her instincts said so.

It was just before dawn when Dorren stopped the cart in a place that smelled only of tilled fields, damp earth and animal ordure. It smelled good to Fox. Dorren opened the tailgate of the cart so that the black darkness of the interior was lessened to a dark grey.

Dorren moved wearily towards Mowl's sleeping body. He shook him, gently.

'Mowl, we are out of Maybury now. I think we're safe here, but I need you to keep watch for a spell.'

Mowl started awake with a cry. He looked around wildly, his hand finding his sword hilt in an instinctive gesture.

'Dorren! Sorry! You made me jump.'

'It's all right, lad. Here, I've some food for us to share. I need to grab some sleep, but you need to keep an eye out. You're not safe anywhere. Do you understand me? It's got so bad that anyone, and I mean anyone, might turn you over to the authorities rather than risk being accused of treason themselves.'

Mowl was beginning to pull himself together. He moved stiffly and tried to stretch. Fox licked the bare skin of his hand encouragingly.

'I don't understand. What do you mean? Who is being accused of treason besides me?'

'Hush! Keep your voice down – you don't want to attract attention. Sound carries a long way.' Dorren paused. 'You've not heard then. There's been trouble – bad trouble. After you'd gone the Militia came for Yani. They brought her to Maybury for treason. The man who came to arrest you claimed she deliberately delayed him to give you time to escape. He also accused her of heresy for allowing a shrine to the Keeper on her land.' The

142

large man's bass voice cracked. 'She would not denounce her beliefs or deny that she knew who you were. The King's adviser, Hale Garnem himself, judged her guilty.'

'I don't understand. What has Yani ever done?'

'That's just it. She's stayed away from court, though the Varls always used to have a presence there. She isn't interested in politics, never has been, but Flane's nervous. There are rumours that Rufin's not dead, that he's planning to take the throne – they've been around for years but something's changed. When the King found out that the Varls had harboured you, that was the excuse he needed. He may try and install one of his cronies on the Varl land. It's over.'

'But what about Yani? We must help her. Can't you do anything?'

There was a heartbeat's pause.

'I'm sorry, Mowl, they hung her at sundown. Yani's dead.'

Mowl was shocked into silence.

'But Yani ...' the sentence hung there unfinished. Mowl could not grasp that the anchor of the Varls, the Goodwife, Leva's mother, Dorren's sister, could be dead. Dorren sighed and it was the saddest sound Karen Fox had ever heard. 'She was very brave. I forced myself to watch. She died very quickly. I think she willed it. We thought she might have been a sensitive when she was young, though she wouldn't admit to it. I think she let her soul free the moment they took her up those steps.' Dorren's voice was thick with the burden of unshed tears. 'They wouldn't let me take the body. They said they'd burn it with the other traitors outside the gates of Maybury. It will not matter because Yani did things her own way, always. She wouldn't care whether the right words were said in the right places. She knew how we felt about her.' He paused and almost lost his tight self-control. 'I don't know how I will tell Dake.'

'Dake doesn't know?'

'He was so convinced that the King would see that Yani wouldn't plot for political gain, that she was only interested in the farm and family and Dake. I don't know how he will bear it.'

'Leva?' Mowl only just kept his voice steady.

'Leva was safe, last I heard. Dake sent her to her husband's family. She's the Goodwife now. He didn't want her taken too.'

Mowl was numb with the shock of it and he'd forgotten Leva was married. There was a dryness in him where there ought to be tears. Yani was too much a part of the fabric of his life as it had always been. He could quite simply not imagine the Varl homestead without her, and her death was his fault.

Karen Fox wanted to say something but didn't know what. She remembered sadness, knew the taste of it in her mouth. She did not think it could be eased by words.

She nuzzled against Mowl's side. He rested his hand on her back.

They stayed like that for a long time, none of them speaking, each with their own thoughts. Dorren lay on the floor of the cart. It was growing less dark by the moment. Karen Fox could see the grief and the weariness etched in Dorren's already lined face. He must have been exhausted because he fell at once into a deep sleep.

'Mowl, I will keep watch outside until he wakes.'

It was a measure of Mowl's own exhaustion that he merely nodded.

Chapter 16

Realising: Day 10 – Day 13 (Dawn)

The woman did not look much like a clairvoyant. She had a blunt, practical face and thick grey hair styled into a no-nonsense bob. She was stout and sensibly dressed in a pleated, checked skirt and pale blue, round-necked sweater. Her eyes were blue too, faded like her hair but her gaze was direct and challenging. Grace thought she looked like a retired teacher or a librarian. Grace found herself to be more nervous than she had expected and not a little embarrassed. George would not approve.

'Karen, my granddaughter, has been in a coma for a while now,' Grace began. She indicated Karen's bed and Karen's pale face with its halo of incongruous brightness, her corona of red hair. As always the sight made her stomach churn. She wiped damp hands on her dress under the pretext of smoothing it over her broad hips. She prayed that this meeting would not prove to be a terrible mistake. The clairvoyant said nothing. The silence was there for Grace to fill. She filled it. 'I just had this feeling that her mind is fine, just somewhere else. I keep dreaming about a red dog. It scratches on the door as if it wants to come in and I get up to let it in and when I get there it's gone.' She shook her head aware that she was rambling, aware that she couldn't even explain the dream to herself.

'Do you think that red dog is Karen, Mrs Rennard?'

Put like that it seemed ridiculous, such an obvious symbol for her red-haired granddaughter, yet in her dream it had seemed to represent something profound. Grace shrugged. 'I don't know and I'm getting desperate. The doctors are talking about Karen having that, you know, persistent vegetative state. I think she's still there somewhere, whole and frightened. I'll try anything.'

The woman smiled briefly. 'Even a clairvoyant.'

'I didn't mean …'

'I know what you mean, Mrs Rennard, and I'm not offended. I'm not a mumbo-jumbo merchant. I see what I see. Sometimes it makes no sense. I don't claim to understand it and I don't have any answers. I haven't got a spirit guide and I don't do automatic writing. I think of it as having advanced intuition that's all. Would anybody mind if I touched your granddaughter? Sometimes it helps.'

'I don't think so. I'm sure it would be all right.'

The clairvoyant sat down on the plastic chair, crossing one ankle over the other and placing her handbag carefully by her side. She closed her eyes and touched Karen's cheek. She sat like that for a couple of minutes and just said 'Karen' a couple of times in a normal voice. She opened her eyes and pursed her lips.

'I see what you mean about the red dog, though I thought it was a fox. Karen and this fox are strongly connected and there is someone else that matters to her. I think you're right. She's somewhere else and still functioning. She is afraid too, but not overwhelmingly. She is still very much alive, just not here.'

'But what does that mean? Will she come back?'

'I don't know, Mrs Rennard. I told you I don't have any answers, just endless questions of my own. She may be in some fantasy world or she may literally be somewhere else, somewhere real in every sense that matters. She's not lost all connection here, though. I'm sure she heard me call. There may be some change in the next few days, if she's ready to come back, but I don't know – and …' the woman hesitated, 'there is always the risk that I've made things worse. It's rare, but I ought to tell you that sometimes calling a person home can cause more shock, more confusion, a kind of splintering of the self. But I think you have cause to be optimistic. She heard me.'

Grace found her eyes were moist. She would have liked to blow her nose but it would have looked a bit obvious.

'Thank you.'

'I think you already knew all this. You must trust your instincts, Mrs Rennard.' She picked up her handbag. Grace hastily groped in her pocket for the clairvoyant's fee. The woman took the money and filed it precisely in her wallet. She put it away and snapped her handbag shut with a decisive click.

'I hope she comes back, for your sake, but it's also possible that she might be happy where she is. You must consider that. She has been very sad here, hasn't she?'

Grace nodded. 'Her mother died. She never got over it. Neither have I.'

The clairvoyant patted Grace's arm. It was a gesture of unlooked-for intimacy that didn't fit with her dispassionate voice and businesslike demeanour. It made Grace want to cry again. 'I so much want her back.' Grace's control broke and the last word was almost a sob.

'I know,' said the clairvoyant and Grace knew that she did.

By the time the sun was properly up, they were back on the road. They had shared some bread and cheese and drunk their fill of cool, clear water from a nearby stream. As the cart rattled on across the primitive roads of Loyrenton, Karen Fox slept. Her hind legs kicked involuntarily as if she ran and, in her dream, she did. She was running on two legs not four. She was running and she was very scared. Something (hair?) got in her mouth and she could taste blood. A voice she didn't know was calling her. The name they called was 'Karen' and she knew that it was her name. She pushed hair back from her mouth with a human hand, felt the dampness of tears on a human cheek, knew that she was Karen and was very afraid. She did not like the feeling and yet in her dream she knew that if she could only get past the fear there was a place for her, a home she could run to, people waiting for her. She whimpered and startled herself awake. Her muzzle rested on her forepaws, pressed against Mowl's warm leg. She was not Karen but Fox, lost. She was struck by the terrible wrongness of her fox being. She should not be a fox. She was a girl, a woman, a person called Karen. She was overwhelmed by the shock of that realisation, the first time she had known for sure who she was. The first time she had remembered anything personal, her name, her hair, the sensation of tears, of running straight and tall. All of those things she had lost. How? Why? She started to shiver and she could not stop. She wanted to weep.

Mowl woke when the cart halted and jarred his

reopened wound. His woollen shirt was stiff with dried blood. It scraped the rawness of his skin where the stitches seeped fresh blood. He remembered about Yani almost at once and at the same moment realised that he had not told Dorren about Fox, about the urgent need to get to Lerry. He clung to that mission, to that purpose because now, more than ever, it was all he had. He reached his hand down to touch Fox's head and noticed that she was trembling. He tried to reach her with his mind but nothing happened. There was a sinister absence where her thoughts should have been.

'Fox?' He could see little in the windowless cart, though some grey wintry light leaked through the gaps between the slats of the tailgate. Mowl did not need to see Fox to sense the change in her. She was no longer fully herself. She had gone somewhere else, a confusing place where he could not find the thread of her reason. Was this the beginning of the end?

'Don't worry, Fox; I'll get you to Lerry. It's a hard walk from the Varl lands, over the other side of the Tear Mountains but I'll get you there.' He tried to hug her to him, for comfort, but her small body was rigid and unyielding. His unease grew. Everything was wrong. Yani was dead. The world had changed. He had escaped death once, twice, but he knew that if the King's men could hang Yani there was no hope of justice. He could not bear it if Fox were to die too. Beneath her thick fur, her bones seemed fragile. She was small and vulnerable. Her heart beat wildly and her whole body trembled to its beat. He felt as if the mystic arl of the glowing aura had shrunk to become this frightened animal. That made him feel frightened too.

There were voices outside. One of them was Dorren's; the other was a male voice, hitching a lift. Mowl tautened and curled his hand around the sword. Surely Dorren wouldn't risk picking up a stranger with Mowl a fugitive in the cart?

Dorren would and did, but then Dorren had never done what anyone expected.

Mowl could not help but listen to their talk. There was nothing else but fearful speculation to occupy him.

'It's right kind of you,' the other man spoke with an exaggerated mountain burr – a farmer?

'It looks like you've fallen on hard times.' Dorren was blunt as ever. 'These new regulations is it? I had to pay a fee to sell my own best wool at market because I wasn't on some list or other.'

'It's getting harder to make a living hereabouts sure enough.' The stranger concurred with a grunt.

'What's your business?' Dorren seemed determined to interrogate the stranger.

'I've been labouring here and there since I lost my place at my sister's farm. I volunteered to go – there weren't enough food for the winter and the temple tax. I

152

can make do.' The stranger seemed to impart that information reluctantly.

'There are a lot more like you around these days. I may be doing the same thing myself in the weeks to come. It's going to be a hard winter. My name is Dorren.'

'Blud.'

'I'm going up beyond Deworth into the hills – that suit you?'

'As far north as you can take me will do me well. I've heard talk there's work there.'

'On one of the temple projects?'

'No, farm work. I don't like being round soldiers, you never know what they're going to take it into their heads to do next. Man I met was run through, just for saying he didn't see the point of all them temples. He wasn't much older than twenty.'

'Like I said – a tough winter.'

'That's for sure.'

The two lapsed into silence. Mowl tried to make sense of what he was hearing. What was Dorren doing? More than that what was King Flane doing? How could such things be happening? How could men and women be killed on the slightest pretext? They were not at war. The crops had not failed. Equilibrium was clearly failing and the descent into chaos that all prophets feared must surely be imminent. Mowl could not order his thoughts into any coherency. Yani was dead, he was a fugitive, Dorren chatted openly with vagrants and Fox, Fox was changing. Mowl readjusted his weight as silently as he could and tried to sleep. Maybe he could find a way to dream of happier times, if his arm would only stop hurting and the pain in his heart would ease.

The cart clattered on. It was at least a three-day journey from Maybury to the Varl lands in Dorren's old cart. Mowl had always wanted to travel that Maybury road. He had done so once already while unconscious. He was doing it again from inside a closed cart.

The cart stopped abruptly. He could hear voices – soldiers. He eased himself away from the dead weight of Fox's head. He found his sword and started to crawl towards the tailgate. He heard Dorren's voice explaining his business.

'Well, you see I went to Maybury – long ride this time of year and the weather's not been good – to sell my wool. You'll have heard of our wool – best in Loyrenton.' It seemed to be Dorren's plan to bore the soldier into letting him journey on.

'Open the cart.'

'Oh certainly. You won't mind the smell – it's just that a sheep died in the back not so long since and …'

'Open it up.'

Mowl dragged the few remaining wool-sacks in the

cart to his new position under the tailgate. If, when the soldier opened the tailgate it did not fall to the floor of the cart, but was propped up a little, it may be possible for him to hide under the ramp. It was a long shot but he could think of nothing better.

He could hear footsteps and Dorren's desperate improvisation.

'Look lads, I'll admit it – I've some goods I've not paid the excise on. How would it be if I gave you half the tax money and we called it quits, eh?'

The soldier was implacable.

'Open the cart!'

Dorren opened the cart. The tailgate fell forward, hitting Mowl a sharp blow to the back of his head. He suppressed an oath. The pain of it was not too bad.

'Where are these goods then?'

Someone was walking across the ramp. Mowl held his breath and pressed himself hard into the floor of the cart. He could feel the weight of a heavy man pressing down on him, just touching his flattened back. Someone was lifting the ramp and he was staring into the face of a stranger.

'What have we—?' The remainder of his question was cut off. The man fell to his knees, a knife protruding from his throat. There was a grunt and a clash of metal outside. Dorren! Mowl struggled to his feet. The soldier in the cart was dead. Mowl carefully avoided stepping on him, blinking at the brightness of full daylight. Dorren was under attack, backing away from a soldier in the King's colours. The soldier swiped at Dorren inaccurately with his sword. He was no swordsman.

Mowl's sword was already drawn and this time he did not know if he could avoid murder. He ran to Dorren's aid and turned to face the enemy just as the enemy crumpled to the ground, blood gushing from a fatal slice to his chest. A tall man, with greying hair, watched the soldier fall with an air of satisfaction. He held a bloodied sword.

'Thanks, Blud.' Dorren's voice shook a little. 'Lucky you're handy with one of them.' He nodded his head in the direction of the weapon.

'Served in a farmstead Militia for years,' the tall man said, wiping the sword on the damp grass. 'It's not something you ever forget.'

There were three corpses to deal with. Blud had dispatched another man while Dorren's knife had seen off the first. It was more death than Mowl had ever seen before. It was more than he ever wanted to see and once more he was to blame. He and Dorren helped Blud bury the bodies but what with Mowl's wound and Dorren's twisted spine, Blud did most of the work. He was fit and heavily muscled, though he was little younger than Dorren. He seemed unsurprised at Mowl's appearance. Dorren merely introduced him as 'Mowl, a friend in a spot of bother'. They were all in a spot of bother now.

They could all end their lives on the gallows for what they had done. Blud seemed entirely unconcerned by that. What kind of farmer killed two of the King's men without a qualm?

The rest of the journey passed easily, though they had lost time in digging the graves. As they were all outlaws together Dorren had no concerns about trusting Blud. They drove through the night, taking it in turns to keep watch in the thickets and woods where they hid the cart by day. They avoided the main road altogether.

Dorren insisted that Mowl rested his shoulder, so he dozed intermittently and tried to reach Fox, find her spiritual emanations. He could not seek out her arl soul. His thoughts grew very confused and most of the time he slept and let Fox sleep, warmed by his body heat. He covered her with his cloak when she was beset by sudden bouts of trembling. He dreamed repeatedly of her dying because he could not get her to Lerry on time.

She lay by his side but, when he touched her, bared her teeth at him. He was growing desperate. Was this the spirit sickness that the Adept had spoken of?

The bone-jarring ride seemed endless.

He could not say how he knew they were back in the Varl lands. It may have been the scent of the familiar hills or some other awareness. He just knew that they were home in the same way that he had known that Dorren was near. They arrived a little after the dawn of the fourth day of their journey. Dorren reined in the horses and opened the door flap. Fox did not wait for the ramp to be lowered; she leaped from the cart, a wild creature, and had gone before Mowl was even aware of what was happening. He could not have stopped her anyway, she was too quick, too feral. Mowl blinked back tears of frustration. She was all he had and she was gone.

Dorren looked terrible, haggard and worried. He had lost weight, his huge frame was gaunt and the hump of his crooked back seemed more pronounced than ever. He helped Mowl from the cart with an unsteady hand.

'I think there are soldiers here – horse tracks. Blud has gone ahead to have a look. Go to your hut. I'll bring you food and blankets when I can. May the Keeper keep you, but I don't like the smell of this.'

'You're a good man, Dorren.'

'Something's not right here, Mowl. Keep that sword out and be ready to run like that hound of yours. Animals have got an instinct for danger. There's nothing for you here. Nothing for any of us if they've got Dake too.'

Mowl patted Dorren's massive shoulder. A terrible sense of loss overwhelmed him.

'I'm sorry about Yani – it was my fault.'

Dorren looked angry. 'Never your fault, Mowl. All you ever did is tend sheep. Should you hang for that? Go! Run! And keep your wits about you.'

Mowl did as he was told. He fell back into old habits

easily. He wondered where Fox was. His wound hurt. He did not have the energy to track her again. Returning to the Varls' clan lands did not feel like a homecoming. The loss of Yani seemed to cast an almost visible pall over the valley. Dorren was right. There was something wrong.

Chapter 17

Confusion: Day 13 (Morning)

Karen Fox ran. She did not know what to do and running was something she was good at. She ran without thought, blindly as if pursued. It was all wrong. She should have had two legs not four. Her eye level was wrong. The scent impressions accosting her senses were all wrong. The world should not smell so much. If she ran far enough and fast enough maybe she could run towards the voice that had called to her. She did not know where that voice had come from, only guessed that it was far away, further perhaps than she could run.

It gradually dawned on her that she was running towards something she had not expected – a farmstead. There were men there – tall men, big men in blue and red. There was shouting and laughter and the desperate sobbing of a woman. Had she smelled her scent before? It was fully light now and there was too much noise and colour, too much sound and heat. There were flames coming from the farmhouse and people, lots of people she did not know, running. They were running and shouting and the smoke got in the back of her throat and it was bad, a bad place, a place to leave quickly. But she could not go. She was transfixed by what she saw. There was a man in the midst of all the soldiers. He was staggering. He was a big man too, but old and covered in blood. She could not see his face for the blood that streamed down it. It was the wrong kind of blood. It did not make her feel hungry, only sick. The soldiers were shouting at him, mocking him, taunting him. They let him run a little, as if they were going to let him get away, though she doubted he could see where he was running through all that blood and dirt. Then they took it in turns to trip him up, watching him fall and laughing with wide, ugly mouths. They kicked him as he lay on the ground. It was horribly, desperately familiar. The man was brave. He tried to fight back. She saw him lash out with hands and feet. She saw him spit blood and curses until he could curse no more. The men laughed and the woman sobbed more quietly, more wretchedly and slipped away. She ran then, fast, although her skirts impeded her. She ran, heading for the hills. The big, bloodied man was dead. Death had its own smell. Had she always known that? The orange flames from the timber-framed house crackled and the thatch ignited. It was damp and the smoke thickened. It made her eyes stream. Someone had let the chickens out of their coop. Karen Fox should have caught one but there was a wrongness in that. That was not what she was meant to do. A person called Karen did not snap a chicken's neck with sharp teeth and savour its warm blood. That was not what she did. The soldiers, still laughing, mounted their frightened horses and galloped away. One threw something at her. She barely dodged it. Something like this had happened before. Something like this, something with blood and pain and cruel laughter had happened before. She moved hesitantly towards the dead man as if searching for a clue; his face was ravaged by cuts and bruises. She looked at him, seeking a memory. Had she known this man? Why did this terrible thing that had happened to him seem so familiar? She did not know him, had never seen him before. She felt unsteady. Her heart beat painfully within her fox's chest. She remembered faces, girls laughing like the soldiers. She remembered blood in her mouth and fear. She almost remembered more. Who was she? Why? It was almost within her grasp. She could taste the answer, smell it. It hid from her like a broken bird in long grass. Something spat sparks at her from the flaming house. The heat was growing intense. Her fox self turned tail and ran, seeking coolness and something to ease the dry burning in her throat. She loped away, easily catching a succession of small mice fleeing the blaze. She started to feel better.

The bad feeling in her chest was going away. She lapped sweet water from the stream and sniffed the air. It was cleaner here and smelled of autumn. It was time to move on. She had a strange feeling that she was leaving something behind, a cache of food? A mate? It was something important, something vital, was it something she had to do, someone she had to find? It was on the edge of memory, but her memory was a poor fractured thing. The scent of the important thing was just at the edge of her perception. She sniffed the air for it, but all she could sense was the burnt, charcoal smell that still wafted her way on the wind. She shook her head, confused. She could remember nothing more than a trace of something too faint to identify. It couldn't have been important. The autumn sun was warm on her back. She was not hungry nor was she thirsty. That would do for now.

'She moved, no, I'm sure it was not the same as before, George. She did move. Do you think she could be coming back?'

George looked at his wife, the way she stood, tense with hope. He noted the way she clutched her handkerchief so tightly it might have been a lifeline. What could he say? He knew he would never see the real Karen again.

'I don't know, Grace. You know, maybe we should just accept …'

He could not finish the sentence. He could not face the hurt, wounded look that would briefly shadow Grace's face. In truth Karen did look a little better in subtle ways. She looked less porcelain white; her hair had more vibrancy. For a moment he too felt a spasm of something close to hope. Maybe she would recover. Grace was watching his face, while pretending to get out her knitting. He did not want his expression to change. He dare not show any optimism. He did not want to give Grace any cause to believe it would be all right. Bad things happened and you had to come to terms with them. His chest felt tight with unshed tears; he was drowning in them. When his lungs and heart were awash with them maybe he would die too. For the moment he would just hold Grace's hand and wait.

'Why don't you come out for a minute and get a breath of fresh air? It's not healthy to stay inside all the time. She's not going anywhere.'

Grace removed her hand and resumed her knitting. 'She might wake up, George. I think something has changed. She had an expression on her face, a real expression. For a minute she wasn't so blank. You go. I'm fine here.' Grace checked Karen's face again. She was sure something, evidence of thoughts, feelings, had flickered fleetingly across that face. That was a change. That would do for now.

Chapter 18

Commitment: Day 13 (Late Morning)

Mowl huddled in the stone hut that had been his home for much of his life. It smelled abandoned, sepulchral. How could he have lived there for so long in such ignorant contentment? He had spent so many hours alone with his thoughts; he ought to be good at waiting. Hadn't all his life been waiting for something to happen? Now it had and the quietness of contemplation was lost to him. He could not calm his beating heart; dampen down the growing sensation of dread. He was worried about Fox. What had happened to her? Where had she gone? Why had she left him? He was also worried about the soldiers and Dorren. What had Dorren said? 'There would be nothing for any of us if they've got Dake too.' Dake Varl could not be hurt. He'd been a soldier himself and a good one, so everyone said. He had a formidable skill with weapons. Dake could defend himself and the farm, why else did they have the Varl Militia? He reasoned that all would be well, but his heart still beat too fast and he clutched his sword so tightly it hurt, but he could not relax his grip. There were footsteps outside, heavy breathing, sobbing. It did not sound like soldiers. He rolled away the stone that blocked the entrance to the hut. It was Dorren and Blud supporting Leva between them. He had never seen her in such a state. Her clothes were torn and covered in soot and grime; her eyes were puffy and red. The men looked grim. They all stank of smoke. Mowl stood aside for them to crawl into his shelter. No one spoke for a moment. They sat huddled together, physically close but distanced. Mowl asked no questions. He needed no special sensitivity to know that something terrible had happened. His dread deepened. Leva sighed and wiped her face on her blackened apron. It made her look er worse but it seemed to make her feel better. She shed hair from her face too and looked at Mowl. How she had changed! It was a very cold look. There was nothing of Leva the mischief-maker, the playful flirt, in this woman's eyes, only a hard darkness that frightened him.

'You! You are still alive then. They took Mother because of you. They hung her, you know. Soldiers rode up from Deworth just to tell us and to hunt for your precious arl!' She stopped her bitter tirade and let out a trembling breath. The three men watched her, warily

166

uncertain. How should they respond? What help should they give her? What words should they say?

They waited for her to continue. She pulled her torn dress down. It was mud-caked and so ragged that the gesture looked oddly incongruous, as if she was at the hearth in the farmstead. She waited a while in the silence. The men waited too, not daring to break it, watching her, praying that she was not broken by this; giving her time. She wanted to talk. She kept her voice even to begin with, conversational, but she twisted the fabric of her skirt between her fingers and rocked backwards and forwards ever so slightly, as a child might.

'It was all right for a while. The soldiers are mainly vagrants and the like but they were well-disciplined to start with. They were even respectful. One of them even looked sorry about Mother; I think he might have worked for the Drays once. Their sergeant asked me some questions about Mowl. I told him nothing. Then he rode off leaving some of his men behind to watch the land – in case Mowl or that creature came back. It was only after he'd gone that things got out of hand – the men started to play.' Leva took a deep breath. 'They taunted me a bit – I'd left Jenn at the Doka farmstead, working. I came alone looking for news of Mother, though I didn't expect the news I got. They went on at me for that – wasn't Jenn Doka up to taking care of a girl like me, ha ha – you can imagine. Then one of them grabbed me and tried to kiss me and ... and my father came in and drew his sword. I've never seen him so angry. Dad cut the soldier, quite badly, but then all of them attacked him at once, they took his sword. They overpowered him and dragged him outside. I think I screamed and the girls and everyone came running from the outhouses but no one had their weapons near and then one of the soldiers threw Mum's good chair into the fire and went mad – lighting the thatch. I screamed to get the kids out and Debb and Neela took them and ran. I think they got away. The rest of the men were too far away to help. They came as quickly as they could, but it was so confused. They were trying to make sure every-one was out of the farm. By the time they saw what was going on with the soldiers it was too late. All I did was scream. I'm so ashamed. I should have grabbed a sword or something but I didn't. There were three, maybe four of them, and they just beat my father and beat him. He didn't stand a chance.' She paused and closed her eyes. No one else spoke. Her voice became dull, drained of colour and feeling, but her words were sharp.

'So that's Dake Varl, the Goodwife and the Varl homestead all gone in two days and it's all because of you, Mowl. All because of you!'

Mowl's eyes were full of tears. It was worse than he could have imagined. Leva opened her eyes. Even in the dimness of the shelter he could see hate burning in them. He struggled to speak.

'I'm sorry, Leva … I …'

'I loved you and I trusted you, cousin. Why did you betray us?'

Mowl was shocked. 'I don't know what you mean.'

It was Dorren who intervened, his beautiful bass voice cracked with dust and anguish. 'I don't think Mowl knows, Leva. You must not believe all the poison the soldiers told you.' He looked at Mowl; the whites of his eyes gleamed, shiny with tears.

'Mowl, Dake Varl was your father's brother. I don't think anyone knew, not round here anyway. Yani confessed it when they came to take her. They said you had been captured. Then today they said you had confessed to treachery and that the two of you, you and Dake Varl, had plotted against the King with the other so-called local traitor, the Adept of Deworth. I think they came here today to kill Dake. His attack on the soldier made sure they killed him bloodily but he was doomed anyway. He is – was, too well-respected here. Men would cleave to him even without Yani. They wanted him gone. They wanted to claim he was plotting too.'

Leva started to sob quietly. Mowl could not take it in. Dake Varl was his father's brother. That explained why he had his father's sword. It also explained why the Varls had taken him in as a baby, employed him as a youth, educated him and done the other uncharacteristically generous things they had done for him over the years. He felt his face go hot when he remembered his relationship with Leva.

'Leva, I had no idea!'

A trembling hand touched his; the flatness was gone from her voice. 'Neither of us knew, Mowl. No one wanted us to know.' Her tone was gentle now and the grief in it tore at Mowl's spirit.

He blurted out, 'You must believe me I was never captured by the King's men. I never plotted against anyone. How could I have betrayed you? What was there to betray?'

'You never knew then?'

'Knew what?'

'Father *was* involved in something – I don't know if you would call it treason. It was to do with your father. Dad gave me some things to keep safe – after they took Mother.'

Mowl remembered the bizarre conversation with Fenn Dale in the inn at Maybury and his meeting with the Adept. Was there really a plot? Was Leva trying to tell him that Dake Varl really had been a traitor to King Flane? He did not know what to think or what to say. He was also suddenly very acutely aware of the presence of the stranger, Blud, listening carefully. In the last few days Mowl had learnt how not to trust.

Blud had fought the King's men to help them but

why? Mowl shut his eyes and sought the spiritual emanations. It was an instinctive thing. He had done it as a child; even then he could tell whether someone was really angry with him. He wanted to know where Blud's sympathies lay. Such emotional emanations must surely lie like a blanket of deep snow on the ether. Strong emotion was perceptible even to those of small gifts. All he could feel was pain from Dorren and from Leva, terrible anguish and loss and loneliness. It hurt his soul to feel it. There was nothing at all from Blud. Either Blud felt nothing in the midst of all this suffering or he was skilled enough to shield his emotions. Neither explanation made Mowl feel very comfortable.

Leva spoke again. 'I am Goodwife of the Varls now. I'm going to rebuild this place. If there was no plot against the King before, there should be now. He murdered my mother and sent his soldiers to murder my father. How can Queen Lin permit this? Does she know what is going on?' She paused. The rawness of her bitterness was painful to hear. 'Would you do something for me, Mowl?'

'What do you want, Leva?' He knew of course what she wanted, because he knew Leva. She had always had a tough streak.

'I want revenge. I want you to be a traitor if that's what it takes. I want King Flane to pay.'

Mowl licked dry lips. He thought of Fox and his

dreams of becoming a scholar, an expert on arls. He thought of Fox and his unexpected Adept's gift of soul speaking. He thought of Fox and his hope of saving her from her soul's sickness that already seemed to have afflicted her. What had he to lose that was not already lost?

'I'll do whatever you want.'

'Swear it!'

'By what?'

'By the Keeper of course, the real Keeper – not the King and his Purple Path.'

Conscious of Blud's cool observation he did what Leva asked. He always had. He could feel his own self shrivelling up under the burden of what she asked of him. He wanted to let her know what he was sacrificing. No Adept could kill directly or enter into the complex emotions of revenge, it sullied the purity of the questing spirit; it locked you into the tier of the natural man. He wanted her to know that he was prepared to sacrifice his dream of becoming an Adept. But Leva had lost her mother, her father, her home and all hope of a comfortable future. What would his sacrifice mean to someone who had lost everything? He said nothing more than she had asked of him.

'I swear by the Keeper of Balances that I will seek revenge for these wrongs.' He fingered his still painful wound and with the still wet blood there, drew the sign of the Balances. He had never felt more abandoned.

After that Mowl, Dorren and Blud waited with Leva in the semi-darkness of the shepherd's hut for a long time. They had fallen into a kind of sleep, a quietness that gave little rest, just stillness. No one wanted to speak; there was nothing more to say. No one seemed to want to go, there was nothing left to go to. It was Leva herself who broke the spell. It had to be. No one else would have wanted to intrude on her grief.

'I must check on the others and make us some shelter for the night.' Leva's voice was flat but businesslike. 'The Dokas will probably take the children, though the Goodwife is rather low on the milk of human kindness. Her sense of duty should make her take them for a day or so. Will you stay Dorren and rebuild? You are the senior man now, apart from Jenn, of course?' she added quickly.

'I'll help sort you out tonight, Leva, then I'll be off with Mowl. He doesn't know the life on the road as I do.'

Leva mulled this over for a moment.

'You mean to join the rebels then?'

'I think I have cause enough.'

Mowl was bemused. How had he lived here and known nothing of a rebellion that seemed common knowledge to the Varls?

'I don't understand,' Mowl said at last. 'It was true

then? Dake Varl was actually involved in a plot? Did everyone know but me?'

There was a long silence. Maybe Leva finally realised the potential danger of a stranger listening to their talk, but she had said too much already to be reticent now.

'I didn't know either. We were always wrapped up in other things.' She glanced at Mowl and blushed. 'My father only told me about it when they took Mother.' She faltered, but managed to continue. 'He never believed your father was a traitor. He had friends in the Militia. He learned a bit about what was really going on. He thought your father had been blamed for treachery that had its root with … well, with King Flane. He wasn't very involved but for your father's sake he took messages and gave talen sometimes.' She glanced questioningly at Dorren who nodded for her to continue. 'Dorren was often the messenger. There is a network, held together by an old friend of his. I don't think my father took it too seriously, he just did what he regarded as his duty to serve equilibrium. He gave me a list of names. Mostly I think they are other relatives and friends of your father who felt the same way.'

She thrust something into Mowl's hand, a small, leather-bound book, of the kind he had heard that scholars used if they were very wealthy and highly esteemed. He didn't take in much of what Leva said beyond the fact that he had more family than he had ever known about.

He was trembling with emotion. He wanted to cry and laugh at the same time. He had always had family. Dake Varl himself was family and he only learned of it now, when he no longer needed the comfort that knowledge might have given him. He had spent his life believing that he was totally alone in a world in which family was all.

'Why did no one tell me?'

'I don't know, Mowl. My father said it was for everyone's protection. Flane made a huge fuss about the horror of your father's deed for a while. Mant Speare's name was synonymous with evil and ingratitude for years. I think Father thought it best to keep quiet about his connection so as not to bring shame on my moth ... on the Varls, but he never believed what they said. That's why he supported the rebellion – in a small way anyway. He never meant to hurt you, Mowl. I think he hoped that this lonely life with the sheep might make you strong. He put great store by solitude.' There was a catch in Leva's voice as she spoke of Dake Varl that reminded Mowl that now was no time to question the motives and failures of the murdered man who had been his benefactor.

'I'll help prepare a shelter for you too.'

'No Mowl, the soldiers might come back. I think you should get away from here and Dorren too. I can cope. Jenn and his brothers will help me.' She tightened her jaw and Mowl guessed that Leva's pride would be injured by accepting help from that quarter. He had no doubt that Leva would do whatever had to be done. Leva was Yani's true heir; tough as an old ewe.

If anything, this second parting from Leva was harder than the first. She clung to him briefly. Under the all-pervading smell of smoke, he recognised the familiar scent of her hair and skin, the sweetness of her breath, his cousin who had been closer to him than anyone in the world. His eyes smarted with tears for what they'd both lost.

'Serve equilibrium,' she whispered. 'I know that none of this is your fault.'

It was good to hear her say it. He needed to know that Leva was still just. He kissed her lightly on the cheek, a mere brushing of lips. She had laid a burden on him from which he could never be free and they both knew it.

'The Keeper keep you, Leva, and comfort you in your sorrow,' Mowl said firmly. Then he turned and walked away.

Chapter 19

Conflict: Days 13 – 16

Fox ran until her paws ached. She did not stop until she came to the river. Only then did she recognise the strangeness of her flight. Where could she go?

She sniffed the air. She could not stay here. There were foxes nearby and they would chase her away. She knew that. Hunger gave her the impetus she needed to run on weary legs, to hunt, to eat and maybe find a dry place safe enough to sleep. Something was wrong. Something nagged at her fox's consciousness. She needed something more than food and shelter but she did not know what it was. There was something (or was it someone?) missing. Her thoughts followed her nose and the scent of field mice. She could not think about anything else. She ran on feeling a strange regret, unable to remember why.

Mowl, Dorren and Blud walked back to Dorren's cart in

silence. It remained intact. The soldiers had left it alone. The air still stank of smoke. Mowl's eyes smarted and tears rolled down his cheeks unhindered. It was growing dark and cold. It was hard to feel enthusiastic for the task ahead. It began to drizzle.

'We'll need provisions.' Dorren's voice was flat, worn out. He looked to be beyond misery.

'Leave that to me.' Blud met Dorren's eye, answering the question he saw there.

'I'm with you. I have heard of the rebels. I was going north to try to find them.'

'Why should we trust you?' Mowl's bitterness at the way his life was turning out made his words sharper than he had intended. Besides, he did not trust a man whose emanations he could not read.

'Trust me because I killed two Militia men for you, Mowl, and will hang as surely as you will if we're caught.'

That was true and Mowl felt obscurely ashamed of his own attitude. It was harder than he had expected to be noble. He resented Leva for what she had made him promise; he gave in to her too easily and he had promised something that could destroy his gift of speaking with Fox, and he hadn't yet given up on Fox. He knew he was behaving petulantly. He forced himself to smile and shook Blud's hand.

'I meant to thank you for that.'

Blud nodded in acknowledgement. 'It's not easy to be

a wanted man. We're none of us free any more and can't be until Flane and Garnem are gone.' It was the first overtly political statement that Blud had made. Mowl looked at him in surprise.

Blud shrugged broad shoulders. 'My family have also suffered at their hands. I'll fight to avenge that.'

Something in Blud's tone chilled Mowl. It would have been so much easier if he too could feel that cold resolute anger that underlay Blud's words. All he felt was a terrible sense of loss and loneliness. He could not sense Fox anywhere.

They drove all through that night. Mowl did not even know if Dorren knew where he was going. It seemed he just wanted to get away from the smoke of his burnt out home, the blackened remnants of his former life. Mowl did not want to stay in the cart without Fox – he missed the warmth of her physical presence – but Dorren insisted and so Mowl slept. He dreamed of a grey place, featureless and lifeless, that sapped his will and his strength. He searched for Fox, trying to track her through the nothingness. In his dream he knew she was there, buried in the shrouding greyness like a creature trapped under ice. He woke less rested than before, overwhelmed by gloom as if the greyness of the grey place had entered his soul.

Only Blud remained cheerful. It was Blud who

insisted that they carry tree branches, moss and earth to hide the cart when they stopped each day. It was Blud who disappeared to return later with pilfered food. Dorren never asked where it came from – he preferred not to know and Mowl did not care.

Mowl cared so little and so obviously that by the second day Dorren finally lost his temper.

'What is wrong with you, Mowl? How can you avenge Leva in the state you're in?' He looked tired and ill and was fighting despair. Mowl it seemed had fallen into it.

Mowl grunted. Dorren drew his knife.

'Listen to me, Mowl Speare, it's not your fault what happened, but you've said you'll make Flane pay. You made a promise to my niece that you're going to keep. Dake Varl always said that his brother was a fighter, a good swordsman, of course, but more than that a brave man and ...'

'And you don't think I'm brave or a fighter – maybe I'm not. What's my father to me? A story, that's all and a story that's ruined my life and everyone else's life – yours, Dake Varl's, Yani's, Leva's, everyone's. Not two sixdays ago I was no one, a clan-less shepherd happy to work for the Varls. Now, I'm heir to a traitor, homeless, hopeless and committed to kill a king I've never seen. We're doomed. How can we hope to avenge Leva by driving blindly into the northern territories? Do we have a plan or are we just running away from the Varl lands? What

180

can three of us achieve anyway?'

Mowl's outburst surprised even him. He was surprised at how angry he felt. He felt even angrier that he had lost Fox and could not now find her, but that he didn't want to discuss.

Dorren did not sheathe his knife and he looked at Mowl without warmth.

'Dake Varl would have expected more of you. Leva is not giving up, why should you?'

Blud saved Mowl from answering.

'Two things we need to think of – first, we're going north because that's where many of Dake Varl's contacts are – is that not right, Dorren? You can check in the book that Leva gave you, and second, if we can find some of these people there won't be just three of us. There's more than you that's angry in Loyrenton. The temple tax is too high. You go to any inn and they all say the same. There's going to be some as can't survive the winter on what's left in the grain stores …'

He didn't finish. Someone was coming. A woman was complaining loudly. Her voice carried clearly in the clear air.

'I tell you someone has stolen half a meat pie and a loaf and I saw someone running in this direction.'

No one breathed.

'Why would anyone run in this direction, woman? We're right at the edge of the forest and if anyone's run in there, I tell you, I'm not chasing them. Did you not hear the wolves baying last night? Now, is there nothing left for my lunch?'

'I tell you, I don't like it.' The two voices receded.

Dorren looked guiltily at the remains of the pie.

'Think of it as a donation. I'm sure they'd support us if they knew what we were going to fight for.' Blud sounded uncomfortable.

'I don't like it, Blud.' Dorren shook his head.

'When I ... I mean when Flane is defeated, I'll find them and we can pay them back. You have my word.'

'We'd better defeat Flane then, hadn't we?'

Dorren sheathed his knife. 'Tonight we go to an inn and pay for our food. We may pick up some good information too. Mowl can stay here. It's not safe for him to be seen. His description has been circulated everywhere.'

'I can tell you some good information,' Blud looked grave. 'The King's elite guard use the wolf cry as a signal. We shouldn't stay around here too long.'

Mowl looked at Blud's smooth, handsome face and wondered what kind of man he was. One thing was sure. He was not a farmer no matter what he claimed.

Fox was tired. Every movement was an effort. She had nowhere to go, no territory to defend, no mate, no cubs. She could not remember how she had got where she now was. All was confusion and wrongness. She had walked a long way, for a long time. She had slept when she felt too weak to run on. She was too weak now. She had done some hunting but she was weakened by exhaustion. As she got weaker it got harder to hunt, as she got hungrier she got weaker still. She was growing desperate. Towards evening she approached a people place. She had been there before. She recognised the smell of it but the detail of memory was lost in that confusion into which her whole past had fallen. There was a man there, waiting for her. He was a big man with a predator's stance and lots of metal and coldness about him. She had sensed him before too. He gave her meat, which was fresh, without taint and water. He talked gently to her and put her in a cage made of wood. He cleaned it up when she soiled it. His tone of voice was not aggressive. He used sounds that almost made sense. She was thoroughly weary in a way that made her grateful to lie in a cage. She knew that was a wrongness, but she no longer cared. It was enough to be still. She ached somewhere that was not in her limbs. She ached somewhere inside that was not her belly. She felt bad and she did not know why. She did not know how to make things better so she lay down and slept for a very long time.

Chapter 20

Another Ally?: Days 16 – 17

Mowl had studied the book that Leva had given him. There was nothing else to do. Fenn Dale was in it; was he a friend or had he betrayed his uncle? It hurt his head to think of it. He knew nothing of plots. There were other names that he recognised – the Adept Laine, the Succeptor of Lerry, King Rufin – of course, and Huta Arn. He had heard Leva speak of Huta and now he learned that he too was his father's brother – more family! Why had no one claimed him when it mattered, when it could have transformed his life? Mowl spent the long hours of the journey reflecting with bitterness on his lonely life at the Varls; he had been grateful for the crumbs from his uncle's table when, by the ancient laws of familial responsibility, they were his by right. He was so angry that at first he overlooked the importance of one other name on the list.

He tried to think of other things, to work out what

day he'd left the Varls, the day he found Fox. By Dorren's reckoning it was over two sixdays ago. Was that the arl's first day as arl? He had no way of knowing.

He dreamed of Fox as he slept in the cart. For the first time since he was a small child he had been in the grey place of meaningful dreaming and had known that she was there too, an invisible presence, imperceptible to every sense, but there. He was sure of it. Only then did he realise – the Succeptor of Lerry was on Leva's list.

'Look the Succeptor of Lerry is in the book, here, I'll show you. Why can't we head there? He's famous through Loyrenton for his wisdom and sensitivity to the emanations of all the tiers, surely he will know what's going on.'

Mowl made his tone as persuasive as possible – he had to convince Blud and Dorren to seek out the Succeptor. If they found the Succeptor, Mowl could find out where Fox was and what needed to be done to save her, without reneging on his oath to Leva. His hope flared – there might still be a chance of saving Fox – before time ran out.

Blud raised his voice slightly. 'I disagree. I think we should stay away from sensitives – they're the riskiest people to approach. Almost all the gifted ones are gone: the Adept Laine is dead; the Adept Hansforth is dead. That old boy in the inn earlier said soldiers took the Adept Illin of Newland Wood. I think we should follow the rumours about your Uncle Huta, Mowl. Two people have said they thought he was heading south. He wouldn't do that on his own.'

Blud was persuasive. He and Dorren had visited every inn they could find in the last two nights. Somehow, though the rumours abounded, they had never come up against the Militia. People were afraid. It seemed to many that Flane was killing off the Adepts so there would be no one to keep the old ways alive, no one who could prove that there were more tiers of existence than the one natural tier, more states of being than that of the natural man. Farmers of a hard land cherished their glimpses of the other tiers – their religion was their private business and not a fit subject for the King's rule. Up in the north, in the High Reaches, it was rumoured that there was a Domus who had insisted that all shrines to the Keeper be destroyed. It was no wonder that the hill people were cagey and suspicious.

Dorren wanted to head east to another village to confirm the rumour that Huta was heading towards Argon in the foothills of the Tear Mountains.

Mowl was not to be persuaded.

'I still think we should try the Succeptor, Lerry can't be more than a day from Argon anyway. We could go there afterwards if we don't learn what we need from the Succeptor. Dorren?'

'Let's see what we can find out at the next large village, Calp, did they say it was called? We should go to whichever place is furthest from the Militia. We've been lucky to avoid them so far – such luck can't hold. Let's be on our way. The roads are bad hereabouts and I want to be in Calp by tomorrow night, while there's still hope of some supper.'

Mowl had no choice but to agree. He tried to bury his resentment. He was beginning to hate the inside of the cart and the strange half-life he lived within it. He let the ragged motion lull him into a semi-contemplative state. If nothing else he could perform his spiritual exercises and listen out for Fox's emanations. This night the ether seemed thick with emanations he could not read. He was afraid. So many Adepts had been killed that there were rumours that Hale Garnem had a special priest, a sensitive, who was seeking out those with the talent and killing them as heretics. Dorren had passed that information on quite gleefully as proof of the unreliability of rumours. Mowl was not at all sure it was a false rumour. He sensed something; some searching something that was definitely not Fox and was nothing like the power of the Adept Laine. He did not dare doze after that, but sharpened his sword and tried to control a growing sense of dread. They had made enquiries about several of the men and women in Dake Varl's book. They had done it as subtly as possible but they must have alerted every spy around to their presence. Too many of those named had been executed or had recently met with accidents. Mowl found it hard to believe in the existence of a rebellion when so many of the rebels appeared to be dead.

It was beginning to look as though they were going to have to avenge Dake Varl and the Goodwife Yani on their own. Their enemies were too powerful.

They arrived in Calp in good time and once more Mowl was left alone in the cold dark, waiting for his companions to return with something to eat. He had left Dorren's cart and decamped to a barn. It was no warmer or more comfortable but he felt that if he did not leave the confines of the cart he would go mad. At least he could pace the barn and stretch cramped muscles, walk around as he had done on the hillside in his old life. He missed Fox, missed her more even than he had missed Leva. The astonishing discovery that he could hear her speak had been the most extraordinary and wonderful thing that had ever happened to him. He dare not listen for her or call to her with all the power of his will and desperate longing. He was too afraid of the forbidding presence in the ether, the searcher who chilled his blood.

There was a sound of movement outside. Mowl reached for his sword in the pitch black. It might be the barn's owner or it might be the Militia. Mowl rolled his shoulders to loosen the joints. His injury was much better but he was not sure it would stand up to a fight. He got silently to his feet. He hoped that the clicking of his cold joints could not be heard outside. He crept outside. It was even colder there. His breath froze in the air in front of him like clouds of smoke from some mythical beast. He tried to breathe less visibly. Someone was moving around inside Dorren's cart. It would not be Dorren; he would have spoken to Mowl. Could it be Blud? Should he declare himself? He waited to see what the dark figure might be up to. If he could find anything to steal in the cart he was doing well. All that was of value in the Varl family had been burnt with the homestead. Only the small leather book with the names of his dead father's supporters was of any value and he had bound that with a piece of cloth over his heart.

Mowl did not think that he had made any sound but suddenly the figure turned and leaped from the cart brandishing something that glinted briefly in the faint moonlight. It was warning enough and Mowl was ready. Following instincts, trained over so many years by Dake Varl, Mowl threw himself to one side to avoid being knocked to the ground. The man who faced him was small and lithe. He landed neatly on the ground, exactly where Mowl had been standing seconds before. He had perfect balance, like a cat, and immediately launched a frenzied attack on Mowl. Mowl's sword was not designed for fighting at such close quarters. The man had sprung at him too quickly for him to swing the long sword. He was wrong-footed, unbalanced by his sideways dive away from his opponent. The knife stabbed at Mowl's heart before he had chance to land a blow. Mowl did the only thing he could; he brought his sword down towards the man's exposed back and sliced, with what little force he could muster. The man slumped forward anyway and Mowl had to dance backwards so that he did not land on top of him. The man's knife protruded from Mowl's chest. He felt no pain, only shock. He did not think he had shouted out, but suddenly Dorren and Blud were beside him with a storm lamp. Dorren's face darkened when he saw the bone-handled knife embedded in Mowl's breast. Blud moved to investigate the condition of the other man.

'I'm fine,' Mowl managed to say despite his shortness of breath. Every part of him trembled and he still didn't feel any pain. It must be shock. He felt light-headed and more than a little shaky but that was all. Surely he should be dead? Dorren took his own knife and carefully cut away the fabric of Mowl's tunic to better judge the damage. He gave a dry laugh.

'The Keeper kept you, sure enough.'

He braced his right hand against Mowl's chest, and, before Mowl could object, pulled the knife from its resting place – Dake Varl's leather book. There was not a drop of blood on its blade. It had not even nicked his skin. The other man had fared less well. The honed edge of Mowl's sword had cut through his clothes and skin so that blood now soaked his tunic. With more force behind the blow Mowl would have severed his spine. As it was, he had caused him pain, but no serious injury.

'What happened?' Dorren kept his voice low.

Mowl scowled, trying to calm his beating heart. He tried to stop himself from trembling – it was unmanly.

'Um. I heard a sound and saw someone searching the cart. He knew I was there and jumped out on me. It happened so quickly … I … I was too slow.'

'Oh, but you were lucky and lucky is even better than fast.' Dorren patted him consolingly on his shoulder and made him wince. His old injury was bleeding again. It was a good job he had not got work with the Militia – they would probably have kicked him out for incompetence – if he'd lived long enough.

Blud had tied the hands of Mowl's attacker with some rope from the cart.

He all but lifted the interloper off the ground as he manhandled him. Blud moved with the same ease and confidence that had characterised Dake Varl.

Dorren lifted the storm light so that it shone into their prisoner's eyes. He was a young man, not much more than four sixyears. He had a small-featured, handsome face and a shock of white hair; not blonde, but white as an old man's and as thick and curly as lamb's wool. His now tattered tunic revealed a lean and muscled torso, slight but strong. He did not look like a farmer either.

'Why were you searching our cart?' Dorren's voice was hard. The other man's eyes remained defiant.

'I was hungry. I was looking for something to eat.'

'Would it not have been wiser to ask at the inn?' Blud's tone was as uncompromising as Dorren's.

'I'm on the run. I didn't want to bump into any soldiers.'

'How do you know we're not soldiers?'

The man's eyes slid to Dorren's humped back and Blud's greying hair, but he said nothing.

'Why did you attack our man here?'

'He might have been a soldier. I didn't have time to ask him.'

The man was very composed.

'Why are you on the run?' Mowl had calmed down sufficiently to be able to trust his voice. A man that quick with a knife could easily be a murderer for all they knew.

'I've been up north, up at Lerry helping out at the quarry. The miners there are a devout lot and when soldiers came and demanded stone for the temple and destroyed their shrine to the Keeper, they fought back. The Succeptor was killed but so were most of the Militia. I'd only been helping out there a half year. I thought it was time to move on. A soldier disagreed and I knifed him.' The man shrugged. 'So I'm on the run. My name is Ponn Gage.' There was a small silence while Dorren weighed this up. It was a too familiar story to be dismissed.

Mowl felt faint. The Succeptor of Lerry, his only hope, was dead!

Mowl struggled not to panic. He forced himself to focus on the matter at hand. For a man so badly out-numbered Ponn seemed remarkably calm and breezy. His dark eyes were both confident and calculating. Mowl did not like him. Something about him niggled at some memory, some bad memory, yet he knew he'd never seen the man before. Mowl could not work it out. Ponn Gage was speaking again.

'I thought I might swing south and join the rebellion. I don't much like what's going on any more than the next man.'

'And what rebellion might this be?' asked Dorren coldly and Mowl saw that he had his hand on the hilt of his own knife. Dorren's malformation made sword work difficult but Mowl had already witnessed his skill with his knife, not that it took much skill to kill a man with his hands tied behind his back. Blud looked bleak but Ponn smiled with cold charm. Mowl looked at him and thought – he's talked his way out of worse situations. He was not a man to underestimate nor a man to trust.

Chapter 21

To Maybury: Days 16 – 18

The young priest smiled his supercilious smile and gazed at the sleeping animal, safely caged.

'So this is your arl, is it, Kreek? Not very mysterious, is she? She doesn't seem to be doing much that's special. She looks like a fox to me.'

Kreek said nothing. He was trying hard not to show his contempt for this man. It took a lot of effort.

Sar Venish did not bother to make the effort. 'My dear ... actually, what *is* your name?'

The young priest coloured a little. He had been trained at court but was far from the status of the aristocratic Second Household to which Sar Venish had at one time certainly belonged.

'My name is Cantus.'

'Well, my dear, Domus Cantus, you must remember from your extensive studies that an arl does not do anything. It does not have to. To contradict your philosophy it merely has to be. This one is in a sorry state. The scholar Varlen once expressed a belief in his lesser-known work '*A Speculation on the Palingenesis of Arls*' that if translated from their natural tier and realm of existence, the very hours of such a profoundly spiritual being were numbered. From the look of this poor creature he was right, always assuming that our noble sergeant has not captured just any old fox that he happened to get his hands on.'

As Sergeant Kreek had suspected, the young priest, Domus Cantus, had singularly failed to keep Sar Venish in anything approaching a sober state. The Domus was embarrassed, but then that had surely been Sar Venish's intention. Kreek would have wished to work for worthier men.

'Yes, how do you know this is the same fox that you claim protected Mowl Speare?'

'She is the same. I would know her anywhere.'

It was the simple truth. Keeper knows, he was not a religious man and not even a very good man, but Kreek's powers of observation were excellent. This was the arl. Her distinctive glow, her aura of otherness was fading. Her fur had lost its luminescence. Her eyes had lost some of the intelligence that had so disturbed him when last they had met. But she was essentially the same creature. Something had happened to her, something had changed her. Maybe the scholar Varlen was right, always assuming that Sar Venish had not simply made him up to highlight the priest's woeful ignorance.

The priest, for all his pompous ways, did not know how to deal with the sergeant. He was afraid of him. It showed in his rapid sideways glances and the unnecessary aggression of his tone.

'Well, if you are quite sure. The sooner you can take it to the King, the better. You still have Sar Venish's missive?' Sergeant Kreek nodded. His silence always unnerved the Domus. 'Well, off you go then.'

'My men?'

'I assure you they are in excellent hands,' the priest intoned, grandly.

Sergeant Kreek wondered to whom such hands might belong. They were a raw bunch, troublesome and undisciplined like most of the new recruits. It bothered him that he had been able to devote so little time to his real job of training the newest of the King's men. He could not see them amounting to much under the leadership of the odious priest and the dissolute Sar Venish. No good could come of such an association. It pained him that the proud traditions of the King's men had been so debased that he had to accept the orders of such men. Technically, the priest was the King's representative in Deworth and outranked him, as even minor nobles did. He did not argue. There was little point. He just turned and, with rudeness that no experienced man would have

196

tolerated, walked away. He fingered the old scar on his right arm, distractedly. He still retained that small core of pride from his days as bodyguard to the old King. He surprised himself with the force of his contempt for both the priest and Sar Venish.

Nonetheless he obeyed his orders. It grieved him to take the arl anywhere she might not want to go. He was glad she still slept as he secured the cage on to a small cart and mounted up. He did not want her to be afraid.

Fox slept for a long time. Kreek was worried; but for the steady rising and falling of her chest, he would have been sure she was dead. Surely even arls did not sleep for two solid days without food or water? He left food in her cage in the hope that the aroma might wake the creature. She looked thinner and seemed to be fading before his eyes. Her ribs were beginning to protrude slightly and her coat had lost its lustrous sheen. Kreek was worried. He even stopped at a roadside shrine to the Keeper to say an awkward prayer for her safe keeping. He did not know what the King, or rather his over-powerful minister Garnem, might do when he got his hands on the arl. Hale Garnem was rather fond of public displays, particularly hangings and floggings. Kreek had heard of more than fifty men and women from powerful families within the territory who had been executed in an effort to 'Protect the State and the King's just aim of promulgating the way of the Purple Path'. It did not seem quite rational to kill an arl in the same way. He was not an educated man but he was not a stupid one either. He knew that according to the King arls were not supposed to exist, so killing one was impossible. He did not want to think too much about what Garnem might do to her instead. He would do something, Kreek was sure, something vile that would illustrate that the body of this fox could not contain an unborn human soul. Kreek toyed with disobeying his orders, or pretending that the arl had escaped him. One look at Fox's immobile body was enough to convince him that she needed him. He would, of course, obey his orders. He was a soldier; he did not know what else he could be.

Grace fought exhaustion. She had to be ready and waiting if Karen's condition changed. Grace had talked to Karen a lot since the clairvoyant had been. Grace had decided to trust her instincts and try to draw Karen back from that other place, try to force a reaction. Billy had been in a couple of times. She relayed their conversation to Karen, word for word. He had gone back out with Tina, because she wasn't a bad girl really, just hard done by, insecure because of low self-esteem. Billy had started doing a counselling course and some other qualifications at night school and was beginning to talk like those American women on day-time TV. Grace couldn't understand half of it. He was trying to persuade Tina to visit Karen. He'd been in to ask Grace if she'd mind. Grace was at a loss. She was too tired to hate Tina as George did. She was too weary to manage any strong emotion any more. She lived in an isolation bubble of failing hope, breathed an air tainted with loss. Not even anger could permeate it. She asked Karen what she thought and argued aloud about the rights and wrongs of such a visit, but it was only to pass the time. It was only words, an argument that meant little. She could not raise any real outrage.

There had been a change in Karen since the clairvoyant came. It was not what she had longed for. Karen was worse. Her vital signs were much weaker. She looked very close to death. It was hard to see her now, covered as she was in an ever more elaborate wreath of tubes and lines. Grace's valiant chatter was interspersed with beeps and buzzers, as monitors registered Karen's failing vitality. More than all that, for the first time Grace began to question whether Karen really did still live on in that frail, diminished form. Grace had lost all sense of her granddaughter and was running out of hope.

Chapter 22

A New Direction:
Day 17 (Night) – Day 19

Blud insisted they leave Calp immediately. He had won the argument. There was no point in seeking out the Succeptor of Lerry. If Ponn had told them the truth then he was dead. Mowl did not argue. He would never find Fox now. Nothing mattered except his promise to Leva and he still had no real stomach for revenge. Ponn lay beside him, bound but not gagged. Blud would have killed him, but Dorren was not so cold-blooded. Mowl allowed the rocking of the cart to lull him to sleep. He tried to seek out Fox but the searching presence was very close. He fled in terror from his own dreams, which were haunted by this faceless threat. He watched Ponn in the near darkness. He was so deeply asleep he seemed scarcely to move. Mowl envied him that oblivion. The night seemed very long, very cold and very lonely, and his bleak thoughts offered him no comfort.

They arrived at the village of Argon soon after dawn. It was a small place of no more than ten simple cottages, clustered at the edge of the tree line and painted with some ochre-coloured, vile-smelling concoction to seal them against the extreme weather. Above the village the bald crags of the ice-crowned Tear Mountains loomed like some malevolent creature of the magical tier; while below the village the deep gloom of the Rye Forest sheltered enough malevolent creatures of the natural tier to make Mowl very nervous. Mowl couldn't work out why anyone would live there. It was cold and the air was weighed down with the promise of snow. It was a place of tangible tensions. Blud seemed anxious. Was he leading them into a trap? The village felt like the kind of place where a trap might be sprung and Mowl did not wholly trust Blud. Dorren had approached one of the larger cottages for food and though they paid well the villagers had been grudging in sparing even poor ale and meat for the travellers and there was nothing that even approximated an inn. Mowl, Dorren, Blud and Ponn huddled together in the cart for warmth, out of the brisk wind. It was too windy to light a fire. There was no other shelter. They stayed there for most of the day, locked in their own thoughts.

The murderer, Ponn, insisted on sitting very close to Mowl. They were so close together that he could smell the man's sweat, his unwashed clothes and another smell, familiar, distinctive, elusive. Mowl did not like the smell and he did not like the man who had so nearly killed him, but his conversation was easy and humorous and before he was fully aware of it, Mowl found himself telling the stranger all about Fox and his one-time hope of being a scholar.

He regretted it immediately afterwards and lapsed into silence. Dorren and Blud said nothing though Ponn kept trying to make them talk. He was very interested in the small leather-bound book that had saved Mowl's life. Ponn's enquiries were met with blank and frankly hostile stares from the older men. Mowl wished he too had stayed aloof and silent in front of the white-haired stranger. Eventually even Ponn gave up his one-sided attempt at conversation. It was too cold. Their breath froze on the air like the emanations of an ice creature or a physical manifestation of their misery. They made very little noise. Then they heard it – a sound to dread, the steady march of feet, horses' hooves, voices – soldiers.

Mowl was terrified. The King's men would find him and he would be hung. It was over. Blud stumbled for the back of the cart and clumsily unhooked the ramp. Sunlight spilled into the cart, illuminating faces tight with worry. Ponn's eyes were shut as though in prayer, his hair shone like a nimbus. No one spoke. No one stopped Blud as he hurried down the ramp and out of view. Had he betrayed them? Nobody pursued him. Their collective will had been sapped by just the sound of unseen men marching towards them. They could have made a run for the forest but they knew what their survival chances would be with winter coming. They just sat there, trying to find enough courage to face the inevitable. Mowl's throat was dry. Who would miss him? Leva? Fox? Only if she was not, herself, dead. He hoped death would not hurt too much and then he berated himself as a coward. He gripped the ever-present sword. It had not saved his father and there was no reason to suppose it would save him, but perhaps he should die fighting.

'Are we going to let them just take us?' he asked. His voice stuck a little in his throat and came out rather more squeakily than he would have wished.

Ponn opened cunning eyes. 'We could ambush them.'

'Some ambush! There's only three of us and Blud has probably told them we're here,' said Dorren, bleakly. He would blame himself for trusting Blud. Mowl noticed that his hand was now curled around the hilt of his knife.

'I'd rather not just wait here to be taken. I'd rather do something even if it doesn't make any difference to – you know – what happens,' Mowl added. It would be easier to die fighting if Dorren stood by his side. Being alone at such time shouldn't matter, but Mowl found that it did. Dorren would be as good a man to die with as any and a better man than most.

'Well, then,' said Dorren, 'let's do it and pray to the Keeper that we serve equilibrium, while we're at it.'

He rooted around up the sleeve of his jerkin and pulled out a second knife.

'Can you fight with two knives at once?' Mowl asked in surprise.

'It's a good time to find out.' Dorren grinned shakily, and that poor joke gave them both a kind of courage.

'Ready?'

Mowl nodded and bounded down the ramp a little unsteadily. The sound of footsteps was closer and with it came the murmur of voices and the smell of an army. Fox might have identified its elements. Mowl couldn't but he knew it for what it was, the scent of many men and animals, blown on the strong wind. He let that wind blow away his fear. He felt stronger, just standing upright with the sword in his hand.

'Are you coming?' Dorren spoke to Ponn who remained in the cart, frozen and crystalline white. Ponn showed his still bound hands and Dorren cut the rope that bound him with a single slice of his lethal knife. Ponn rubbed the pink marks where the rope had chafed his pale skin.

'I'll follow,' he said. Dorren nodded. He did not think that Ponn was the kind of man for futile heroics. Maybe Ponn would get away to the forest and take his chances there. Dorren thought he would rather have a clean death than slow starvation and exposure, but it was not a great set of choices.

Mowl and Dorren walked side by side towards the sound of the army. Some two sixties men and maybe the same number of mountain ponies filled the stony lane that linked the houses of Argon. Whoever they were they were not dressed in the livery of King Flane. They were not dressed in any way Mowl had ever seen before. Most wore mountain men's goatskin jackets under heavily padded, quilted tabards. They were made of thick undyed wool in shades of white from clean snow white to dark oatmeal white and elaborately embroidered with multicoloured thread so that each was different, each with its own complex arrangement of swirling patterns. The tabards were long, reaching to below their wearer's knees to cover the tops of thick fur-lined boots. Mowl could tell they were fur-lined because they had a cuff of fur turned over at the top. Each man wore fur-lined gauntlets of goatskin and a close fitting, fur-lined hood that covered most of their faces, showing only their pale eyes shadowed by their hoods. On top of his fur-lined hood each man wore a pointed, steel helmet, swathed in a turban of oatmeal cloth decorated with bright embroidery. Each man carried either a huge double-headed axe, or a sizeable long sword, strapped across his back. One man, Mowl noticed, had a mace and a coil of iron chain, barbed with spearheads. Almost all of them were as tall as Mowl but in their bulky clothing all looked at least twice as broad. They stood in line and waited. There was very little chatter. Mowl did not know what to make of them. Were they friend or foe? Blud was talking to the only short man there. The man would have been stocky even if he hadn't been wearing his strange costume; padded as he was, he looked almost as broad as he was tall. Mowl gathered his courage. If he was going to fight these men he would try to give a good account of himself, but his stomach roiled and churned and his legs felt as weak as water.

Blud waved cheerfully at Mowl and Dorren. They gripped their weapons tighter and advanced.

'Mowl Speare, Dorren Varl, this is Huta Arn. Our problems are over. I think we have just found the rebel army!'

Mowl tried to control the sudden trembling that afflicted all his muscles. They seemed to recognise what his thinking self could not quite grasp; he did not have to fight this army; he did not have to die just yet. Huta Arn was brother to his own father and to Dake Varl. Huta Arn, however, gave no smile of welcome; his face was a mask of hostility.

'So, you are the treacherous murderer?' His voice was as hard and cold as Mowl's sword. It cut through his sudden relief and turned his spine to ice. Blud was bemused.

'What do you mean?'

'The Succeptor of Lerry was knifed three days ago. His assistant managed to let us know that before he died he had offered hospitality to my nephew, Mowl Speare. Speare had gone before they found the body.'

'But this man here was with me three days ago, he is not responsible, I swear it!' Blud seemed outraged that Huta could even think that Mowl might be a murderer. Mowl felt a pang of guilt. He had distrusted Blud.

'Do you know what this man looked like, the one who claimed to be Mowl?'

Huta shrugged. 'Some of my men here knew the Succeptor. It's possible they saw the man.' Huta paused. 'I am glad it was not the work of my kinsman. It makes more sense for the murderer to be a King's spy. I will find out who did it – they'll pay, don't you worry.' His smile was brief and savage, then he extended a huge, gloved hand to Mowl. 'In the mountains we embrace a kinsman – it is one way to keep warm. If you are truly my brother's son, I will gladly share warmth with you.'

He enfolded Mowl in a hard embrace. Mowl did not know how to respond. He had experienced terror, relief, fear and now this new, unfamiliar emotion in a matter of heartbeats. Now, the only feeling that mattered was the sudden warmth that engulfed him when Huta called him kinsman – a warmth that had little to do with his external temperature. Huta himself was not unmoved.

'Mant was a good man and the only man ever to beat

me in a fair fight. It grieves me to march on my own King and bring more strife to our already troubled land, but I would be proud to have my brother's son by my side.'

Mowl had to turn away so that Dorren and Blud did not see how close he was to tears.

'I am afraid I have little avuncular comfort to offer you this night, nephew, just a hard march until we reach the shelter of the forest and a cold night by the campfire, but you will understand what we have to do here. I heard about Dake and I will grieve for him only after I have seen the head of King Flane separated from his spineless body.' Huta turned his attention to Blud; even so, Mowl hesitated to move away.

'Now, I have a problem. I was expecting word from Fenn Dale. I have heard nothing of him for weeks.'

Mowl kept very still and listened. That name again. Was Fenn Dale friend or foe?

Blud scowled. 'Many of Dake Varl's contacts are dead. Maybe too many of Fenn Dale's men have suffered the same fate. Have you heard nothing?' Blud dropped his voice conspiratorially so that Mowl had to strain to hear what was said next.

'I do not know if the Queen is with us, no.'

'You cannot march under her banner without her permission.'

Huta shook his head. 'It will be harder to attract men

to the cause without it.'

'What will you do?'

'We can march under King Rufin's colours.'

Blud shrugged. 'I doubt that many men would rally to that flag.'

Huta grinned, showing sharp, brown-stained teeth. 'I don't know. He was not so bad as Flane. Sometimes it's not what you stand for but what you stand against that counts.'

Blud nodded. 'When do we march?'

'Now.' Huta turned to give an order to a gigantic fur-clad figure just behind him, and Mowl found himself being guided, with Dorren, towards the middle ranks of the army. There was no time for discussion. Someone unhitched Dorren's carthorses and brought them to Mowl's side. They left the cart at Argon; it was of no use to them in the forest. Dorren and Mowl walked together in stunned silence as the cold day became a bitterly cold night.

'Did you see what happened to Ponn?'

Dorren shrugged. 'He could be anywhere. I think he did follow me. I heard his footsteps. How d'you think Blud knows Huta?'

Mowl shook his head. He did not know anything. He did not know where Ponn was and didn't much care. More importantly he didn't know where Fox was, who Blud was, or what Fenn Dale was up to. He also could not work out why, after the brief embrace of a kinsman who had ignored him all his life, he felt a strange glow of unexpected happiness. They walked on in silence. The mountain men set a brisk pace. The snow did not fall. Mowl did not know whether that was good or bad. His bones ached with the tension of trying to keep warm.

They walked for a long time. Mowl moved beyond tiredness to a state of stumbling exhaustion. He had scarcely walked at all since his injury. Dorren's limp became more pronounced with every step. Mowl knew he was in great pain. He would have offered a helping shoulder if he had not feared to offend Dorren's pride. They carried on, reduced to a mindless shambling. The order came through to make camp in the glade and Mowl halted then. The troop may have been small but it was well organised. The horses were hobbled and watered, fires were lit, food shared and crude shelters made in no time. Everyone had a task to do and did it with quiet competence. Even the watch roster seemed to have been prearranged. Mowl and Dorren were poorly equipped for a forced march having nothing but their weapons and the clothes they stood up in. Mowl was afraid that they would both prove inadequate. The mountain men were taciturn to a man but before Mowl had really understood what was going on, someone had taken the reins of the horse from his hands, which were numb with cold. Food and extra items of clothing found their way to the two newcomers and space was made by the fire, under a tepee of branches. It was impossible to know whom to thank and thanks did not seem to be expected. Mowl was just grateful to have survived the day. His clogs had never been designed for marching. His feet were blistered and bleeding, every part of him ached. He could not think about what would happen when they reached their destination. He would probably be required to die. He sank into sleep almost as soon as he finished his food. He still had equilibrium to serve but he took comfort in the fact that in the rebel army he had found people who might know how to go about the duty of revenge.

When they woke short hours later it was only to march some more through the Forest of Rye at an unrelenting pace until, exhausted, they camped again outdoors in the company of the tireless mountain men. Dorren and Mowl stayed together, exhausted beyond speech, beyond thought. The world had contracted into the rhythm of the horses' steady gait, their own feet and the jingling of harnesses. They ate what they were given, grateful that it was a stew that needed little effort to consume. Dorren was asleep almost before he had finished, his face grey with fatigue and pain. Mowl tried to look for Ponn amongst the crowd of mountain men, but it was hard to care too much about his whereabouts when the pain from his injury nagged at him in the cold and he ached all over. His last conscious thought was of Fox. They were walking rapidly south, towards Deworth. He could begin to hope that he might see her again.

Chapter 23

On Watch Duty: Day 19

It was with great foreboding that Kreek cantered up to the castle stables and passed the reins of his horse to the groom. He dare not disobey his orders and he had a superstitious fear of involving himself in this business. Who was he to judge how equilibrium could best be served?

The duty guard escorted him towards the presence of the King himself. Two of the King's own bodyguard carried the wooden cage to the audience chamber. The creature did not even stir. Had he had the power Sergeant Kreek would have summoned an Adept to investigate the fox arl's condition, but he had heard that it was not just Domus Cantus who killed Adepts without provocation. Rumour had it that at least half of the executed 'traitors' had some Adept's gift and training. The King or Garnem or both did not approve of Adepts. He recalled with regret the cowardly slaughter of the Adept of Deworth. It pained him to think of that.

Kreek did not much like the coldness of the stone walls or the eerie quality of the coloured light that filtered through the many, narrow, stained-glass windows. To Kreek, glass windows were an affectation that made the castle harder to defend. The light and the enclosing stone made him feel as if he was leaving the tier of the natural man altogether and entering the tier of the magical; something else that King Flane did not believe in.

As they neared the audience chamber the corridor grew crowded with courtiers and petitioners, an anxious buzzing throng of people that made Kreek rest his hand on his sword hilt and loosen his belt knife from its sheath. He did not like crowds. He did not like the stench of too many spiced and perfumed people in elaborate clothes, any one of whom could have concealed a weapon under a velvet sleeve. Strangely, his first thought was for the arl. He hoped she would not wake and be disturbed by the press of the milling crowd. He unconsciously opened wide his chest and adopted a fighting stance. He was a bodyguard again, braced to defend his prisoner. The armed escort and his own forbidding face cleared a way through the crowd. The sleeping arl brought silence in her wake. He saw fear in more than one face. All courtiers had converted to the Purple Path but Kreek could see in their eyes that they liked the idea of a caged arl about as much as he did. The silence was awed and reverential which was odd as most of those present professed that arls could not exist. He permitted himself a grim smile, which swiftly evaporated as the King's crier announced their presence in the audience chamber.

The chamber was a miracle of arching stone, elaborately painted with such art that it took his eyes a moment to distinguish reality from illusion. It seemed as if the King and Queen sat together in a wooded valley carpeted with lush grass on a summer's day. Kreek blinked and realised that the King sat in austere black against a painted wall of extraordinary beauty. The King was a surprisingly small man with plain features and a large crown. He needed it. Without it no one would ever have taken notice of him. He looked earnest and serious and unremittingly ordinary. The Queen was still as he remembered her, scarcely touched by the years, a woman of unusual loveliness but with a vague abstracted air as if she was scarcely present in spirit. It was a look he had only seen before on the face of the Adept of his home village. It made him deeply uncomfortable. Queen Lin used to be regal and commanding.

There were other figures present whose livery of the Second Household made them seem part of the huge painting. It was one of these who spoke to him. Kreek had seen him before. He was the King's own adviser, Hale Garnem, a man with much power and no scruples.

Kreek began to focus as he did in battle, slipping into a kind of heightened awareness. His instinct for danger warned him, 'Think!'

'Sergeant!' Hale Garnem did not speak in High Loyrenton but in the common language of the people. Sergeant Kreek was relieved. His grasp of the court tongue was tentative.

'Sar!'

'Explain! What are you doing coming before us with this creature?'

'Sar, I was instructed by Domus Cantus of the Purple Path to bring this fox before you. Some people have described her as an arl.'

'You know, of course, that there is no such thing.'

'I know that is the teaching of the Purple Path and I believe that is why he wished me to bring this fox to you.'

The King looked forward and squinted at the sleeping animal. When he spoke his voice was light and melodious. He too used the common tongue, though somewhat awkwardly.

'Is this the creature who was linked with the traitor, Mowl Speare?'

'I believe so, Your Majesty.'

The King stepped forward and approached the cage.

'As I suspected, this is but an ordinary fox. Is that not so, Hale?'

'Indeed, it seems probable,' replied the King's adviser.

The Queen suddenly seemed to wake up to the proceedings. She shed her vagueness as if it were some garment she no longer needed. She looked at Kreek with a focused directness that took him aback.

'Did you say that you believed this fox to be an arl?' Her voice was precise and resonant.

'People have thought so, Your Majesty,' Kreek replied carefully.

'Why does she sleep?'

'I don't know, Your Majesty, I think perhaps she is sick.'

The Queen indicated that the cage should be unlocked and, ignoring the presence of her husband, gently lifted the sleeping creature from her temporary prison and carried her back to the throne. She sat for a moment stroking the fox's sleeping form, the dreamy look returning to her face.

Kreek saw the expression on Hale Garnem's face alter. He had no power over the Queen. After several minutes of silence the Queen spoke.

'I am tired. I will see no more petitioners today. Do carry on without me. Sergeant, please accompany me to my chamber. I would know more about this creature.'

She left through a different door and, with a brisk salute to the King and his adviser, Kreek marched after her. The two soldiers of the King's Guard followed at a discreet distance. Did they think he would harm his Queen?

The Queen carried the fox in her arms as if she were a baby. The fox showed no sign of being aware of anything. The Queen flashed Kreek a hand signal that startled him further. 'Stay close.' He recognised it from his service with King Rufin's Guard as a young soldier. Could the Queen have recognised him? It did not seem likely. The Queen swept through the corridor at an altogether unregal pace. Kreek was almost at her shoulder. The King's men were a little behind. It would be unseemly and undignified for them to run.

'When we get to my room, bar the door immediately.' The Queen spoke in an undertone. Kreek felt his spirits sink. There was trouble coming. It was suddenly clear that the King's guards were not keeping a watchful eye on him but on the Queen herself. By the Keeper and all the tiers of being, he did not want to get mixed up in whatever was going on in the castle. It could prove a very quick way to die.

Kreek bolted the door carefully and moved a heavy carved chair in front of it for good measure. He did not know what to expect. The King's guards were outside the Queen's chamber and he was inside. Without fully intending to it seemed he had been forced to make a choice and for better or worse he was the Queen's man now. When he had finished securing the door he saluted the Queen.

'Your Majesty.'

The Queen looked at him thoughtfully. She had seated herself on another carved chair, the twin of the one now abutting the door. The fox, still asleep, lay on her lap. She stroked her as one might a pet cat.

'I'm afraid that by asking you here I have done you a disservice.'

Kreek made no reply.

'As far as my husband and his odious adviser are concerned, you will no longer be above suspicion. I'm sorry, I'm not in the habit of kidnapping soldiers but I find myself in somewhat desperate straits.' She sighed, then was again the decisive, businesslike leader he recalled from his youth.

'I will get straight to the point. King Flane has chosen not to believe in any tier of existence but this. Under the influence of Hale Garnem he has decided that our lives would be more efficacious if we all concentrated on the here and now and not on other modes of being and other tiers of existence. He supports the philosophy of the Purple Path because it is concerned only with the world of the four crude senses: sight, sound, taste and touch. He believes only in what he can hold in his hands. It would be very inconvenient if other people believed in this arl. She is proof, if such a thing were possible, that there are other tiers of existence and that the adherents to the Purple Path are wrong. There would be no need for temples and no need for the temple tax, which largely funds our enormous Militia and without the Militia, Hale Garnem is merely an adviser. You understand what I'm saying?'

Kreek nodded.

'Forgive my frankness. I don't have the time or energy for dissembling any more. This creature is in grave danger whether she is an arl or not. She is of enormous use to the King's enemies even if she is only a dumb fox. I want you to promise to protect her, with your life if necessary, and get her out of here. I have compromised you now. Do not think of going to tell the King what I've told you. He will kill you because he will think that I have sent you. I'm sorry to put you in this position, but I have few options.'

'But you are Queen!' Kreek could not help but say it.

The Queen sighed weakly. 'Things have changed since Rufin's day. As you know, Flane is only King because Rufin died and I married him. Loyrenton still holds to the ancient tradition of inheritance through the female line, but at the moment I am Queen in name only. Hale Garnem has the army, the ear of my husband and most importantly my daughter, Lenya. I am a prisoner. My daughter is *protected* by those loyal to Hale Garnem. He keeps her as far away from me as possible in the King's wing of the castle. If I were to try and discredit him – and make no mistake, Garnem, not Flane, is ruler now – he would kill her. I would lose my beloved child and the security of the Royal Succession. I am as trapped as the arl was in her cage.'

'And now – will he not kill her if you help this arl to escape?'

The Queen shook her head.

'I have other plans, but it's not a risk I take lightly.' The Queen's bravery touched a reserve of sentiment Kreek did not know he possessed.

'What would you have me do, Your Majesty?'

'It would be easier if this fox were awake. What did you give her?'

'Truly, Your Majesty, I gave her nothing. She has slept for almost three days.'

The Queen looked thoughtful again, dreamy and distant as she had in the council chamber. Realisation struck him. The woman was an Adept. He wondered if Hale Garnem knew.

'I cannot say if she is truly an arl, though I do not think she is entirely a fox. Something has happened to frighten her very badly. Her soul has gone to ground; she has buried herself in unconsciousness. To wake her we will have to lure her out.' The Queen spoke almost to herself. 'I haven't got much time. The guards will insist on entering here very soon. I know that you are honourable and brave, I recognised you even under that monstrous beard and I remember.' Kreek lowered his eyes, like any soldier he had done too much of which a sensitive man might be ashamed. He was not sure he was still honourable and brave. A lot had happened since the young Kreek had saved the Queen from an assassin's knife. Kreek fingered the old scar on his right arm. For years it had reminded him of better days and filled him with remembered pride and shame.

'I cannot do what I need to without your help. To whom do you owe allegiance?'

He answered honestly and unhesitatingly.

'The crown.'

'Would you swear personal allegiance to me? I will pay you well from my own fortune if I live. If I die, you may pledge allegiance to whomsoever wears the crown.'

Kreek did not have to think about it. His head was not easily turned, which was why it still remained on his shoulders, but in truth he would have done anything for this woman, from the moment he had first seen her some twenty years before. Besides, by all the laws of Loyrenton, she was the crown and his soldier's oath had always been hers.

'My allegiance has always been to the crown, Your Majesty, but if you wish it, I promise to serve you with my sword, my honour and my life, for as long as you live.'

The Queen's eyes were suspiciously moist and she glanced quickly away.

'As you've probably noticed I have some of an Adept's

gifts. I never trained properly – unfortunately, it wasn't thought seemly – but I have affinity with this creature. You say she was with Mowl Speare, Mant's son?'

Kreek nodded and blurted out, 'I'm afraid I tried to kill him.'

Kreek never knew why he said that, maybe he wanted her not to think too well of him. He knew he didn't deserve it.

The Queen raised one delicately arched eyebrow.

'Why did you not succeed?'

Kreek nodded at the fox.

'I saw her. She seemed all aglow and … I was afraid to harm one she protected.'

The Queen nodded her approval.

'If I'm going to lure her out of her wilful unconsciousness, I am going to have to try and enter the Adept's trance state. I need you to watch over us both.'

Kreek drew his sword and belt knife as the Queen settled herself, cross-legged on the floor in front of the fire. She gave Kreek a smile of unexpected brilliance and closed her eyes. Kreek suddenly felt very alone. For all he knew he was the Queen's whole army against the might of the King and the power of Hale Garnem. It was not a comforting thought.

Exhausted beyond the strength of her seventy years, Grace slumped in her plastic chair at Karen's bedside.

She was pale herself and a passing nurse, seeing her so deeply asleep and in such an uncomfortable position, paused to check her breathing. Grace still breathed, and grieved and waited. The nurse wondered which would cease first.

Chapter 24

Choosing: Day 19 (Night) – Day 20

*I*t was grey and misty in the place where Fox wandered. *Nothing seemed to have a clear outline, a discernible texture or an honest scent. It was a place of vagueness and uncertainty. She had been there for a long time, without food or rest, without the warmth of sunlight or the reassuring hunter's cloak of night. She was lost and alone and so numb with the nothingness of it all she almost didn't care.*

She did not know how long she had been there without anything happening, when, quite unexpectedly, several things happened at once. First, an owl appeared flapping through the deep greyness. She could not eat it for she couldn't catch it, but it didn't matter. There was something right about not being so alone. The owl watched her, but did not seem to be a threat. It seemed a familiar, comforting thing. It made her want to remember something, something that had once been important. Fox sat down near a tree just to be near something else in all this hazy nothingness. Next, just as she was beginning to enjoy the silent companionship of the owl, a beautiful, exotic bird appeared on another hazy tree. This too was out of her reach and did not smell as though it would be good to eat, carrying with it a pungent, spicy scent. The exotic bird brought colour to the grim place and Fox was content to watch it and take comfort in the presence of the friendly owl. It was nice to have company. Then, suddenly, a third creature, another fox materialised a few metres in front of her. It offered her no challenge, just sat and watched her. It might almost have been her own reflection, but it did not flick its tail when she flicked hers. Fox was nonplussed by this, by all of it. She decided to wait and see what would happen next.

'You can't just wait, you know, you must decide,' sang the exotic bird in a high, piping voice. 'Choose, choose, choose.'

Fox thought it odd that the bird sang words she understood; perhaps in this strange place that was the way things were. She had a pretty voice.

'Come home, Karen, love! Come home!' hooted the owl in a voice that was old and tired and full of love.

'I need you, I miss you, come back please, Fox,' said the fox, facing her with a look of such sad appeal in its dark eyes she thought she might cry. Something strange was going on here, something important. She knew these creatures, or she had once known them. She knew the owl who called her 'Karen'. The name opened the floodgates of memory.

'Grandmother!'

The owl flapped her wings excitedly and hooted. 'Come home, love, come home!'

The exotic bird sang again. 'You choose, you choose, you choose.'

The fox barked. 'Don't go! Don't go! I need you! Come back! Come back!'

The owl and the fox tried to drown each other out, while the exotic bird trilled high above them in a kind of elaborate descant. 'You choose, you choose, you choose.'

Karen Fox remembered all of it.

'Grandmother, I love you!'

The owl flapped its wings wildly and a silver tear dropped from its glassy eyes.

'I want to come home but I have some things to do here.'

The other fox was begging her now to stay and it was hard to resist another creature so like herself. Karen Fox was on her feet and walking towards that other fox. He spoke with Mowl's voice and with that recognition came the memory that she had abandoned him, that she had run away and left him when he had needed her. The strange place was getting stranger; a dark mistiness settled like flakes of soft soot and muffled all sound. The owl and the bird sounded fainter and further away.

'Grandmother!' Karen shouted as loudly as she could through the stifling blanket of shadow. Even the fox, that might have been Mowl, was hard to see. The owl and the exotic bird had completely disappeared. She panicked, calling wildly, 'Gran! Gran!' but the mistiness deadened all sound. Karen started to sob and, through the suffocating darkness, thought she still heard far away the owl's voice, cracked with sadness, hooting through the gloom, 'Be happy, Karen, love, be happy!'

She woke in an alien room to find her fox face wet with tears.

Dorren woke to a flurry of snow and an awareness of cramp, cold and stiffness in every joint. What rest he'd had hadn't been enough. The camp had all but disappeared and everyone but himself and Mowl were ready to march. He had not slept well on the cold ground. His limp was very much worse. Blud had sought them out and brought them some thick oat biscuits and a handful of blackberries to break their night's fast. He shared them out, stamping his feet on the frozen earth to get warm. The biscuits were hard to chew and the blackberries were sour, but Dorren was glad of them. He shook Mowl awake. He was very deeply asleep, but when he came to his senses he smiled with unadulterated pleasure.

'Fox is still alive. I dreamed about her. I think she's still in Loyrenton.'

Dorren mumbled something grumpily noncommittal but Mowl did not care.

The world was suddenly a less bleak place: Fox lived.

Somewhere in the part of himself that could launch his thoughts into the ether, he could feel the steady candle flame of her spirit still glowing brightly. Mowl felt his spirit expand with joy. The shadow of the unseen searcher was gone and Fox was still alive!

Mowl's high spirits encompassed even Blud. He was glad to see the older man.

'I meant to thank you for defending me to – my uncle.' It still seemed odd to have a family.

Blud shook his head as if it was nothing.

'What you doing here now – had enough hobnobbing with the command?' Dorren asked grouchily, though the grin with which he accompanied his words removed much of their sting.

Blud still looked uncomfortable even so.

'I wasn't quite honest with you before. I served as a mercenary abroad for many years – I've met Huta before and with him not being a professional soldier, there were things he wanted to ask me. I'm sorry I was not more honest before but ...' he trailed off.

Mowl was in an expansive mood and nodded encouragingly as if he believed it was perfectly all right to mislead close companions. They gathered up their things and joined the rest of the mountain men in companionable silence.

Blud looked around.

'Where's Ponn then?'

'Ponn? We've not seen him since Calp – we thought he was with some other group. 'Why?' Dorren limped stiffly; every step made him wince. He hoped he would loosen up as the day went on.

Blud swore inventively under his breath. Mowl, who had been watching Dorren's awkward progress with concern, turned his attention back to Blud.

'What's wrong? Oh, Ponn? He must have run for it after he followed me. In this cold, without a blanket or means of lighting a fire he's probably dead by now.' Mowl didn't feel too much regret for the loss of Ponn – there was something about his presence that oppressed him and made him uneasy.

Blud had gone very pale. 'I've been a fool,' he said simply.

'What— ? ' Mowl began.

'Ponn said the Succeptor was killed by the Militia, didn't he?'

Mowl nodded – he remembered the conversation well. He would not easily forget his feeling of despair after that revelation.

'Well,' said Blud impatiently, 'that was a lie; wasn't it? Why lie if he did not have something to do with it and if he had something to do with it he was probably an agent of Hale Garnem!'

It was Mowl's turn to look stricken. He should have thought of that himself. He ought to have made more of an effort to look for Ponn.

'He will betray us to the King!' Dorren's tense face creased into a frown.

'It's worse than that. Was he following you when I spoke with Huta – you know, that first time?'

Mowl shrugged. 'Blud, I didn't notice. I thought Huta was a King's man – I was too worried about dying to care about anything else.'

Blud gave Mowl a swift appraising look. 'I'm sorry I hadn't remembered that. But please try and remember! It's important.' Blud's voice was both more urgent and more commanding than Mowl had ever heard it before.

'Why does it matter?' Mowl couldn't see why Blud should be so insistent about the detail – Ponn had gone to warn King Flane of their whereabouts. What more did they need to know?

Blud seemed mildly irritated by Mowl's slowness, but spelled his concerns out syllable by syllable. 'Because if he followed you, he would have heard us talking and if he's an agent of Flane he shouldn't have heard what was said.'

'And what was that?' Mowl felt stupid, but his memory of the whole conversation was somewhat over-shadowed by his overwhelming relief that he wasn't about to be killed. 'That Huta was awaiting news of the Queen from Fenn Dale.'

'So? I don't understand.' The cold seemed to have numbed Mowl's thoughts. He couldn't grasp what Blud was talking about.

'First, King Flane does not know that the rebels are looking to the Queen to lend them her support. We have heard that Flane is keeping her and the Princess virtual prisoners.' Blud swallowed hard. 'Look, while the Queen is by his side, or at least, in the palace, Flane can claim to be the legitimate ruler. If enough people were convinced the Queen was against him, he would be in a difficult position with his subjects and if the Queen could publicly denounce him, his rule would be unlawful. Rather than risk that,' Blud looked deeply concerned, 'He might kill her. Second,' Blud paused, uncertain whether he should continue. He continued: 'Fenn Dale is the main organiser of the rebellion *and* King Flane's spymaster!'

It took a moment for this intelligence to make any impact on Mowl. Fenn Dale was on their side, in spite of all his doubts. Mowl felt very cold. If he'd stayed with Fenn Dale he would still be with Fox and he would not be bound by his promise of revenge. Blud had already begun to move away.

'Where are you going?' Mowl asked.

'With fast horses and no rest Ponn could be in Maybury by late tomorrow. There is a route through the Calley Rift that leads straight to Maybury through the forest. It's hard terrain for an army but I've ridden it once. The Queen, Fenn Dale and the rebellion are all at risk! Maybe Huta can send a man that way to warn the Queen!'

Blud disappeared in the direction of Huta, who led the rough column of men. Mowl squinted after him. At least Blud seemed to understand what was going on. Mowl most certainly did not. If only he'd trusted Fenn Dale, he would never have lost Fox. By the Keeper, running away had been a mistake. He couldn't afford to make any more.

Chapter 25

Unexpected Developments: Day 20

Karen's vital signs were stronger, the tubes were gone, and George was bemused by his wife's grief.

'She's not coming back, George, I know there's something else that's pulling her away from us.'

'Grace, use your common sense. You have some kind of mad dream about a red fox and you decide that means Karen isn't going to get better. That's not like you, Grace, to be so fanciful. You don't know anything. She's got a medical condition. That's got nothing to do with dreams.'

'But you don't believe she's going to get better either, do you?'

The question stung him. He didn't want to say those words. Until he said them he could pretend to share his wife's hope.

'I don't know anything about medical stuff but the nurse said she was improving. Her colour's better.'

But Grace was not to be consoled.

After George had gone, Billy came round with his usual large bouquet of roses for Karen.

'What if she is afraid to come back? Because of Tina and everything. Maybe if Tina could apologise, Karen would know it was over.'

'Does Tina want to come?' Grace spoke flatly. It was hard to focus on Billy's conversation.

'No way, but I've told her she has to face up to it and face you – I don't know about George, he might try to kill her.'

'George would kill her. I don't know, Billy. I don't want to see her; you never know I might kill her myself. Look what she's done to my girl! I'm not sure I'm strong enough to forgive her.'

She looked at Billy's earnest face. She knew he loved Tina and wanted Grace to forgive her. She really didn't think she could.

'Look, bring her in tomorrow at about eleven o'clock. I'll go and have a coffee in the canteen. Don't ask me, Billy, I can't see her, even for your sake. She's taken the only thing in this world I care about, apart from George. It's too much to ask me, whatever your psychologist counsellor people tell you. It's too much.'

And after Billy had gone she sat and wept, as she had

not allowed herself to do since the whole nightmare had started.

It was dawn by the time the Queen opened her eyes. Kreek had been worried. He allowed himself to relax, imperceptibly. He had been afraid that she might not wake. She had looked so still and lifeless. Kreek was relieved to see that the fox was also awake. The light of intelligence was back in her eyes. She snarled at him and would have gone for him with her sharp, vicious teeth if the Queen had not caught her and pulled her firmly back.

'She remembers me.' Kreek kept his voice steady, though he was startled by her response.

'It would seem so.'

'She hasn't eaten for a while, Your Majesty. She must be hungry.' It was ridiculous that Kreek, battle-hardened veteran that he was, should be so concerned for the condition of a skinny fox. He couldn't help it. He *was* concerned about her.

'I think we will have to let the King's guard know that all is well. Hold her and I will send for some food!' It struck him then, for the first time, that the Queen had no servants at all, only guards. She was right. Things had been very different when she had been with Rufin.

Fox would not permit herself to be held by Kreek. She turned into a snarling bundle of muscle, teeth and claws when he tried. The Queen could not hold her either, but half dropped, half laid her on the rug-covered floor. Kreek knelt before the fox like a supplicant before his Queen. He did not speak much High Loyrenton but he did what he could with the common tongue.

'Noble arl, I see that you remember our last meeting. It grieves me greatly to recall it. I am sorry I harmed your companion. I had been ordered to kill him as a traitor. I know now that I was wrong. The Queen has instructed me to protect you. I have given her my word that I will serve her and protect you. I give you that same promise.'

Kreek spoke in total earnestness. He had made his own mind up about her and nothing had happened to change it. She was more than a fox, even if she turned out to be less than an arl. Somehow in his own mind being accepted by Fox was all tied up with the restoration of his honour. He could not have explained how, even to himself.

The Queen looked surprised by his speech and his action, the more so when the fox ceased baring her teeth and stepped towards the sergeant. The fox opened her mouth. The Queen and Kreek both wondered if she intended to bite him. Kreek did not move but met the fox's green-eyed gaze with his own steady, chilly stare. The fox bowed her head and quite deliberately licked Kreek's nose.

The Queen laughed out loud. The sergeant grinned but he had a lump in his throat that he could not easily swallow down. He would make himself worthy of her forgiveness.

Kreek unbarred the door and stood between the Militia and his Queen. The arl stood by his heel, ready, though for what she could not say.

The King's guards did not challenge Kreek. That worried him. They brought food for the arl and for the Queen. They gave a large tray to Kreek, who accepted it warily, and with one hand. He had to keep his sword arm free. The guardsmen kept their expressions blank and Kreek did the same. At any moment Kreek expected a knife in his guts. He had inadvertently become the Queen's own and only bodyguard, in a castle full of the King's – or Hale Garnem's – men. He did not yet know if the King's men and Hale Garnem's men were even the same. Was there dissent in the ranks? Were all the King's soldiers loyal to him or to their captains or to some other faction? There were too many imponderables. Dare he ask the Queen what was going on? When the soldiers took up their sentry posts on either side of the door, Kreek closed it behind him with his heel. Sweat trickled down the inside of his jerkin. He prayed that he did not glow with it. The whole situation made his skin crawl. He did not think he had long to live.

The Queen shared the food out silently as if she had

been a serving girl in a wayside inn, though her hands were cleaner and she took more care. Fox ate hungrily. The trembling in her limbs ceased almost at once. As the food, the very good food, hit her stomach she was able to think. She started to think. That in itself was a change. She knew herself now. She was Fox but she was also Karen. She had dreamed herself back into existence from the limbo of near nothingness. She remembered her grandmother and her life as Karen. She remembered her attack and her escape. She remembered all that had happened to her as Fox; the sounds, the smells, her feelings. Now she could look back and interpret them as Karen. She felt reborn. It was good to see, to smell, to hear but it was even better to know that she saw, that she heard, that she was herself. It was a new kind of joy, this feeling. For the first time ever, she was happy to be herself.

She pushed all the many questions from her mind, the hows and whys and wheres. They mattered less than they should have done. Now she would try to help Mowl. She had chosen Mowl. Somehow in the strangeness of the dream place, she knew she had been given a real choice. She had chosen to be Fox and help Mowl rather than go home and be Karen. In this alien room, with two strangers, it seemed like a perverse choice.

'What now?' Kreek asked. It was a good question and one Karen Fox would have asked if she could.

The Queen put her fingers to her lips and pointed to the wall.

'Spyhole,' she mouthed.

Kreek frowned, then nodded to show he understood. He looked around for something with which to make a noise loud enough to drown out the Queen's words. He saw the Queen's lute in the corner and handed it over for her to play.

'That will do fine, sergeant,' the Queen said in her normal voice, presumably to give the eavesdropper something to listen to. The Queen had a beautiful voice, high and clear and commanding. Fox had heard it before she'd woken here, in this room. How had she heard it before? She had heard it singing. It had sung out, 'You choose, you choose,' from the mouth of an exotic bird. What was this Queen doing in her dreams?

Who was she? Could she help her to help Mowl? The blue-tinted light from the stained-glass window gave a strange sheen to the Queen's lovely features. She was beautiful but not like any human Karen could remember. Her face was not thin but curiously angular, her neck and limbs elegantly elongated. Her pale hair looked silvery blue and was swept up in an elaborate bun, held in place with small silver daggers that glinted ominously in the light from the fire. Kreek's face was almost expressionless. His face could have been chiselled from granite; the planes of his face were flatter and more pronounced than she had noticed before. She had chosen to be here, chosen to stay with Mowl. Were these people even human as Karen had once been?

The sergeant sat cross-legged on the floor as close as possible to the Queen, and Fox noted for the first time how abnormally broad was his back and massive his hands. As the Queen began to play an unfamiliar melody full of semitones and odd dissonances Fox grew really afraid. She felt a sudden visceral aversion to this alien place. The hairs of her neck and back prickled erect. She wanted to run away. She knew there was nowhere to go. She closed her eyes instead – to block it all out. She had chosen not to return to her Grandmother. God, what had she done?

Chapter 26

Meeting: Day 20

Huta's army left the shelter of the Rye Forest a little after dawn. Blud had returned with the news that Huta had sent a man to intercept Ponn through the Calley Rift. Blud had clearly wanted to go himself but had grudgingly accepted Huta's right to send one of his own men. Blud was angry, frustrated and far from being easy company so it was something of a relief when he made his excuses and left to rejoin Huta at the head of the troop. It was also a relief to be out of the constricting trees. Huta gave the order to mount and Dorren and Mowl scrambled on to the backs of the Varl carthorses. It had never felt so good to ride. Dorren smiled with the sheer pleasure of it and slumped forward over the horse's broad neck to release the tension in his malformed back. Huta was speaking. They all strained to listen.

'Now it begins. We march now in a state of battle readiness. We march to Maybury. At every village we pass we will recruit men to our cause or, if need be, fight them for the freedom to march on. I know you are tired, I know you are hungry, I know we still have a long way to go, but you are the best in the Kingdom and it is only fitting that it should be you who liberates it!'

Huta finished and the men let out a short, disciplined cheer before forming into precise columns. Blud had been lent a short mountain pony and rode alongside Dorren and Mowl. Mowl felt his stomach begin to churn; by the look on Dorren's face he was not alone.

Within the Queen's chamber in the fortress in the walled city of Maybury, the Queen of Loyrenton played her lute and murmured to Kreek in a low voice. Fox's sharp ears had no difficulty in hearing her.

'I need you to get the fox out and to find Fenn Dale.'

'Fenn Dale? You trust him?' Kreek scarcely spoke aloud at all, but mouthed the words in evident surprise. As far as he was aware Fenn Dale reported to the King and was a man to be avoided wherever possible. Fox pricked up her ears at the mention of Fenn Dale, grateful that Kreek had posed the question she could not.

'We trust him with our life. Tell him ...' The Queen paused and appeared to concentrate on a complex combination of notes that made Fox shudder. 'Tell him we support the rebellion.'

Kreek's eyes widened but he nodded again.

'We leave at nightfall.'

'How?'

'Trust me. I have a plan. Sleep now. I will keep watch.'

Kreek bowed his huge head. If he was about to argue he thought better of it. He lay down where he sat and was instantly asleep. Perhaps that was a soldier's gift.

The Queen smiled fondly at the huge recumbent figure. For all his size he looked vulnerable. The Queen rose gracefully and opened a large wooden chest from under the window and took from it a richly coloured cloak of emerald green. She covered Kreek and returned to her chair.

'Sleep, noble arl, it is not yet time to act.'

Fox did not want to do as she was told and at first paced the room, anxious to get out, to find Mowl. She sought out his mental presence, but felt nothing. There must be a knack to this type of telepathy that she had not yet grasped. She did not know how she had managed to meet him in the grey land. She was sure he was somewhere outside the castle but she could not find him. The stone walls of the chamber were oppressive. The richness of the tapestries that hung in the room did not distract her, for though they were beautiful, colourful depictions of men, women and animals they all smelled the same; of dyed wool, damp, mildew, candle smoke, old grease, tallow and the cold stone which they covered.

Fox wanted to leap out of the high arched window

that was the source of the room's steely, winter light. The window was glazed with a complex symmetrical pattern of pale cobalt blue glass. Like the window of the tavern in Maybury it did not open. Fox could not smell the fresh air, and the staleness of the enclosed space depressed her. She watched the blue light grow bleaker as the day faded. It gave the marble fireplace and silver mirror, the polished table and the carved desk and chair that furnished the chamber a strange, almost metallic quality. It was not cosy at all. It felt more alien than anything Fox had yet experienced. The design of things was also strange. The table was triangular, the desk was supported by two interlocked equilateral triangles. The marble overmantel was arched so that nothing could stand on it. The mirror that hung above the green-tinted flames was formed of three triangular pieces of glass so that it fitted perfectly above the arched mantelpiece. It struck her again, forcibly, that this was not her native world. She had never seen objects like this before. They were like the things she had seen at home but subtly, and incontrovertibly different. It was warm in the room for all that it was made of stone. The hangings on the wall and rugs on the floor insulated them from the uncompromising rock of the fortress. Kreek still slept, the Queen was busy writing something at her desk by the fire. Karen Fox lay down.

She had felt so sure of her choice when she first woke.

Now she was no longer sure. Where was she? She thought through the events that had occurred since she first found herself in this alien fox body. Why did she trust Mowl? He had after all drugged her once, no, twice. She remembered with a shock the strange-smelling stuff he'd given her just before his encounter with Kreek. After that she had thought she could speak to him. After that she had felt close to him. Had that stuff made her loyal? Did she really know what was going on here and was any of it real? In spite of herself, Karen Fox began to doze.

Mowl had forgotten how tiring riding could be. The pace was relentless. His joy at communicating with Fox had ebbed slightly. Even if he found her, how could he save her? She had been in fox form, by his calculations, for at least twenty days and the Succeptor of Lerry who might have helped her was dead, probably at Ponn's hand. Almost as worrying was the fact that they had ridden for hours through land that was largely deserted. It seemed inconceivable that Flane and Hale Garnem could not know of their existence. Garnem's network of spies was famous yet they rode on unchallenged. Huta was getting edgy, fearing an ambush. The men grew tenser by the hour. They had covered a lot of ground since dawn, eating dry rations as they marched. Even the mountain men were flagging at the tireless pace. When they approached Bengale Wood, not two hours' walk from the Varl lands, Huta ordered that they set up camp, rest and prepare a hot meal before they marched on Deworth. He knew there were Militia in Deworth, and ambush was possible. They may have to fight at Deworth and the men would need to be fresh.

Mowl slumped with his back to a tree. He was too tired and too miserable to be hungry. He shut his eyes and at once drifted off into a deep sleep.

He knew he was dreaming, though the place of his dreams was not unlike the real Bengale Wood except that everything was shrouded in the suffocating mist of soft shadow. It was warm at least, and he was unsurprised to find himself in the body of a fox. The question of why he should be unsurprised to find himself in the body of a fox did not occur to him. He padded on silent paws through the soft ground of the dream forest until he found what he'd been looking for, the arl, Fox, curled up under a tree. She looked well, if rather thin. Her coat glowed with the luminous russet he associated with her. He was very relieved. The weight that had burdened him all day, lifted a little. At the very least she still lived. She looked up when she saw him and snarled.

'It's me, Mowl.'

Fox bared her teeth and growled at him.

'What did you do to me in the forest, when we hid from sergeant Kreek?'

Mowl was bemused, so much had happened since then. He

could not understand why she should suddenly be so aggressive. She had changed. She had never been aggressive before. Was this some corruption of her soul, some dissolution that might be a precursor of her death?

It took him a moment to understand what she was talking about.

When he realised what she meant, he struggled to remember exactly what had happened. The memory of that time was coloured by fear and anxiety. He struggled to see back through that distorting glass of distress, to describe what had really happened.

'When I was in Deworth, the village by the river, some of the men took me to the Adept there. I told her about you.'

That must be true. Fox distantly remembered the strange sensation of being sought and found by something she could not identify. There was something else associated with that, a great wrongness, a nasty sense of being violated, of something scrutinising her very soul. She shuddered. That memory belonged to a time of great confusion, when she had given herself up to the fox side of her nature. Nothing from those days made much retrospective sense. Mowl carried on, screwing up his fox face in a curiously human way, as he tried to remember precisely what the Adept had said.

'She said we were not in alignment, but we might be able to find the same resonance if we each had a few drops of this liquid she gave me. She seemed concerned for you and I trusted her. Perhaps it was foolish but I do not think we would be able to meet now and understand each other without it.'

'How do I know this is not a dream? I may just be imagining you telling me this?' Fox now sounded less angry than frightened. She still seemed different. There was a new clarity about her thoughts, a new clarity about her fear. Mowl wanted to put his arm round her to comfort her but he had no arm. He licked her muzzle instead and she did not object. For a moment some fox instinct he did not know he had, awoke. He calmed himself and pushed such thoughts away. Fox may have experienced the same unexpected surge of feeling because she jerked away from him quite suddenly. They were both breathing hard. He forced his thoughts back to her question. How did they know it was not a dream? Mowl had an idea.

'Where are you?'

'Here.'

'No, I mean are you sleeping somewhere?'

'The Queen's chamber inside a stone place – it feels like a fortress. I don't like it.'

'Fox, if I told you that the Queen was in danger and you later found out that she was, and what I had told you was true, would you believe that this meeting was not just a dream?'

Fox paused from the nervous licking of her forepaws. She nodded.

'It wouldn't prove that I wasn't dreaming all of this but …' she tailed off, unwilling to pursue the thought. She seemed to fade a little when she was in doubt. Mowl wanted to cry out, as he had before, 'Stay!' but he was afraid to scare her. She seemed a more fragile creature suddenly, beautiful yet fey.

'I am with the rebels who want to depose Flane. They were waiting for word from Fenn Dale about whether the Queen was on his side. Fenn Dale is really a rebel leader but he works for the King. I think that's why you didn't trust him. There is a man called Ponn. He was here, but he's riding to the fortress. He's a small man with white hair – but not very old ...' Mowl pictured Ponn in his mind and, perhaps because he spoke in the guise of a fox, suddenly remembered his smell. 'He smells of that stuff, that bitter stuff the Adept gave us.'

As he said the words Mowl had a sudden flash of insight. Ponn! Was Ponn an Adept or one who sought out Adepts? Had he known that Mowl could speak to Fox? He had felt oppressed all the time that Ponn was near, and yet he had told him about Fox! Why had he not seen such an obvious thing before? Had Ponn himself muddled his thinking so that he could not see the obvious? He dare not worry about that now. Fox was looking at him with concern. With an effort he pushed away that fear. He continued, 'Ponn is going to tell the King that the Queen is plotting against him and that Fenn Dale is a traitor. He could be there by tomorrow. He might be an Adept.' Mowl was very afraid that none of this would make any sense at all to Fox.

She surprised him.

'The Queen gave Kreek a message to give to Fenn Dale. She said, "Tell him we support the rebellion."'

Mowl could see Fox's red coat paling visibly.

'What's the matter?'

'I'm afraid. I don't know what I've got involved with…'

'Do you trust me?'

Fox looked into Mowl's eyes. Even in the guise of a fox they were Mowl's own grey eyes. What did she know about this person? Did it matter? At her very core she trusted Mowl, without reason, without understanding. It was an instinct. It was a conviction. In her soul she had chosen him. Of course she trusted him.

'I trust you,' she said.

'We're coming to save you from Flane. We are coming to save everyone. Warn the Queen and Fenn Dale about Ponn!'

Could Mowl save Fox? He was very afraid that even with an army, considerably bigger than Huta's small band he could not save Fox at all. They dared not touch. They just looked at each other.

'Keep safe, Mowl,' Fox said and disappeared.

Chapter 27

Making Progress: Day 20

Mowl thought about his dream as he ate the hot stew Dorren forced on him. He had been so certain that it had been something more while he dreamed it. Now he was not so sure. He had accepted Leva's demand for revenge. All that he had read suggested that talent and vengefulness, indeed talent and any fierce emotion that upset equilibrium, were incompatible. Maybe the vengefulness had not worked through his nodes of being yet; maybe he *had* experienced a true communication with the arl. How could he be sure? He remembered the way he had felt when he had touched Fox. That disturbed him. Such an encounter could not have been truly of the spiritual dimension. He had felt like a male fox confronted by a vixen. That was not the way things were supposed to be. He was sure of that.

All around Mowl, Huta's troops were gathering their equipment together for the march on Deworth. Dorren was massaging his weak leg, lost in his own private battle against pain and physical frailty. Mowl did not want to disturb him. He respected both Dorren's indomitable courage and his pride. The light was beginning to fade and snow was beginning to fall. Mowl wondered at the wisdom of marching in the dark. He wondered at the wisdom of the whole enterprise – they were so few to save a kingdom.

Should he tell Huta of the Queen's message, or not? He did not want his uncle to think him a fool. Adepts were not so common that it was a small thing to claim their gifts. He looked for Blud. It was strange how since he had met Huta, Blud seemed more commanding, less reticent, the kind of man who knew what to do. He also seemed to know an awful lot about the way this world worked. He made Mowl feel young and ignorant. No, not ignorant; he knew something that was important, he had a duty to share it. Mowl approached Blud shyly.

'Mowl.' Blud nodded a greeting.

'Blud, I want to ask you something.'

'Yes, Mowl.' Blud's cool appraising gaze weakened Mowl's resolve. He did not want Blud to think him a fool either. He began tentatively. 'Blud, if I said that I had reason to believe that the Queen agreed to Fenn Dale's plans what would you advise me to do?'

'What do you mean, Mowl?' Blud's brow was furrowed with concern.

Mowl had led them a little apart from the rest of the men. Mowl was uncomfortable. He did not want to be thought self-aggrandising in claiming talents that were rare. 'You know I had a fox with me, when we went to the Varl land. Did you notice her? She ran away as soon as we arrived. Anyway, I believe she is an arl. The Adept of Deworth also thought she might be.' Mowl did not feel that this was going well. Blud's face was stony. 'She can talk to me – I think I might have had the talent to be an Adept if things had been different – I spoke with her last night. Fox is in the castle with the Queen. She said that the Queen wanted to get a message to Fenn Dale saying that she supports the rebellion.' Mowl felt very foolish and struggled through the tale with growing embarrassment. It sounded an unlikely story.

Blud's face was carefully impassive.

'What did you tell this arl of our plans here?'

There was an unexpected coldness in Blud's voice but he did not challenge Mowl's story.

'I warned her about Ponn – I thought she might be able to warn the Queen.'

'Did you tell her about the army?'

Mowl nodded, suddenly understanding Blud's concern. 'She is on our side – how can she not be? She is an arl or something else Flane's people won't believe in. Do you think they will let her live? They have killed Adepts. She is not on their side. She could not be.' Mowl surprised himself with the passion of his answer.

Blud nodded. He looked a little less tense.

'Thank you for telling me. You are right, there is little risk that she can harm us.

Mowl had not thought of that. Blud knew altogether too much about the thinking of Mowl's enemies for Mowl to be entirely comfortable.

Blud forced his face into a smile.

'It's good news about the Queen. It will help us attract more supporters.'

Mowl had rather hoped that they already had some more supporters waiting for them in Maybury.

'Is this the whole rebel army?'

'Fenn Dale is supposed to have a network of supporters in the city but we haven't been able to contact him. No one has heard anything from him for too long.'

'He is on our side, is he? All the people in the book are dead – he couldn't have betrayed them could he?'

Blud's smile this time was genuine. 'Fenn's on our side. I'd trust him with my life.'

'You know him?'

'By reputation.' Blud looked discomforted.

'I should thank you, Mowl, for trying to warn the Queen and telling me this. I wouldn't mention your … talent to anyone else. I've heard that Hale Garnem has men in his employ dedicated to killing Adepts. I am glad men like you are on our side.'

Mowl wondered if Blud himself had some small gift, enough to recognise it in others and to prevent his own spiritual emanations from leaking into the ether.

'I think Ponn might have been one of those Adept killers.'

'What?'

'I can't explain it, but I did feel strange when he was around, and don't you think it odd that none of us thought to look for him for days? I've read about people who could do that – you know, influence people.' Since meeting the Adept Laine, Mowl was a lot less sceptical about the possible applications of the spiritual arts. 'There was another thing too – he smelled of something that Adepts use.'

Blud looked grim. 'It fits. Well, if he is what you say, better make doubly sure you never fall into his hands.'

Mowl nodded. He felt afraid. He didn't want to fall into anybody's hands. He hadn't even considered the possibility of meeting Ponn again. Something inside him turned to ice at the thought.

'Blud, you know what I promised Leva?'

'I know. I think you will have your chance for revenge.'

'Will you help me?'

'I have scores of my own to settle, Mowl. I might be racing you to have a go at Flane and Garnem. Don't worry, when it comes to a battle you'll get your chance.'

Why did that assurance not make Mowl happier?

Fox woke abruptly at a bang on the door to the Queen's chamber. Kreek was on his feet and ready instantly. Fox with her honed survivor's instincts was a little before him. As always happened when she didn't have time to think, her fox self took over and she went to ground, under the desk.

'His Highness, The King Keeper of the Purple Path, His Holiness, King Flane requests the presence of Queen Lin, and the counterfeit arl, in his private chamber.'

It was a courtier in elaborate court dress, flanked by six guardsmen, sonorously intoning his message in High Loyrenton. The man stank of perfumes and tooth decay.

The Queen rose gracefully from her seat.

'The hour is late, Sar Hayson. Please pass on our compliments to His Highness, the King Keeper of the Purple Path and the esteemed consort of Her Royal Highness Queen Lin of the ancient Royal House of Rayl. We have been long at our theological treatises this day evaluating an appropriate test to determine the nature of this creature – a task of which we know our husband will approve. We would gladly meet with His Venerable Holiness to discuss this matter further, after His Majesty has completed his most pressing matters of state, tomorrow afternoon.'

It was clearly not the answer they expected or wanted but Sar Hayson had little choice but to bow and murmur pleasantries. He dare not arrest the Queen. That was a treason much deeper than merely supporting the claim of an alternative Royal consort. Sar Hayson looked a little sick and one of the younger guardsmen went noticeably pale. They left unhappily, but they left.

'They will come back but perhaps not for a while,' said the Queen quietly as she stoked the fire to cover the noise of her voice. 'We must get Fox away. It is time to go.'

Huta's army walked on. Snow turned to slush under the horses' hooves and the white landscape shone with an eerie luminescence in the dying light. Blud had spoken with Huta. How he had persuaded him of the truth of Mowl's communication, Mowl did not know. It didn't matter. He was sure again. He had an Adept's powers and his dream had been true – in all the ways that mattered. Huta raised the Queen's standard and the stoic mountain men cheered as it unfurled, a gold crown on a sky blue background, bright against the dark sky.

There were a number of homesteads on the route towards Deworth, though none belonged to anyone Mowl knew well. It was a more fertile land this side of the forest and it supported many more families than the rugged mountain land. They were not sure what reception they would receive. It was fully dark as Huta's army of mountain men marched towards the first building they had seen since they had left Argon. It was a poor-looking place, shuttered against the night. As they approached, Mowl could feel the tension among the men. There could be King's men there. This could be the ambush that Huta feared. A few men reached for their weapons but Huta stopped them with a signal. The householders must have heard the noise, but there was no movement. Were they lying low, hiding from a force that might be the Militia or were they themselves the Militia?

Huta signalled and the first and second six ranks of men peeled away and surrounded the cottage. In the darkness their pale coats caught the moonlight and made even their bulk seem insubstantial and wraithlike. The silence was as absolute as a large body of men could make it. Huta drew his axe. There was a rasp as sixty men unsheathed swords and unhooked war axes. The silence was sinister. Mowl was beginning to speculate on practicalities. Dorren was too close by his side to allow him to swing his sword. He could not see how his weapon or his skill could be much use in such close formation. Huta walked up to the cottage door and knocked upon it authoritatively. Two huge mountain men flanked him with swords drawn; ready to defend him should the cottage shelter King's men. The door opened and a bewildered Goodwife with grey, unbound hair opened the door, a candle flickering in her hand.

She balked at the unsheathed swords but brandished the stick she was carrying in her other hand with conviction.

'What do you want?'

'We are the army of Queen Lin, come to liberate Loyrenton from King Flane. We are looking for recruits. Will you join us?'

The woman peered outside at Huta's men.

'Bah, you think you could beat Flane with them!'

A tall boy of about sixteen stood beside his mother, armed with a meat cleaver. He too squinted into the darkness.

'Show me your flag.' The woman's voice was firm. Pale light just illuminated the banner and caught the gold thread of the crown so that it glinted like the real thing.

'Is that the right one, Mother?'

The Goodwife peered at the flag.

'That's her flag all right. Your father fought under that banner. I should know it. But I don't know about the truth of what they say.'

She paused and dragged her boy back behind her. She was a substantially built woman.

Her voice was harder now. 'If you take my sons who'll keep us all fed this winter? The Militia took our stores, you take my boys and you might as well bury me now.'

'We'll not take anything, Goodwife,' said Huta, pronouncing the unfamiliar lowland dialect with care. 'We are fighting to prevent the Militia taking your stores again. We are an army of volunteers, we'll not press anyone to risk their lives. Join us if you want to be free of the Militia. Otherwise we'll leave you be.'

'You'll not slaughter my pigs to feed your men?' The woman's voice was both incredulous and challenging at the same time.

It was obvious that she already had some experience of armies. It was, of course, exactly what Huta wanted to do, for the men were hungry and he could hear the animals grunting and snuffling, disturbed by the noise.

He hesitated for a moment, weighing the situation. The woman eyed him shrewdly. He indicated that his guards should sheathe their weapons. The rest of the army did the same. The boy did not drop his cleaver.

'We'll not take what you don't give. We are not the Militia.' He turned round with great dignity hoping that the young man had enough sense not to plant a meat cleaver in his back. He signalled for the men who had surrounded the house to return to the ranks and get ready to march on.

At a signal from the woman some fifty men emerged from the trees and bushes that surrounded the farmstead. Mowl gulped and grappled to unsheathe his sword again.

The men fell into line by the cottage. They were armed with longbows and home-made arrows. A long hunting knife hung from each man's belt. The Goodwife spoke again.

'I'm not sure I'd trust you to beat the Militia. I could have killed you all where you stood.'

'You knew we were coming?'

'We're not fools, mountain man, we'll defend our own as well as the next man. We heard what happened at the Varls and up north. We're not fools to the Purple Path hereabouts. I've had men tracking you since yesterday.'

'Will you join us?'

'Aye, but I'll lead my own men. I don't trust a mountain man to lead archers.'

She turned to her son.

'Slaughter a couple of the pigs. We'll not be here to eat them. The Militia grow fat on what they take, and a starving army fights like pig slop. When you're in the castle, Huta Arn, I will expect payment for my pigs and the winter harvest that won't be gathered because men are away fighting.'

Goodwife Sale, for that was the formidable woman's name, had not only organised a defence force if she found that she did not trust Huta, but had also anticipated the needs of his army's stomach in the event that she did. They rested then, after a fine meal of bread and pork and ale. When they were done there was not a drop of ale left in any of the neighbouring homesteads. Blud, who proved himself the modest owner of hidden talents, took careful note of every morsel donated to the army and every jug of ale given so that she might be recompensed. The Goodwife Sale did not consider the possibility that they might lose. After they had eaten Huta allowed the men some rest. The Goodwife's confidence in their ultimate victory seemed to give him heart.

'No one round here will stand for what Flane and that Hale Garnem are doing. Every man, woman and child makes his own way with the Keeper. No man tells us what to believe and worse than that, that we have to pay to believe it! Besides,' she added in a voice that was as hard and steely as Mowl's father's sword, 'if we don't stop it now, while we still can, by the spring there'll be too many soldiers, too many men profiting. People will be too frightened to fight back. We win now or we'll never win. Flane is bad enough but Hale Garnem! He's not an old man. He's got years in him yet. I'm going to shorten his days for him, if I die trying.'

Mowl could sense the anger in her, a slow fire that would burn everything in her way. Goodwife Sale's sharp practicality reminded Mowl of Yani. She would have approved of the Goodwife avenging her. The Goodwife lent courage to them all.

Chapter 28

Mysteries: Day 20 (Night)

Queen Lin had lived in the castle all her life. Her family had built it generations before and it had secrets. Every family had its secrets, Kreek knew. There were things only the Goodwife and the heir would know, trade secrets, craft secrets, family secrets – how to make a particular poultice, a certain way of mixing the dye or making a sauce, or shaping a horseshoe. The castle's secrets were numerous and had been designed almost for their current situation – to keep those of the House of Rayl safe, even when surrounded by enemies. The Queen banked up the fire noisily and Kreek stoked it.

Fox stayed close to the Queen, waiting for a chance to warn her, somehow, of Mowl's fears and to hear the Queen's own quiet words. It was closer to the fire than she wished to be; it singed her fur and the hot smell of burnt wood brought back too forcibly the burnt ruin of the Varl house and the pain and confusion that followed.

'The castle is not all it appears. It is very ancient and my ancestors who built it had skills that we've lost. I'm going to open one of the secret ways to get you away, Kreek. It is a last resort. It is many years since I've tried it – it's rather a frightening experience.' In truth she seemed nervous. She picked up the emerald cloak from the floor where Kreek had neatly folded it and put it round her shoulders, her hands trembling. She took another cloak of thick grey wool from the window chest and gave it to Kreek. He took it without question. Both Fox and Kreek watched the Queen intently, wondering what it was she had to do to unlock the secret way. Had they not been watching so intently they probably would not have noticed. She began to pace up and down the room in an agitated fashion, twisting the largest and most ugly of the many rings she wore. She looked anxious, distressed even, pacing up and down faster and faster. Fox exchanged a very human look with Kreek. Had the Queen lost her grip on reality? Then, suddenly, she seemed to relax. She smiled. There was a flash of white light so bright it dazzled Fox and the floor at the centre of the room dissolved, disappeared to reveal steep stone stairs descending into blackness. There had been no visible mechanism to account for this, no grinding or groaning as the great stone flags of the floor opened. The floor had merely vanished, as silently and as sweetly as melting ice. Solid objects did not behave that way. It did not accord with Fox's concept of the physical universe. They hurried down the steps. The floor reformed above them and they were plunged into darkness.

'What the...?' Began Kreek but he did not have the words to express his astonishment.

'It is to do with the displacement of one tier of existence with another.' The Queen explained.

'My ancestors experimented for years to build this, the pinnacle of their achievement. It is why I have never doubted the existence of other tiers. This place exists in more than one tier at the same time – it's a very arcane branch of practical philosophy, which is easier to demonstrate than it is to understand. I've never understood it. My ring is from another tier, holding it helps me to picture the other castle and then – it's a knack, an inheritance passed, like everything else, through the female line. Maybe anyone could do it if they had to practise as much as I did. We practise switching between tiers from birth pretty well.' Her face darkened. 'I always hated it. I got lost once, when I was about six. It's not something I ever wanted to repeat.' She sighed. 'Anyway it's easier with the ring, though not much. If anything happens to me – see that Lenya gets it will you?'

Kreek nodded, then realising that it was too dark for his gesture to be seen said firmly, 'Of course,' then, after a decent interval, 'So, where are we now?'

They were descending stairs in the dark and nothing

smelled of anything, not of stone, nor of damp, nothing. Fox hated it.

'I don't know exactly. Technically we're probably not in Loyrenton. This castle doesn't inhabit the same space as my castle – there is some displacement of the components of being. I can't claim to understand it properly, you have to learn it like a maze. Although we're going down these steps they will take us up to the upper floors of my castle.' She grinned nervously, obviously little more comfortable with the strangeness of it than Kreek. 'The two castles connect in unpredictable ways. I think the ancestor who built it had a perverse sense of humour – what is a privy here is the throne room of Loyrenton.'

The stairs stopped abruptly and Kreek stumbled, but a trickle of light from an unseen source enabled them to follow a stone corridor to where a ruined wall allowed the light of early morning to spill into this castle. It was very disorienting. It was night in Loyrenton and the castle there was whole and well-kept. Here it was after dawn and they stood amidst the ruins of a different castle where a light sea-scented wind ruffled fox's fur. There was nothing to see out of the crumbling window but tall trees and a distant ocean. 'Not all of this other castle is ruined either, parts of it seem quite lately built,' said the Queen, conversationally, letting the clean wind blow loose the tight arrangement of her hair, breathing in the salt smell.

This was a different kind of wrongness. It confounded Karen's intellect and confused Fox's senses. She started to feel quite odd. Kreek noticed first.

'Your Majesty, look to the arl!'

Fox was fading like a badly dyed garment, dissolving like the floor of the castle had done.

'She is too far from her own tier of being. We must get her back to Loyrenton!'

The Queen scooped up the unresisting fox and, wrapping her firmly in her cloak, ran along a further corridor, up a flight of wooden stairs and through a chamber decorated with breathtaking opulence in gold leaf and precious stones. She twisted another of her many rings, made of silver mined in her own Loyrenton, and thrust Kreek and the Fox through a swiftly evaporating section of wall.

'You are in the stables of your own Loyrenton castle. Be aware, I think there's been a time slip. I'm so out of practice with this. I think we've lost a day between tiers. Time can run differently here unless one is skilled at making the transitions. By the Keeper, I'm like a girl of six again. Go! Find Fenn Dale. I have to find Lenya and bring her here. I can hide here indefinitely. Go!'

'How will you know if it is safe to return?'

'You would know all your Queen's secrets in one day? I will find out, Kreek. Don't worry! Keep Fox safe. All my hopes go with you. Find Fenn Dale, Sergeant, and I am in your debt.' The Queen spoke gently but the shove she gave Kreek was very firm. He steadied himself and walked into the dimly lit stable, within the fortress walls. By the time he turned to say goodbye, the Queen and the gilded room were gone and one of the King's men was staring at him in amazement.

Huta's army, the Queen's men, flying the Queen's blue and gold banner were on the march in the still, cold dawn. Goodwife Sale had sent her boys out to ride with news of their coming and before they broke camp their ranks were swelled by men and women from the wider region. It was a mixed bag but there were a smattering of tough old farmers and former soldiers who'd fought for the southern kingdom when Queen Lin first came to her throne, twenty-five years before. They were outnumbered by the young farm hands and younger sons, who saw a chance for honour and glory. There was less hope and more resignation in the eyes of the veterans. More than one of these did not expect to return home. It was their choice to serve equilibrium and end their days as they'd begun them, at war, fighting under the banner of Queen Lin.

The mountain men sang now as they rode. They sang old songs about love and battle, songs that filled Mowl with longing for something he could only glimpse. The mountain men sang of battles where men fought to preserve their homes. In the language of the mountains the word for home meant more than a farmstead. It meant 'the place where the soul belonged'. Mowl might find it easier to fight for that than for revenge. He tried again to count the days of his journey from the Varl farmstead. He had done it several times before. Whichever way he worked it out, it was nearing the end; the fourth sixday. According to Varlen of Boyaine and the Adept of Deworth, the fourth sixday marked the end of an arl's allotted span before Transformation or death. The knowledge was a cold rock of grief.

Mowl had sought Fox since their dream meeting. He could no longer feel her presence. He was very afraid she had died already. He marched on among the singing men out of duty to the cause of Balance, but his hope was gone.

Chapter 29

Deworth: Day 21

The Rebel Army reached Deworth by late morning. The villagers were already up and about their business. If Goodwife Sale's boys had warned them of their coming they gave no sign. There was no welcoming party to greet them on the river road; just the stench of the soldiers' barracks which almost overwhelmed the stink of gutted fish and the fresh salt wind from the open sea. In the sixdays since Mowl had been there much had changed. The badly built barracks now rested on the shingled plain of the River Varla, alongside the few blocks of stone and roped off foundations that marked the infelicitous beginnings of the temple. At the sound of their tramping feet, the soldiers tumbled from the barracks; half dressed, badly equipped and only half awake. They were young, outnumbered, poorly disciplined and suddenly very afraid. A young man, unkempt and dishevelled, tried to take control. He looked like he had been drinking heavily the night before and his breath reeked of sour ale. He watched with growing trepidation as Huta and his men marched in.

With fear in their eyes, the townspeople were gathering along the river to watch what was going on. Every man, woman and child carried a weapon, even if it was only a stick or a broom. The carpenter, and his Goodwife, who had hastily secured the lace cap of her respectability on top of her unpinned hair, walked past the other villagers towards Huta's troops. The carpenter stepped forward.

'Sar, what is your business at Deworth?'

'We are a liberating army, Sar, to free Deworth from the yoke of the Militia. We serve Queen Lin and in her name plan to free all of Loyrenton from the unjust rule of King Flane.' There was a gasp at that. Too many men and women had been hung of late for suspicion of the treachery now openly spoken. The carpenter waited for silence.

'And what do you plan to do with this … scum.' He spat at the feet of the unkempt Militiaman. By way of reply Huta addressed the young man directly.

'You will surrender your arms to us immediately.'

The young man looked into Huta's grim face, saw the hot anger and contempt of the carpenter and the hard eyes of the Goodwife, glaring at him from the front rank. He silently let his weapon drop. His men did the same, all trace of their thuggish bravado disappearing with their weapons.

Dorren tensed as he watched the surrender from further down the column.

'That's the man who killed Dake Varl,' he whispered to Mowl. One of the Goodwife's archers heard him and bellowed.

'That's the man who killed Dake Varl!'

Now that they were more certain that Huta's men were truly on their side the townspeople grew more confident, even bold. Several of them began to shout out, 'Hang them!' and 'String them up!' They banged their makeshift weapons on the floor and bayed for the soldiers' blood with growing confidence.

'Silence!' Huta yelled, red-faced.

He nodded at Blud who stepped forward. Blud's voice, less its exaggerated country burr, carried easily. People hushed each other to listen.

'We are the Queen's men. We are here to liberate Deworth from the King's Militia. We do not execute our enemies on a whim. We stand for the old ways, the rule of law and respect. If there are charges to be brought against any of these men, I will write them down, but they *will* have a proper trial. We are an army, not a lynch mob. Those soldiers who have no accusations against them may take an oath of fealty to the Queen and join us. Those people of Deworth who want to join us are welcome. We will rest here for one watch-space then start our march on Maybury. We fight for Loyrenton, Queen Lin, and her people!'

The townspeople cheered at that. Blud was a better speaker than Huta, whose strong mountain accent made his speech sound clipped and surly. Blud was relieved at the people's response. It was the only sign of any enthusiasm for their cause that the villagers had shown.

The rebels broke ranks and relaxed on the green open space that was the town's market square. Goodwife Sale spoke with the women and in a short space of time preparations were underway to prepare broth for the army.

Blud called Mowl over.

'Mowl, you can read and write?' Mowl nodded. Blud continued, 'Several of the villagers want to lodge complaints against the Militia and against the priest here. They are claiming that he killed the Adept Laine. We've taken him prisoner as well as most of the soldiers and Sar Venish, the scribe. Will you take statements from them? I think the Militia men are safer under guard – they've made too many enemies here.'

Mowl walked towards the inn, uncertain of his feelings. There was Balance here of sorts – he was back where he had started not a month before. As then he was without Fox and time was running out.

*   *   *

Kreek took a deep breath and tried to stay in control of his wits. Nothing was quite as it had seemed just days ago. He was faced with a King's man whose shocked expression probably mirrored his own. Kreek was about to draw his sword, ready to fight the bemused guardsman, when he remembered – he still wore the uniform of the King's Militia. No one was likely to know of his change of allegiance. Hale Garnem expected him to be guarded with the Queen in her chamber. He may be able to bluff his way out of the fortress.

'You! Saddle me a horse and be quick about it, I have business with Fenn Dale.'

At the familiar accent of authority, the guardsman forgot his confusion and did as he was ordered. He must have dozed off for a second for he had not seen the big sergeant arrive. In such circumstances it was wiser not to mention his surprise. Something was going on in the castle and the officers were edgy and quick with a punishment detail, or worse, a salutary thrashing.

'You haven't seen Fenn Dale, have you?' Kreek asked casually. Using only one hand he mounted the well-groomed cavalry horse that the guardsman had hastily saddled, balancing the fragile weight of the fox under his arm.

'He rode out to the town, Sar, just as the watch changed. I don't know no more than that.'

Kreek nodded his response and, carefully placing Fox

275

in front of him across the saddle, he rode for the keep. It was ludicrously easy to leave the way he came. He wore the King's colours. There had been no alarm raised about the fox and he doubted whether the yawning guardsman who took his salute even noticed the muffled bundle of blanket. He did not imagine that it would be so easy to get back in. He hated to leave the Queen but the castle protected her far better than he, one solitary swordsman, ever could. The most important thing was to get word to Fenn Dale that the Queen agreed to support the rebellion. He accepted the fact that he was a traitor now with surprising equanimity. He had been unimpressed with Flane for a long time; saving the Queen and Fox restored his self-respect. Everyone had to die sometime and he had chosen his allegiance with his soul.

Chapter 30

The Problem of Mercy: Day 21

Grace sipped too strong tea, bitter with the taste of tannin, in the hospital canteen. She found it difficult to force herself to sit down. She was agitated, angry, and all too aware that Billy had brought Tina to see the damage she had done. Grace checked her watch and then the canteen clock. It was eleven o'clock. The hands moved with excruciating slowness. It only took her four minutes to sip her tea and wish she'd chosen coffee instead. It took only three minutes to quickly scan the tabloid paper left on the table and wonder that everything went on exactly as it had before Karen's coma. It was ten past eleven. They would be there now, at her bed. Grace did not want to see Tina, could not bear to see her and yet could not bear not to. If Tina had to face what she had done maybe, she, Grace, had to face the fact that Tina had done it. Grace had to face the fact that Tina was not a horned devil, not an inhuman monster, but a sad, angry, desperate creature, who had done a terrible thing and now had to live with it. Could there be pity? Could there be forgiveness? Grace thought not. Could there be understanding? No. Never. Could there be acknowledgement that Karen's condition had changed everybody's life? Maybe. Should she face Tina? She didn't know.

Her feet took her back to the ward, to the curtained bed and the sound of a woman sobbing. She heard Billy's voice gently soothing and felt sick. Karen no longer sobbed; Karen was no longer soothed by kindly voices. Tears spilled once more from eyes that she had thought were dried out. She could not face Tina; Tina who still walked and talked and sobbed and lived. Grace could not face any of it – a crisis was looming. She knew it in her bones. Karen was not long for this world.

Mowl was not happy. He had listened to a litany of complaints that made him heartsick. The soldiers had returned from the Varl homestead, wild and full of bloodlust. They had tasted power; the power to terrify and they took pleasure in exercising it. While the others rested Mowl listened and made notes with Sar Venish's parchment and inks, neatly writing out the crimes the soldiers were said to have committed. Mowl believed the villagers. There was no doubt that the soldiers had done all of which they had been accused. Mowl struggled to write it all down and still keep his knife sheathed and his sword unbloodied. The soldiers, men little older than himself, had behaved like animals. They had beaten several of the younger men, almost to death, for failing to work quickly enough, or for looking at them with insufficient respect. They had robbed the villagers of their valuables and tried to force themselves on one of the villagers' daughters but the priest had intervened. The priest himself had killed the Adept, he admitted that, and smashed every village shrine to the Keeper with his own soft hands. Mowl wrote it all down carefully. The soldiers were fearful, guilty men. They feared a lynch mob with good reason. Mowl did not know if Blud was right to keep them safe. These men had hurt his Leva. Did his vow to her mean he should kill them? Who was responsible? These thugs or their absent leaders? He had no answers. But he felt a greater certainty that he fought on the right side. These terrible acts must be stopped.

By noon they were back on the road. They left behind one mountain man to guard the prisoners, and added to their ranks a further sixty men from the farms by Deworth. More would catch them up outside Maybury. Mowl bowed his head in friendly acknowledgement at former neighbours; men and women of the Drays, the Corners and the Hayns and fell in beside Dorren with relief. It was good to march until his limbs ached, good to do something practical, something useful. They were marching on Maybury. He felt a new determination. They were going to fight and they were going to win.

It was late and Kreek was lucky to find himself a bed at a decent inn. Fenn Dale would be asleep now, somewhere in Maybury. Kreek would draw less attention to himself if he found him in the morning. He was exhausted. He had ridden into Maybury a free man with a captive fox, now here he was an escaped captive with a free fox. Was this Balance? At least the fox was still all right. He'd checked her and she had regained her solidity. He could feel her heart beating strongly under his hand as he carried her, still wrapped in a blanket, to his room. He kicked off his boots and lay on the bed and was instantly asleep.

Karen Fox was more cautious. She lay by the door and listened. She stood by the open window and sniffed the air. She had to find Fenn Dale. She had failed to warn the Queen, and Mowl depended on her. She listened to Kreek snoring on the lumpy bed and felt the first faint stirrings of something like affection for the burly soldier. She had arrived scant weeks ago and yet she was already bound to this place by more ties of honour and affection than had ever bound her to her real home. She thought of her grandmother and her grandfather with a pang of guilt, she knew they loved her and she loved them back, but the scents of this night enticed her. She had never felt that way at home. It was so much more real here. She glanced at Kreek. He slept so deeply he would not miss her, she wouldn't be gone long. With a quick movement she had leaped to the window sill, was through the half open shutters of the unglazed window and out into the night. It felt good to stretch her legs and smell the damp streets and the fresh wind and all the scent messages they brought her. It would be easier to find Fenn Dale in this quietness, when she could taste the air at her leisure and hunt as her fox self was born to do. It gave her deep satisfaction to explore Maybury under the bright moon in the silence of the empty streets. She liked it here. She was happy.

Chapter 31

Fenn Dale: Day 22

K aren found Fenn Dale just before dawn. He was staying in the inn to which he had taken Mowl. Karen wanted to warn him about Ponn. She considered the Queen safe enough in her castle between worlds. Karen Fox slipped into his room behind the pretty servant girl, who delivered his polished boots then left a moment later. He looked old as he slept, old and tired. He slept with his large hands round the hilt of his sword and his boots on. He also slept lightly. He opened one eye when she padded silently into the room. He did not relax his guard even while he chatted amiably to her.

'You're back then? I saw you go with Dorren. I trust you found my old friend, Dake, well? I wonder what you're doing back? If I find that Mowl...' She tried to cut through his rambling and speak to his mind as she had with Mowl. Obviously he had a mind but she could not find it. She shook her head vigorously as an alternative attempt at communication, but Fenn Dale seemed to regard this as an eccentricity. Now that she remembered, he'd never taken a lot of notice of her. He offered her milk and water and some of his leftover supper. She ate this and indeed drank the offered milk, only because she might not have time to hunt much later. It was clear that Fenn Dale regarded her as a pet fox and she was not going to be able to warn him of anything. When she had finished her meal, which was satisfyingly tasty, she ran back to find Kreek. He, at least, might make an effort to understand her, and would pass on the Queen's message. It would have been so much easier if Mowl had been there. She missed him badly.

Kreek was already up when she returned. He greeted her with a relieved grunt. He was removing his beard with a cut-throat razor and could not do more than acknowledge her presence. Without his beard he looked younger, less baleful. She wondered if his new look was intended as a disguise.

When he had wiped his face, he turned to scrutinise her more closely. He seemed to be checking her out for injuries.

'Noble arl, you should not have gone out without me. If King Flane or Garnem learns that you have left the castle, every Militia man in Maybury will be after your hide. I am your sworn protector, you should not have left without me.'

Karen hung her head in a gesture of exaggerated repentance. Kreek seemed unconvinced. He tossed her a lump of bacon from his half eaten breakfast and poured milk from a stoneware pitcher into a dish for her. She delighted in the taste of it.

Kreek had done what he could to spruce up his appearance. He had found a brush from somewhere and brushed his uniform and polished his sword, scabbard, helmet and chain mail till they shone. His leather boots also gleamed with a shine that spoke of careful effort. He did not look like a renegade, she was sure that too was his intention. When he was properly dressed he turned his attention to Fox. He checked her paws carefully to ensure that she had not cut herself and ran gentle fingers over her neck and back. Finally satisfied that she had come to no harm he stood up.

'It's time to find Fenn Dale.'

She nodded her head vigorously and ran from the room. She waited by Kreek's horse with as intelligent an expression as she could manage. Kreek was not a stupid man, he expected her to try to communicate.

'You know where he is, don't you?' Kreek said when he had caught up with her. She bowed her head. 'Then I will follow you, noble arl, but stay out of the way of the Militia. If I have to fight to protect you, I will declare myself an enemy of the King. I would rather not do that just yet.'

He made sense. Karen waited in the shadows while he paid the innkeeper and readied his horse.

Maybury was a very different place by day. The sound, sights and smells were far more confusing in their multifarious complexity than in the sweet clarity of the night.

Kreek spotted her easily where she hid and indicated by a flash of his eyes that she should lead. His skin looked raw and sore where he had shaved it. It was pale too, and becoming spotty, like a plucked chicken.

Fortunately, Karen's memory was good and, though she had to take a more circuitous route than before, she found Fenn Dale's inn without difficulty. She paused outside the inn to let Kreek catch her. He tethered his horse to a hitching post outside and was about to go in. He looked at her for confirmation and she shook her head. There was a scent here that she did not like. It hovered on the edge of her memory, the bitterness of gall and that potion that the Adept had given Mowl. In that moment she knew; her dream had been true, Mowl had been right and that man, Ponn, was here before them. How could she warn Kreek? Her repertoire of signals was limited by her lack of hands and the immobility of her fox face.

She jerked her head to one side and Kreek scowled. She knew he had understood when he turned away from the door and started purposefully fiddling about with the horse's tack. With a quick glance backwards with all her highly tuned senses to check that she was not observed, Karen trotted into the inn. There was a dog in the small chamber that served as the inn's main room. Karen put all the warning she could muster into a savage glare in his direction. For whatever reason he cowered under the table. No one else noticed as Karen scaled the stairs, her soft paws making little noise, but her sharp claws clattering slightly on the bare wooden boards. The smell was very strong now as she approached Fenn Dale's room. She could hear voices. She hesitated slightly at the door. She had no clear plan of action. What could she do to make Fenn Dale recognise his danger? She was given no chance to think; the door swung open and the man she knew to be Ponn stood before her.

'Ah, if it isn't Mowl Speare's arl.'

Fox could feel the power of this man's mind boring into her own, invading her secret thoughts as the Adept of Deworth had done. This time her human will rebelled and she screamed. She thought she was screaming with her mind, for Ponn reeled backwards as if she had struck him. She also screamed like a human woman in a cry that froze the marrow of every man in earshot; 'Fenn Dale, run!'

She was vaguely aware of the less than agile Fenn Dale leaping out of the first floor window. There was the sound of rapid footsteps running heavily up the stairs. The water jug on the table shook. Kreek burst into the room, his sword ready. Ponn recovered quickly from the shock of the arl's response. The bright metal sheen of his knife flashed towards her. He was ready to plunge it into Karen's heaving chest. She saw the danger but could not cease her long, keening cry. She cowered before him, unable to run as her fox nature dictated. Kreek ignored Fox's distress as if a fox's scream was commonplace. He was utterly focused on one end, to protect her. He acknowledged no distraction as, with single-minded intensity, he brought his long sword down in one clean perfectly balanced stroke, on to Ponn's pale, unprotected neck. Ponn's body crumpled with the force of it and crimson blood gushed from his severed neck. In that fraction of an instant he was dead.

Fox was silenced. Kreek quickly checked the room. Fenn Dale was not there. With one quick, decisive gesture he picked up the trembling fox, tucked her under his arm and ran. He did not want to stay to explain himself. He was shaking a little, his mind and pulse racing with the aftershock of combat, however brief and unequal the fight. Whoever the white-haired man had been he'd been granted a clean, swift death and may the Keeper of Balances accord him the place that balanced the deserts of his soul. Kreek swung his powerful bulk into the saddle of his borrowed horse and rode, not so fast that he would attract suspicion, but fast enough to put space between himself and the scene of his crime. No one from the inn dared follow him. He was a soldier in the livery of the King. Such a man could pretty well murder whomsoever he pleased. He understood then, when no one gave chase, just how bad things had become in Maybury. He was ashamed to wear the livery of King Flane.

He had heard Fox's strange, articulate cry, a chilling thing. He was shaken by it. She was an, unearthly creature indeed.

'It's all right now, blessed arl, you are safe! I don't know how you did that, but it was well done. Now we must find Fenn Dale.'

Kreek whispered to the trembling bundle in front of him. He stroked her head gently as he rode and whistled a popular ballad. Guilty men never whistled.

Chapter 32

Readying: Day 22

Fox shook with the shock of it; the malign power of Ponn. Her inner self quaked and in the depth of her distress she broke through some barrier within herself, some inhibition that had trapped her. She called out to Mowl and Mowl heard her.

'Fox! You are alive! Thank the Keeper! What is wrong?'

'Ponn! Ponn read my thoughts! He hurt me! He's dead but, Mowl, I cannot explain how he made me feel!'

'Don't worry, Fox, hold fast, dear Fox, I'm coming. I'll find you. Please don't be afraid!'

Kreek rode through the city. Fenn Dale had run at the fox's command – how could he not? Kreek reviewed what he knew of Fenn Dale. Kreek thought that Fenn Dale had always been the right arm of Hale Garnem. It was a shock to discover that he served the Queen. Kreek searched his memory. Years ago, when last he had served in Maybury, Militia men used to joke that Fenn Dale kept a mistress in the Rye Forest, because of his habit of disappearing for long rides alone. A small strip of the once vast Rye Forest had been declared sacred to the Keeper and used by the royal hunt. In just this one place the forest had been preserved in its totality by royal decree. It extended from the coast to the Tear Mountains as a reminder of the deep forest wilderness that once covered the whole land and from which the toughness of the Loyrenton people was derived. The southernmost tip of this forest lay just outside Maybury and there was a place in the forest that would be a natural meeting place for rebels – Kreek knew of it, could never forget it. It was the site of King Rufin's murder.

It was a crisp, cold day and frost sparkled on the winter boughs. Kreek stopped singing and listened. Sound could carry a long way on such a morning. The ground was hard and his own horse's hooves struck the ground with a clear, clipped sound that he feared could be heard for a great distance. He thought he heard another horse cantering a little way ahead. The branches were lower as he moved deeper into the forest; he had to dismount and set Fox on her own four feet. She seemed to have recovered from whatever had so frightened her. She did not speak nor show any sign that she could. But she sniffed the air and loped off. Kreek followed, enjoying the crystalline clarity of the morning, the scent of the earth, and the cold air chilling his face. He had not walked for long when his instincts told him to be wary. He unsheathed his sword. The scrape of metal against metal sent birds hurtling from the trees. It was far too loud in the quietness, but he had not been exactly silent before. There was a sound behind him. He turned and swung his blade. It met another man's long sword with an echoing metallic clang. It was Fenn Dale.

'I need to talk to you,' Kreek said, nonchalantly.

'Oh?' the older man was breathing heavily at his sudden exertion, but his grip on his sword was certain. He was strong and steady as a rock.

Kreek did not move, though his left hand held his knife ready.

'I came with the fox, the arl that warned you.'

'An arl you say, some would doubt that. Is she your prisoner?'

'No, my charge, I am supposed to be her protector. I serve Queen Lin.'

Kreek could see Fox just ahead of him sniffing around in the decaying leaves, taking no notice of the confrontation between the two men. Sensing his eyes on her she looked up and shook herself in a way that communicated impatience. Fenn Dale had noticed her too.

'Does *she* know that?'

He lowered his sword and Kreek did the same, though they continued to regard each other warily.

'I have a message from the Queen. She says that she supports the rebellion.'

Fenn Dale narrowed his eyes.

Fox trotted up to them.

'*Ponn had found out you served the Queen – he was about to betray you and the Queen.*' Fox contrived to speak without opening her mouth, but both men heard her clearly. Kreek licked his lips, afraid now. If she had been able to speak before, he had not been able to hear her.

Fenn Dale looked aghast.

'You are an arl?'

Fox shrugged. '*I don't know. Does it matter? I know that there is an army riding towards us, here.*'

Karen couldn't have explained how she was suddenly able to project her words in such a way that Kreek and Fenn Dale could hear her. It was not quite like it had been with Mowl. It was as if she was shouting. It made her head hurt. She had found out the knack of it from Ponn. He could do that thing with her thoughts that the Adept had done, only he did it more roughly and more completely. She shuddered when she thought of his mental touch, insinuating itself into her awareness, demanding that she tell him things. It had only taken half a second but the memory of it would be with her always. Mowl had been right about him. He was a vile man. She was glad that Kreek had dealt with him. She shocked herself for a moment with that thought. It was not a Karen thought but a ruthless Fox one.

Fenn Dale was looking at her as if she were some kind of monster. Maybe she was.

'I did not know the army was on the move. I have heard nothing from Huta Arn for weeks. I sent someone up through the Ridge last week but I've heard nothing back. Hale Garnem has in own spies – I fear for my own network. How do you know this?'

Karen said nothing. She did not want to tell this man about Mowl. She remembered too clearly Fenn Dale's knife against Mowl's throat.

Kreek looked at her with something like appeal in his eyes. He wanted her to cooperate.

'*I can talk with Mowl – he's with the army. He warned me about Ponn. Was Ponn your agent?*'

Fenn Dale looked uncomfortable.

'Yes and no. I work for King Flane and I listen to his spies. Ponn was sent to find out what was going on in the Tear Mountains because Hale Garnem had wind of some talk of rebellion there. I also talk to those who do not support the King. I walk a narrow path but …'

It sounded as though Fenn Dale might have a lot to say on the subject. Kreek did not have time to listen. He did not show by a flicker of an eye that the information about Ponn and Mowl and the army was news to him too. He took charge and cut in.

'We have heard about that. The important thing is;

can you raise an army to support this group Mowl is with?'

Fenn Dale's eyes widened. Karen Fox did not think he'd ever believed it would come to this.

'Maybe.'

'Why not *yes*?' Kreek's eyes were hard. Perhaps Kreek did not entirely trust Fenn Dale either.

'Hale Garnem is a powerful man with a tendency to kill people who disagree with him. Many of the men and women who might help have their clans to think of, their position ... people are nervous – more now than they have ever been. Many of my contacts have been either hung or found dead with their throats cut. A spymaster without his spies is a worthless individual.' Fenn Dale sounded deflated, weary, sad. It couldn't be as bad as he said.

'*I think the Queen expected better of you,*' said Karen, suddenly afraid for Mowl. How many people were with him? How were they armed? How many men did Flane have? Did they stand any chance against Flane and Hale Garnem?

'How soon will the mountain men be here?' Fenn Dale said crisply, with one of those swift changes of mood he'd shown when Fox had first met him.

'*Mowl did not say.*'

'Can you find out?'

She did not know. Her head hurt and she suddenly felt

294

very tired. She looked soulfully up at Kreek who some-how took her meaning.

'Fenn Dale, you speak to a blessed arl of the spiritual tier. Do you not have men who will tell you what is going on in the rest of the country?'

'I did but I wouldn't trust it now. I think Hale Garnem is winning the espionage war. Anyway if what you say about Ponn is true, I'm not sure it is safe for me to return to my office. If Ponn knew about my other role – he may have sent a message to Garnem or Flane. You will have to take messages for me. I think perhaps something can be done. I do not know how quickly.'

'Fenn Dale, I fear I may also be a wanted man and my place is with the arl.' Kreek indicated Karen who had curled up under a tree with her tail tucked under her. She had begun to doze.

Fenn Dale, thought for a moment, the light of a calculating intelligence glinting from behind keen eyes.

'Just to satisfy my curiosity, how did you know where to find me?'

Kreek was a little taken aback by the question before he realised that Fenn Dale asked it as a kind of test.

'Long ago, I served with King Rufin as a bodyguard – I remember you, though you are unlikely to remember me. I was with the cohort that came to recover the bodies of Mant and the King. We only found the King's burnt corpse and with my own hands I helped to build the shrine that now marks the spot. I knew that you often rode in the forest. When I found out that you too served the Queen, I guessed that you might come here. Few people even know it exists any more. I thought it might have been an appropriate meeting place.'

'Good.' Fenn Dale said enigmatically. 'You are right, it has been a meeting place for we rebels for years. The shrine is here, but it was never for Rufin. It's Mant Speare's body that lies here. King Rufin lived to fight another day.' Fenn Dale's eyes were gleaming. 'It's been eighteen years. I knew then what Garnem was like. I've waited so long to make him pay for murdering my friend and attempting murder on my king. I had hopes that after years of my constant persuasion King Rufin might return. He would never believe that King Flane was a worse King than he was. When Flane started his latest spate of hangings and burnings I thought I might be able, finally, to convince him but I think my messengers or his messengers or maybe both have been killed. I've had no word. So I spoke to the Queen – my last throw of the dice – I never expected her to agree. I half believed that she would tell Flane and I'd be hanged like the rest.' He turned to look at Kreek with the wolfish grin of a much younger man. 'Eighteen years is a long time to wait for revenge, I thought perhaps it was too long. Now I see that if we can't persuade more people to rally to our cause, it will not have been long enough.'

'Sar Dale, I am only a sergeant. I know nothing about spying or plots, but I have sworn allegiance to the Queen. The Queen is a prisoner in the castle – I will do all I can to set her free. If that involves taking orders from you, I will do that just so long as it does not hinder me from protecting the arl. Tell me, what do we need to do?'

Kreek rarely had that much to say. He shifted uncomfortably when he'd finished, regretting that he hadn't found finer words to say what was in his heart. The Queen needed him and he'd die before he'd fail her.

Chapter 33

The Tension Builds: Day 22

Karen heard Kreek's voice in the background as she drifted into sleep. She had no choice in the matter; her mental resources were exhausted. She needed to find Mowl again. She needed his reassurance. Without knowing how, only knowing that she had willed it with all her strength, she found him. It was almost as if she could smell his uniqueness with her mind. She tried to call to him as she had before but now she could not tell what he was thinking. She could not make him hear her. *Mowl!* She called out to him with all her faded strength.

Mowl was riding now in the direction of Maybury. The Goodwife Sale and Blud between them had talked up almost another army. The ranks of the flint-faced mountain men were swollen not just by the Goodwife's archers and the good citizens of Deworth, but by people from almost the entire north west of the Kingdom. The word had gone out and the Queen's blue flag fluttered at the vanguard of an army of six sixties at least. Not all were well-armed, but all were willing to do whatever was necessary to free Loyrenton from the yoke of King Flane and his loathed adviser, Hale Garnem.

They kept up a steady pace, even though most of the newcomers were on foot. They brought carts of food too and ale, for three hundred and sixty men could not just knock on doors and beg for their supper. Emotions mingled; anxiety and determination, fear and excitement. It was a heady mix. They rested periodically and at one such stop Mowl had the strong feeling that Fox was close by again. She had sounded so distressed when she'd contacted him before. He was torn between joy that she was still alive and sorrow that he had failed to protect her from Ponn.

The feeling that Fox was nearby was so strong now that he desperately searched the vicinity for the tell-tale flash of luminescent red. Then he upbraided himself for being a fool; he who had wanted to be an Adept and yet could not even distinguish the distant emanations of the spiritual being from the plain everyday fact of Fox's physical presence. He closed his eyes for a moment to try to clear his thoughts, to relish the discovery that she still lived and was startled to find himself trapped in the soft, grey forest of a waking dream.

Fox was waiting for him, like before, not sleeping this time but pacing the ground in agitation.

'Mowl!' she ran to him and once more he longed to put his arm round her. He sniffed her musky scent. He had missed her so much. She still seemed fit and well in spite of her experience with Ponn.

'Are you well, Fox?'

'I miss you,' she replied without looking at him. 'Ponn was—'

'I'm sorry!'

'At least I can speak now – to other people, not just you!'

'Oh!' Mowl hid his disappointment and berated himself for his selfishness. He had wanted to be uniquely able to talk to her. 'I should be in Maybury soon – by noon tomorrow.'

'But Ponn got here this morning!'

Mowl shook his head.

'There was a faster way but we didn't take it – the way we've come has let us pick up more supporters. We are six sixties now but Huta is trying to recruit more people all the time.'

'Fenn Dale hasn't got a rebel army yet – lots of his people have died. I don't know if he can gather one! Will that be enough?' Karen tried to hide her doubts. She feared for Mowl. Hesitantly, she licked his muzzle. Mowl was distantly aware of movement all round him and a quick, sharp flash of pain across his nose.

'I have to go. Keeper keep you, Fox.'

He woke to find Dorren slapping him sharply across the face.

'You were out cold. What happened?'

Mowl touched his stinging cheek.

'I must have dozed off. Are we moving on?'

He took a rapid gulp of bread and ale and clambered to his feet. He had to let Blud know of this new intelligence from Fox. It was not good news if Fenn Dale was not able to raise more men for the army. Mowl should have been worried but he was not. All he could think of was the fact that his beloved arl was still the same, undamaged by Ponn, and that he could still speak to her: his soul was not yet sullied by his oath to Leva. He was suffused with sudden and unexpected joy.

When Karen woke it was late afternoon. Fenn Dale and Kreek were talking tactics. Something had changed, for there no longer seemed to be any doubt that people would rally to the Queen's flag. Fenn Dale, seemed to have put whatever worries he might have had to one side and exuded competent confidence. He was a strange man, Fenn Dale – never any one thing for very long. Fox stretched and yawned and almost went off to hunt before passing on her important information. Even though she now knew herself to be Karen, the insistent demands of her hungry fox body were frequently overwhelming. She managed to put her hunger aside for a moment. She padded towards the two men who were drawing maps with sticks in the now thawed soil.

Kreek looked up and bowed his head respectfully.

Fenn Dale merely looked uncomfortable. The remains of food from Fenn Dale's saddlebag captured her attention. She had difficulty concentrating. Fenn Dale waved at it. 'Please, noble arl, do finish it.'

She did not need to be asked twice. She felt better almost at once, more human, able to sequence her thoughts. She projected her thoughts as clearly as she could and the men listened.

'Mowl says the army will be here tomorrow round noon. They have six sixties.'

Fenn Dale scowled. 'It's not long, is it – eighteen years and a day and a half to assemble an army!'

Kreek grinned briefly at him, recognising the older man's strange humour. His talk with Fenn Dale had convinced him that Fenn Dale was not the old fool he'd feared he might be. He knew his business, but the situation was grave.

'I'm worried Flane will attack us before we're ready. They must be suspicious of you – they've killed and maybe tortured your contacts and if Ponn did get a message through to Hale Garnem surely they will want to move quickly, before you can join up with Huta's army?'

Kreek was most worried that Flane's Militia could nip the rebellion in the bud. Three hundred and sixty men was a start, but the Militia numbered thirty sixties, when last he'd heard, and it was recruiting, often forcibly, all the time.

'It is hard for them to do much quickly at the moment. King Flane is so taken with this new status of Keeper of the Purple Path he is taking less notice of Garnem. Garnem is the power there, but he still needs the King, or the Queen if she was not so much more difficult to manipulate. He has no personal right to power. For months now there has been conflict brewing. The King wants to build his temples, Garnem only ever wanted the temples to be an excuse for raising money to fund the Militia. King Flane believes he is saving the souls of his people, Hale Garnem doesn't believe in anything. My hope is that Garnem won't be able to act as quickly as he'll want to because the King will object to bloodshed. Garnem's only got away with so many hangings because he's claimed they were needed to wipe out the twin evils of heresy and treason. Don't be put off by the numbers, Kreek. If the Militia don't take the initiative today or tomorrow we have a good chance.'

Karen wondered if a good chance was good enough, but said nothing. She was relieved that Fenn Dale seemed to be the Queen's ally, in spite of his connection with the King's men. Kreek seemed happy with the plans he was outlining and Kreek seemed to her to be a competent soldier. She would put her trust in him. She loped off in search of something more to eat.

The rest of the day was very strange. She could feel the

tension growing. It was a palpable entity; fear and excitement. She felt it in her bones when she was near Kreek and Fenn Dale. It was disturbing to her as she had no obvious way of dealing with it. It made her want to bite someone or run fast for a long way. As neither was a particularly helpful response she stayed out of the way. Kreek rode off into Maybury, returning later to debate with Fenn Dale. Karen would have liked to have been more involved, but she didn't understand much of their talk. It was about people and things she knew nothing about and she was constantly distracted by the scents of the deep forest and hunger and the urgent need to get on with her fox life. Existing had become a pleasure the old Karen had never recognised. She savoured every moment of it, as if in some deep part of herself she knew it was going to end, soon. She did not try to contact Mowl. She did not have to; as he came near she could feel his presence, familiar to her as her own shadow. She knew that he was coming closer with the army and with every hour she felt the nearing of the inevitable. There was going to be a battle, it was unavoidable. She had to hope and pray that they would survive it.

Chapter 34

Gathering: Day 23

From dawn of the next day Fenn Dale's army began to gather at the forest site, near the shrine. Fox could not avoid the smell of male sweat and fear, of human hair and breath, of wool and leather, metal and grease. Human sounds filled what was rapidly becoming a military camp. There was no way she could leave. She curled up as close as possible to the familiar protection of Sergeant Kreek and listened and watched and noticed as quietly as the old Karen would have done.

There were all kinds of men gathered. Kreek and Fenn Dale had called in town traders and itinerant pedlars, carpenters and stonemasons, couriers and scribes, grooms and leather workers, a couple of farriers, several recent deserters from the King's Militia and then representatives of some of the most powerful families in the land, their personal guards and household retinue. There were, as Mowl would have calculated it, five sixtys of men, variously armed, and a smattering of women, mainly armed with bows and hunting knives. Sergeant Kreek, she noted, talked to each one in turn, to find out their experience and particular skill. He sorted them into groups of six, picked a leader for each group known as the sixman, then further into groups of thirty and then into sixty. He spent the morning explaining the chain of command and introducing the various leaders to one another. He also picked one fast runner to join each thirty, as both messenger and medical assistant. Kreek was clear that their first duty was to take messages and the second to help a wounded man. He told them frankly to ignore the seriously injured and to forget the dead. Kreek's instructions, bluntly and clearly expressed, left no one in doubt as to the seriousness of the operation. The distinctive reek of trepidation and fear clogged Fox's nose. It was hard to scent anything else.

At noon Huta's men arrived with a little under seven sixties of men to add to the rebel tally. Karen wanted to fling herself at Mowl, like a pet dog greets its master but she could not. Now that he was there she felt shy. She found it easier to see him as the fox figure of her dreams than this tall, grave-faced man. She approached him hesitantly, her eyes seeking his, the only feature he had in common with the fox of the grey place. They spoke silently in the emanation only they could hear.

'*You are safe then, Mowl? You look tired.*'

'Yes. It's been a long march, but it is good to see you. You look ... fine.' She could not smile at him in welcome, or hug him as she so much wanted to do, but she rubbed herself against his leg, glad to touch him, to find him solid and real. He stroked her red pelt reticently. They should be of the same kind. This difference between them felt wrong. He wanted to say how sorry he was about the Succeptor but he didn't. He didn't think she knew that an arl's days were numbered. He wanted to throw himself at her and sob an apology for his failure – his failure to save her from her arl's fate. Instead, he turned to inspect her appearance more closely. She did not look like she was dying. She was looking sleek and fit and she still glowed as she always had.

A sudden cheer interrupted their reunion. Fenn Dale was kneeling by the side of the shrine. At first Mowl thought he was bowing in obeisance to the Keeper, but then he realised that Fenn Dale was bowing to Blud, which made no sense at all. People everywhere were cheering and bowing. Blud was smiling in a kind of pleased, embarrassed way. What was going on? Mowl and Fox moved closer to hear Blud's words.

'It is good to stand here eighteen years on, at the very place where my courageous friend and bodyguard gave his life to save mine. It is long past the time that we should remember the bravery of Mant Speare, with gratitude and respect. It is eighteen years since I left this land. I have had eighteen years in which to think of the things I failed to do as King and consort to Her Royal Highness Queen Lin. I have spent eighteen years away from this beloved country, fighting in other wars. It is time I fought for my own land at last, to free it from the tyranny of men who feel free to murder and terrorise their own people. I do not wish to lead you as King Rufin. I abdicated that right when I escaped from here, barely alive, those eighteen years ago, but I do wish to lead you. I wish to lead you as a man dedicated to restoring the Kingdom, to putting Loyrenton back into the hands of its Queen. I will lead you into a fight against King Flane. Will you follow?'

There was a resounding cry of affirmation from the army that made the hairs lift on Karen Fox's pelt. She had been in larger crowds, but she had never been anywhere where the feelings had run so high, or where so much had been at stake. Mowl looked flabbergasted.

'Blud is really King Rufin?'

Dorren was suddenly by his elbow. 'I always knew he wasn't a farmer!'

Mowl was still reeling from the shock of it when Blud, or rather King Rufin, called him over. Fox followed. Mowl's uncle Huta was looking very pleased with himself; presumably he had known all along.

'I wanted to tell you, Mowl, how much I regret what happened to your father. He was a dear friend in those far away times when we young. We had a lot of fun, your father and I, and I know that you haven't had much fun at all as an orphan in Loyrenton. I wanted you to know, if we win, and we will, and I am in a position to return favours I will honour your father and you.' Blud looked earnest and Mowl could not help but be moved, especially when he continued, 'I knew your father well. I have only just met you but I know you are as brave and as resourceful as he would have wished you to be. Mant was so looking forward to the birth of his son – he kept talking about what he would teach you.' Blud looked away. 'It's eighteen years ago, but being back here it hardly seems it, then I look at you and the weight of those years overwhelms me.' He shook his head as if to rid himself of an unhelpful thought. 'Is this the arl?'

'*Your Majesty*,' said Karen respectfully and the King could not have been more startled if the trees had spoken.

Kreek who had been consulting with Huta and the Goodwife chose that moment to reappear.

'Your Majesty.'

'Kreek?'

'Yes sir.' Kreek could not disguise his grin of pleasure to be recognised after so many years. 'Your Majesty, there is no sign of any movement of troops from the castle or, as far as we can see from the region. According to one of the Goodwife's sons, who has been riding round the region for the last four days, a lot of former Militia men are just burning their uniforms and pretending never to have been involved.'

'Thanks for that, but we both know the professional core will fight and fight well. I assume they are still trained in the same way?'

'Yes, Your Highness, Hale Garnem still has charge of that.'

Blud glowered a little at the name.

'We camp here tonight. Can you sort out the watch? You better call yourself Commander or some such, a mere sergeant cannot run my army. You'll need another day to get organised I suppose? The Goodwife will sort out rations and weapons, liaise with her. You won't find a better Chief of Staff in the Militia or, come to that, in all the tiers of being. We'll work out our campaign in the morning. It's very good to see you again, Commander Kreek.' Rufin stepped forward and embraced his former bodyguard. 'It's even better to see you on my side!'

Kreek glowed with embarrassment and pride, the years of his service to Flane seemed to drop away and he was, once more Rufin's loyal bodyguard. He hurried away. The years had improved Rufin, he was more like a King than he had ever been. The fun-loving young man obsessed by hunting and gaming had changed beyond recognition, but then he had needed to change; King Rufin had been a spoiled, idle man. Kreek liked Blud better.

*　*　*

Fox and Mowl found a quiet place away from the others. They had a lot to talk about. Mowl was afraid that Fox would die on the twenty-fourth day of her fox incarnation. Karen was afraid that Mowl would die in the fighting. They did not talk about those fears. They spoke about their lives before. Mowl was shocked and intrigued and delighted all at once by all that she could tell him of her own world and agreed that if she did indeed come from the tier of the spiritual, it was most inappropriately named. After sharing a meal with others in Mowl's six they slept. Fox curled around Mowl's leg like a common or garden pet.

Karen dreamed of the owl calling to her in the grey place. 'Come home, love, come home!'

And when she woke in the stillness of the night, it was with tears and an aching sense of loss. She did not think she would ever see her grandmother again.

Chapter 35

Approaching Crisis: Day 23

The tension mounted. The rebel army made its preparations. Men sharpened sharp swords, checked kit, gambled and squabbled and sat thinking, and prayed to the Keeper. They fingered lucky charms and talked of their families. They ate and they drank and caught sleep when they could. They ate and slept in their sixes, that were fast becoming close as brothers. They practised and waited together, and the waiting seemed as long as childhood. They knew they were outnumbered and that if it came to a siege few of them could afford to remain in Maybury. The usual winter food stores had been heavily depleted by the Militia and there was not enough spare food in all of Maybury to keep starvation at bay for long. They needed to find King Flane's granaries. Kreek was certain that the provisions were kept within the castle wall. King Rufin was worried that Hale Garnem and King Flane could and would remain in the castle indefinitely and it was the besiegers who would starve first.

The men were very edgy. They were keyed up for a fight that Rufin was beginning to fear would not happen. He did not know how he could look them in the face if they were obliged to slink home in a few weeks' time, vanquished by hunger and not by King Flane. Everyone had an opinion on the best strategy. No one had any real answers. They examined the problem from every angle. Rufin wanted to get it right. They would only have one chance. He did not want to waste it.

'What if we could smoke them out of the castle? A few sixties at a time to keep the King's men confused and divided,' Karen asked Mowl thoughtfully. They sat a little apart from Mowl's six. Like the others in Huta's army he had been interviewed by Kreek, an odd and uncomfortable experience, and requested that he be given no responsibility except to protect Fox and to fulfil his oath of revenge. He could see failure at both tasks looming.

'How do you intend to smoke them out – with fire?' Mowl looked at her as if she was thinking with her tail. His tone was unusually scathing.

'No. I meant scare them away from the castle, into the hands of the army.'

'It would take a lot to scare Hale Garnem and his men out of a comfortable billet. Why should they fight us? They know we can't take the castle – the walls are as thick as a man's arm is long. I suppose there are the windows but even so …'

But Karen Fox had started to use her neglected human brain; she was sure the answer lay with the Queen. Quietly she explained the beginnings of her plan to Mowl. Reluctantly, he agreed to go with her to find Kreek. The cold-eyed veteran was catching a moment's ease, eating bread and cheese and poring over a map drawn in the mud.

Mowl found it hard to look at him without breaking out into a sweat and remembering the powerful swing of Kreek's sword arm that had nearly ended his life. Only the warmth of Fox's presence and her assurance gave him the necessary courage.

Mowl briefly outlined Fox's plan. She still found it tiring to speak for herself.

Kreek listened attentively. 'I could not betray the castle's secrets – it would be to betray my Queen,' said Kreek slowly, after a moment's considered thought.

'*We don't have to say how we will get the men into the castle, just that we will get men into it,*' said Karen. '*I am an arl, after all, and nobody knows what an arl can do.*'

Kreek nodded at that and gave Karen Fox a respectful look. *He* didn't know what to expect from her and he had seen more of her than most.

'It would mean splitting our force,' Kreek said, thoughtfully. 'I don't like the idea of that. We're too few to start with.'

'If we were clever, couldn't just a few of the best men

and maybe some archers give the illusion of many more?' Mowl was growing more enthusiastic by the minute. Fox's plan made sense.

'What makes you think there is a way in from outside the walls? I had to make my escape from the gatehouse.' Kreek was still uncertain.

'*But the Queen was in a hurry and got me out by the nearest route, not necessarily the best route,*' said Karen firmly. '*There has to be a way out of the castle and a way in, to allow a member of the family to escape if they absolutely had to.*'

Kreek nodded. 'How are you going to contact the Queen?'

This was the least certain part of the plan. Fox licked her lips and Mowl stared at the ground.

'She is an Adept. We'll have to try and find her in our dreams,' said Mowl.

Kreek was about to laugh dismissively, but something in the intent faces of Mowl and Fox prevented him.

'Could you pick men to go into the castle and have forces ready to meet Flane's men as they come out by, say, dawn?'

Kreek nodded. 'I will put it to King Rufin and the others. It could be a good plan, if …' He did not finish the sentence. He hardly needed to.

Mowl and Fox exchanged glances. It was up to them. All the lives here might depend on what they would do tonight. Fox shivered, but did not flinch from the responsibility. She had chosen Mowl. She would do what she could to help him.

It was full dark now and the smell of cook fires and roast meat filled the air. The night was cold and clear. Karen gazed at the hard, bright light of the unfamiliar stars through the lattice arc of branches. The universe was vaster and weirder than she had ever imagined. It was also more beautiful and more perfect than she had ever appreciated. She was part of this intricate universe, part of the incomprehensible mystery of it. She had never felt part of anything much when she had just been Karen. Fox was a much more rooted creature. It was good to have been Fox – whatever happened.

She and Mowl walked in silence to a place away from the fires, a dry hollow by the sculpted roots of an enormous tree. They had already eaten and even Karen's ravenous fox belly was satisfied.

'*How are we going to do this?*' Mowl could hardly see Fox in the dark. He laid his hand on her back for reassurance, his not hers. He knew she could see him quite clearly.

'*I thought you knew how to do it?*'

Mowl shook his head in the darkness.

'*Can't you call to the Queen, Fox, like you called to me, when you pulled me into your dream?*'

'I was asleep.'

'Perhaps you should go to sleep again.'

'Just like that?'

'Why not?'

'Because it's cold and I'm afraid and if this doesn't work, if we don't defeat Flane, they'll catch you and hang you and, even if we do fight Flane, we could lose or you could be killed or ...'

'It's going to be all right, Fox. We serve Balance and Balance will always be restored.'

Mowl did not speak about his own fears. There would be no point. If the Adept had spoken truly, he could not save her. He knew that now. He could only hope there would be time to say goodbye.

Mowl stroked her coat comfortingly and Fox snuggled down into the hollow under his warm soldier's cloak. She was Fox as well as Karen and she made herself take pure animal pleasure in the warmth and kindness and the safety of Mowl's presence.

She fell almost instantly asleep.

'Mowl!' she called urgently. Summoned him with all her force of will into the grey place to be with her. His fox form appeared almost before she'd finished the call.

'That was easy,' he said, looking pleased with himself. She was momentarily distracted by the fine intelligence in his grey eyes, the luxuriance of his thick winter coat, but she forced herself to focus on their task. How did one call a Queen?

Dreaming, Fox closed her eyes and pictured the exotic bird, her bright colours and her clear, sweet voice. She wished to see her again so badly that suddenly she was there, in all her multicoloured splendour, on a part of the greyness that formed a tree. The exotic bird appeared startled but otherwise seemed much as before.

Before she could fly away, Karen Fox and Mowl Fox had her cornered.

'Don't fly away, Queen Lin, Your Majesty, we need your help to get us into the castle.' Between them they tried to explain their plan to the Queen in her guise as exotic bird. Her attention span was not as lengthy as they might have wished, but they managed to put together a simple plan. They would meet at dawn at the back of the castle, by the gargoyle shaped like an eagle, by the glass window designed like a sunflower under the carving of the Keeper's scales. They repeated it several times, to be sure that the exotic bird had understood. The exotic bird was so unlike the competent Queen that it was puzzling. They were still talking when she flew away, out of the greyness, as abruptly as she had arrived singing, 'At dawn, at dawn, at dawn.'

Mowl and Fox looked at each other once she was gone. There was a temptation to stay a little longer, vixen and fox, Karen and Mowl. The thought did not need to be spoken.

'We need to get ready for the dawn,' said Karen regretfully.

'There will be other times,' lied Mowl, trying to keep the

sorrow from his voice. He was sure of his chronology now, he'd checked it with Fox. Dawn would mark the twenty-fourth day of Fox's incarnation. He did not want dawn to come.

Chapter 36

The Beginning of the End: Day 24 (Dawn)

They waited. Mowl's six, another six of men-at-arms, good swordsmen all of them, hand-picked by Kreek, Kreek himself, Fox and thirty archers. Fox looked as she had ever looked. She glowed like a jewel in the pink dawn.

Rufin led the main force. A ring of archers encircled the fortress, but waited under cover of the trees at the rear of the castle and the walls of the town. Behind them what heavy cavalry they had filled the streets with large horses armoured with stiff hide and plate metal, stamping iron-shod feet against the cobbled streets. Their riders, sweating even in the cool dawn under the weight of mail, prepared themselves, ready to ride down Flane's men as they crossed the broad space of the killing ground, the clear plain between the fortress and the town. The mountain men were with them, though by preference they did not fight mounted. They hefted their war axes and hummed their war songs under their breath. It made an eerie drone, like warrior bees. It made Mowl shiver. The townspeople had largely evacuated. They had taken their children, their valuables and the tools of their trade and gone, quietly in the night. A few of them armed with farm implements or ancient pikes took their place with the infantry sixes.

There were no sounds of life from the castle. The battlements seemed empty and there were no extra men lining the walls, ready with their burning oil or their sheaves of arrows to tear out the throats out of their enemy. It was odd. It was inconceivable that Flane did not know that forces loyal to the Queen packed the stone streets of Maybury and waited.

It was as well that the exotic bird (Karen could not quite regard her as fully Queen Lin) had been so specific about the exact meeting place. Rings of garishly painted sculptures, gargoyles, stone carvings and small arched windows, wreathed the higher reaches of the castle's walls like a cross between a cathedral and an over fanciful wedding cake. It took them awhile to spot the exact place for their rendezvous and while they searched they were at risk from any sharp-eyed observers from the battlements. There seemed a dearth of any kind of observers from the battlements. It made Kreek and Mowl nervous. What was Flane playing at that he had not readied his men? Ice almost stopped Mowl's heart when he suddenly feared that their dream conversation with the exotic bird might have been overheard, but Ponn was dead and he did not think there could be another like him. Could they have caught the Queen? Could they have tortured her into participating in their meeting in the grey dreaming place? It did not seem so. With no warning, no sound, a small section of wall roughly the size of two tall men walking abreast, suddenly dissolved like a castle of air. The men almost bolted but Kreek, who had experienced this phenomenon before, steadied them.

'Don't be afraid. This is the secret door I told you about. You will see strange things as I warned you before, but hold on to your weapons and follow the Queen.'

Displaying greater confidence than he felt, Kreek led his small party into the barren ruins of that other place.

The Queen and Princess Lenya were both there, white faced and anxious.

'What is it, Your Majesty?' asked Kreek, concern colouring his voice.

The Queen looked harrowed. She had lost weight and deep lines of stress creased what, only days ago, had seemed a face unmarked by age or life.

'I am glad to see you, Kreek. It is, as I told you, like being a lost child of six again.' She leaned a little against his arm and he could feel her trembling. 'Hale Garnem and the King argued. We heard them from one of the spying places. Flane did not want to loose the Militia on the townspeople, or on the rebels. He wanted to stay here and wait for everyone to go home. Garnem wanted to launch an immediate pre-emptive attack. He wanted to kill every man and woman who had rebelled and mount their heads over every window in the castle.'

Princess Lenya, moved closer to the Queen and stroked her mother's hair. It spilled in disarray from its dagger clips and hung in thick, brittle grey coils to her waist. Princess Lenya looked strained and unhappy. She whispered to Kreek over her mother's head, 'It's very hard living between worlds. It unsettles. It's hard to remember things, to keep track of days. The Queen has made thirty or forty transitions to make sure she can take you where you need to go. She is exhausted and distraught.'

The Queen heard that and straightened her back. 'We are fine but the news is not good. Garnem's men told of your planned attack. The King forbade Garnem even to man the battlements. He does not think he needs him any more. Garnem is getting desperate. He is not a good man to anger.' The Queen faltered. 'The King's own bodyguard had to step between him and Garnem or I swear Garnem would have knifed him. I fear for the King's life.'

She paused and made an effort to calm herself. When

she spoke again it was with her habitual cool control. 'Garnem has control of the Militia not the King. Garnem has given the order to man the battlements. He will march out soon in good order and the King cannot stop him. There's a lot of confusion at the moment but the minute Hale Garnem starts throwing his weight around – I'm sorry, the rebels are doomed and we will have Hale Garnem on the throne of Loyrenton. If he beats you he will dispense with the King. Flane has become a hindrance to his plans.'

She said nothing about the increased vulnerability of her own position. She did not have to, it was written clearly in her tense face.

'Don't worry. We won't give Garnem time to get organised.' Kreek sounded calm and firm.

'Take us first to the barracks. If we can persuade those not yet kitted out to run, the rebels will have less to worry about.'

Mowl swallowed hard. Men were about to die.

The Queen and Lenya led them a complicated route through curiously decorated chambers, up and down ruined stairwells where mildewed stone supported crumbling steps and ivy twisted round grandly curving banisters. They hurried along walkways open to the wind and rain to end in a small room with the cosy air of Karen's grandmother's sitting room. The men lined up. The archers notched their arrows.

'Now,' said Kreek gently.

The Queen twisted her ring, and focused her will and her 'knack' as she had before. The wall dissolved. Every one gave a sharp, surprised intake of breath. It was disorientating. They had arrived in the barracks. Two or three sixties of off-duty soldiers were relaxing round a game of dice. Kreek's heart sank. He might know these men. He could not consider that. His orders were clear. 'Fire!' Arrows rained into the room and found their target. Men went down. Guardsmen shouted and made a grab at weapons but Kreek gave them no time. 'Charge!' he said and, as the small group of rebels advanced, the guardsmen ran, bootless, stumbling over fallen men. As far as they were concerned the walls of their barracks had disappeared and an army had attacked them out of nowhere. Kreek would have run too. What would have happened if they had turned and fought? The Keeper only knew. The guardsmen ran from Mowl and the twelve other swordsmen as if they were denizens of the spirit world. Kreek did not let them draw breath. Like Mowl he was shaking with fear and exhilaration.

Kreek urged the Queen to move on and she led them again through a procession of rooms, up a narrow spiral staircase to a painted walkway that opened on to the corridor outside the audience chamber. It was too easy. The archers struck and then, before the King's Militia had time to draw breath much less their swords, Kreek led the Queen's swordsmen in a charge. One brave man turned to fight but Kreek cut him down with one swift swing of his sword. The sound of metal against flesh and the soft thud as the man's body hit the floor made Fox feel ill. She felt herself fading. The door to the audience chamber was unguarded. Mowl stepped forward, all his previous reluctance forgotten in the passion of the moment: 'If he's in there he's mine, for my father, for my uncle and for Yani Varl!'

Kreek nodded tersely and they marched in. The King's bodyguard had formed a protective wall around his throne. Hale Garnem and three other men stood directly in front of the door. Mowl's six formed a ring around the archers who fired into the armoured guards. Their bows were accurate as rifles and almost as effective. Four men were down and three injured before the swordsmen crossed their blades.

Fox watched through blurring vision. The Queen and Lenya had grabbed swords from the fallen soldiers in the corridor and, in spite of their elaborate court clothes, looked like they might know how to use them. They took their places in the circle of men around the archers, releasing more men to join the bloodier battle in the centre of the room. Only one guard now protected King Flane. The others had joined Hale Garnem's men in attempting to repel the rebels. Mowl's face was covered in blood but it did not look like it was his own. He was concentrating all his will on staying alive against the experienced guardsmen who blocked his every blow. One of Mowl's six was down, slashed across the heart, with a deep gash from which dark blood briefly welled. Mowl had downed his opponent.

Karen could not see how. The moment was lost in the mêlée of blood and bodies. The man was not dead but blood pooled around him where he lay and groaned.

Fox wanted to stop her ears from the cries and grunts of effort and the ringing clash of weapons, from the agonised, heart-wrenching cries of the injured. Kreek was still alive and fighting like a man possessed, a mirthless smile fixed on his face, his eyes dark with some unreadable emotion. Mowl was running for the King, running and almost slipping on a floor, red and slippery as an abattoir. The last of King Flane's bodyguards had crumpled to the ground, an arrow through his eye. Mowl, crazed with a kind of battle madness, charged in obedience to his oath. Hale Garnem got there before him and before Mowl's horrified eyes beheaded the King with one massive swingeing stroke of his heavy sword. Flane had denied him the power he needed to crush the rebels. Thanks to Flane everything was lost. Garnem watched with a curious expression of satisfaction as the King's head landed with a muffled thump on the carpeted step of the dais. Transfixed with horror Mowl could not take his eyes off it. Fox saw Hale Garnem's sword rise again and leaped with all the speed in her lean, balanced body towards Mowl, a fox's inhuman cry all the warning she could manage. She threw herself at the dead King's adviser, the force of her assault all but knocking him over. Mowl turned; his mind focused again, both hands clasping his own rising sword.

Karen Fox felt a fiery shaft of pain, the hot metal taste of blood, the stench of Hale Garnem's mead-sweetened breath. She saw Mowl's face contort in slow motion fury. She saw his sword falling as she fell. She did not see where it landed.

In the grey place, the owl swooped and flitted over Fox's bloodied, prostrate form.

Fox found the words, sent them like the owl's own white feathers to float towards her grandmother from the other side of pain. 'Goodbye, Gran, I love you.' She smiled a fox's smile. There had been time to say goodbye. She had not expected that.

Chapter 37

The End: Day 24

Grace woke with Karen's voice in her head, her words vibrating in her memory, like the sweet, high note of a violin. Grace's cheeks were wet. She had cried in her dreams and her throat ached with the sobbing she hadn't done. She opened her eyes and gave a little cry of shock. Karen was there, on her bed, her eyes open, alive, smiling! Smiling! Grace blinked and she was gone. There was nothing there. No Karen, no body, nothing but the white sheets and the indentation in the mattress left by her form. In reverence and confusion and shock, she touched the bed. It was still warm. She was alive. Grace knew that, knew that the last sight she'd had of her had been true. She was still alive but she'd gone. The sob that had caught in her chest and had filled her mind all night built and grew until she could no longer hold it in. It became a wail, a cry, a great instinctive primal scream, somewhere between loss and triumph. It shook the walls of the small bare cubicle. It reverberated through the cool, pale, paint-ed corridor, echoed off the green lino floor. It shocked the ward to silence. Nurses ran in from every direction. Outside, George started and guessed a part of its import. Karen had gone. Grace's darling girl was gone! But some-where she lived and she loved her still.

Kreek heard Fox's unearthly scream. There was some half grown bodyguard of the King blocking his path. Kreek despatched him with callous ease. He had been young. Hand-to-hand experience told. Kreek saw Mowl fighting for his life against Hale Garnem. Blood spurted from Mowl's shoulder; his old wound, Kreek assumed. Blood and sweat streaked his face. There were few of Garnem's men still standing. The headless corpse on the throne told him all he needed to know about the King. He strode to Mowl's aid, then hung back. An oath of revenge was an important thing, let Mowl fulfil it if he could. Kreek's eye was suddenly caught by a flash of red in his peripheral vision. Not Fox? He felt cold. Not the arl? There, lying on the floor just behind Mowl, was the bloodstained body of a young woman. Red hair the colour of Fox's pelt spilled round a delicate face, as pale as the white cotton shift she wore. The shift was splat-tered with the violent red, the crimson of her blood. The woman still breathed. The arl had Transformed.

* * *

Rufin's men fought on. It had been easy at first. The first frightened unarmed men who ran from the fortress had been easy pickings for the archers and the cavalry, and their bodies littering the way put fear in the eyes of those that came after. They had been armed and well-trained and frightened but desperate too, desperate to avoid being trapped in the pincer movement of a great army. Many had died and many had run. Rufin's men were tiring. There were many wounded. He saw the Goodwife rallying the archers, collecting arrows from the dead, screaming vengeance and victory and anything else that helped lift the spirits of men tired of the grim business of shooting to kill. The sun was halfway to midday when the flag was raised. It was the Queen's flag, raised on the castle flagpole. It was victory! Those Militia men still in the castle surrendered. Rufin, flanked by Fenn Dale and the Goodwife, marched triumphantly back into his former home. There had been casualties; Huta was injured, though not fatally. About a fifth of his army was dead or injured. They had triumphed – at a cost.

The cost became clearer inside the castle. Bodies littered the corridor outside the audience chamber. Inside, the audience chamber looked like a slaughterhouse. Rufin took in King Flane's headless body and the corpse of Hale Garnem lying nearby. Kreek still lived, as did the archers. Then he saw her. The Queen was embracing her, crying with relief; Princess Lenya, his only child was alive and unscathed. He wanted to run to her and beg her forgiveness. If he'd been a decent King, Hale Garnem would never have got a toehold in court, Flane would never have bewitched his Lin with his intellectual charm. His triumph turned to ashes in his mouth when he saw her, his Lenya, so like Lin in her youth. What a fool he'd been. The Queen saw him and paled. 'Rufin?'

He fell to his knees before her.

'Your Majesty, I am so sorry for all this, for what I've done to this Kingdom.' He had thought he had shed all his tears of regret long ago but seeing the worn beauty of his once young wife he felt only guilt for the long, lost years, when he had been free and she had fought to rule her Kingdom. He could have helped her, should have helped her.

He hung his head in shame. Queen Lin found it difficult to breathe. She had grieved for this man and believed him dead for eighteen years. Only years of self-discipline enabled her to regain her equanimity. She was suddenly aware of the state she must be in, her wild hair and her haggard looks. She wanted to straighten her hair. She wanted to embrace this man she had once loved to assure herself that he still lived. Instead, she found the remnants of her dignity and gave him her hand. He kissed it.

'You've saved us, I think, and as for the rest.' She dismissed the past with a flick of her long beringed hand.

'For all the rest, she paused, suddenly overwhelmed by the memories of herself when she had been young and arrogant, far too quick to criticise and far too slow to forgive. 'We too must bear some blame.' She turned to her daughter who was observing this performance with some bemusement. 'Lenya, this is your father, Rufin. It seems I was quite wrong about him, he lives still, after all.'

Mowl was impervious to everything. He had killed Garnem. He did not know how. He sat now, slumped on the ground, blinking back tears. He was sure that the killing had sullied him. He did not like the way it made him feel to see Hale Garnem's dead eyes staring up from his lifeless corpse. There was loss in that, but he could not believe what he gained. His noble arl, his beautiful, luminescent, perfect fox had transformed. She had not died, she had Transformed. On the twenty-fourth day of her incarnation she had saved his life and Transformed into a beautiful, luminescent, perfect woman. She had opened her eyes and smiled and he had known, known that she was the same; still Fox, still his and that they would be together for however long she lived.

Epilogue

King Rufin ruled as consort to Queen Lin for thirty more years of peace, prosperity and religious freedom. Kreek remained commander of the Queen's Militia, and the Goodwife Sale became chief adviser. Fenn Dale retired to new estates, granted by his royal patron, and Dorren returned to the Varl lands to rebuild what had been destroyed. Leva was the kind of Goodwife her mother would have been proud of. She brought up five sons and two daughters quite happily with Jenn Doka, though she was never able to like his mother.

Karen and Mowl were happy, very happy. King Rufin granted lands and gifts that allowed Mowl the freedom to become, if not an Adept, a man of talent and learning respected throughout the Northern Kingdom. All their four children had red hair and a preternaturally acute sense of smell. Karen never forgot the intense pleasures of sight and sound and scent and never quite lost the sharp perceptions of her fox persona.

She still dreamed of roaming in her fox form, and on clear nights Grace often saw a red fox watching her through the open curtains of her parlour window. Grace always smiled and waved and left it milk. And in her dreams she, the grey owl, flew to many a secret meeting in the grey world where the red fox spoke and played with her four delightful cubs.

George never believed the strange tale his wife told him. He insisted that the hospital launch an enquiry into their security and filed a complaint against the local Hospital Trust. Yet, when he saw the red fox, as he sometimes did when he watered the garden late at night, he'd whisper softly so that Grace wouldn't hear, 'Miss you, Karen, love, be happy!'

And, of course, she was.